Praise for
Becoming Us

"Robin has an ability like no other to write a story that not only captures your attention but your heart. That's exactly what she's done yet again with this must-read, *Becoming Us!*"

—CAMBRIA JOY, author of *Look Inside*

"Robin beautifully tells a story of friends who walk through the realities of
life ⋯ ⋯ ⋯ ⋯ ⋯ oks
lik ⋯ ⋯ ⋯ ⋯ ⋯ der-
sta ⋯ ⋯ ⋯ ⋯ ⋯ veet
cir ⋯

"I ⋯ ⋯ ⋯ ⋯ ⋯ and
fri ⋯ ⋯ ⋯ ⋯ ⋯ that
wi ⋯

"E ⋯ ⋯ ⋯ ⋯ ⋯ God.
Th ⋯ ⋯ ⋯ ⋯ ⋯ oup
of ⋯ ⋯ "

"A heartfelt story of the power of faith and love, *Becoming Us* is hard to put down. Once again, Robin Jones Gunn has created believable characters who struggle with everyday problems and emotions that we all face. Her ability to weave beauty and hope into the complicated life of Emily Winslow and her newfound friendships, a delightful circle of women, renewed my faith in God's good plans for my own life and relationships. A must-read!"

—AMBER LIA, best-selling coauthor of *Triggers* and *Parenting Scripts*

Becoming Us

BOOKS BY ROBIN JONES GUNN

SERIES AND COLLECTIONS
Christy Miller
Sierra Jensen
Christy and Todd: The College Years
Katie Weldon
Christy and Todd: The Married Years
Christy and Todd: The Baby Years
Glenbrooke
Sisterchicks

NOVELLAS AND HALLMARK MOVIES
Finding Father Christmas
Engaging Father Christmas
Kissing Father Christmas

NONFICTION
Praying for Your Future Husband: Preparing Your Heart for His
Victim of Grace: When God's Goodness Prevails
Spoken For: Embracing Who You Are and Whose You Are
A Pocketful of Hope for Mothers

ROBIN JONES GUNN

Becoming Us

A Novel

MULTNOMAH

BECOMING US

The characters and events in this book are fictional, and any resemblance to actual persons or events is coincidental.

Trade Paperback ISBN 978-0-7352-9075-4
eBook ISBN 978-0-7352-9076-1

Cover design by Kelly L. Howard; cover photography by Schon & Probst

Published in the United States by Multnomah, an imprint of the Crown Publishing Group, a division of Penguin Random House LLC, New York.

MULTNOMAH® and its mountain colophon are registered trademarks of Penguin Random House LLC.

Library of Congress Cataloging-in-Publication Data
Names: Gunn, Robin Jones, 1955– author.
Title: Becoming us : a novel / Robin Jones Gunn.
Description: First edition. | New York : Multnomah, 2019.
Identifiers: LCCN 2018035288| ISBN 9780735290754 (trade paperback) | ISBN 9780735290761 (ebook)
Subjects: LCSH: Domestic fiction. | BISAC: FICTION / Contemporary Women. | FICTION / Christian / General. | FICTION / Family Life. | GSAFD: Christian fiction.
Classification: LCC PS3557.U4866 B43 2019 | DDC 813/.54—dc23
LC record available at https://lccn.loc.gov/2018035288

Printed in the United States of America
2019—First Edition

10 9 8 7 6 5 4 3 2 1

To my creative sister, Julie, who has taught me how to be a haven maker in every season of life. And to my darling nieces, Amanda and Ashley. Thank you for making every gathering a time of beauty and sweetness.

Chapter 1

J had no problem finding Jennalyn's house that windy night in early December. The two-story charmer stood out from the other Costa Mesa ranch-style houses on Ventura Street. I even made it as far as the welcome mat by her front door before a rising sense of panic pressed in on me, causing me to stop and draw in a deep breath.

You don't have to do this, Emily. You can leave now. No one inside knows you're here.

My gaze went to the meandering red ribbon that looped through the fresh evergreen wreath hanging on the door. The wreath had an artistic assortment of bright silver bells, clusters of holly berries, and strategically placed starfish—a charming blend of beachy, artistic, and classy. Just like Jennalyn.

Nervously, I pulled her handmade invitation from my shoulder bag as if another glimpse at it would bolster my courage.

Come to a

Favorite Things
PARTY!

December 5, 7:00 p.m.

Jennalyn's new home

Bring a plate of Christmas cookies
and
4 gifts of your favorite thing that costs under $5
(No whiskers on kittens or
bright copper kettles, please)

It was all so cute. The idea, the invitation, and now the charming wreath on Jennalyn's front door.

Why did I say I would come? I can't do this. I won't fit in with these women.

My feet didn't move. In my pounding ears, I could hear the echo of my husband's calm voice right after we moved to California. He had to coax our daughter out of the car on her first day of fifth grade.

"You gotta be brave, sweetheart. You've gotta take the first step. Truth is, I don't know anyone in this wide world who wouldn't want to be friends with you. Go on, you can do this."

Audra had taken that first step, and she had made lots of friends at school over the past three months. Now it was my turn. If Trevor were standing beside me, I knew he would slip into his most adorable southern drawl and say, "Go on, Emily, darlin', ring the bell. You'll be glad you did."

You better be right, Trevor Winslow. You better be right about a lot of things.

I rang the doorbell and waited. When the door opened, cheerful Christmas music spilled out. Jennalyn's dark, silky hair hung over her shoulders, and she smiled at me in her welcoming way.

"I'm so glad you came! Come in." She offered me a pregnant-mama side hug.

I held out my plate of cookies with an apology. "They're not homemade. I hope that's okay."

"Of course it's okay." She took the plate and led the way past the garland-festooned staircase. The fragrance of fresh pine mixed with cinnamon and cloves hung in the air.

I could hear the other women's voices coming from the large open area at the back of Jennalyn's beautiful home. They were laughing the way friends laugh when they know each other well.

I hung back slightly, my heart pounding. The conversation paused when we entered. I counted the women seated on the plush sofas. There were only three, but they were all looking at me.

"This is Emily." Jennalyn placed her hand on my shoulder. "We met at the grocery store a few weeks ago and ended up having such a great conversation, I knew I wanted to include her for our Favorite Things party."

A chorus of greetings followed as each woman said her name. I gave a nod and a "hi" and placed my gifts on the end of the long marble kitchen counter where the other gifts were. Jennalyn added my plate of cookies to the snacks.

"Would you like something to drink?" One of the women had stood and was now coming toward me. Her long hair had a pretty nutmeg-brown tint to it and was tucked behind her ears. Her oval face seemed to be framed like an open window with the curtains pulled back to each side.

"I was going to make some hot tea," she said. "We have cold drinks too."

As she came closer, I read in her distinct blue-green eyes a gentle sincerity. Or maybe it was compassion, as if she instinctively knew how nervous I was.

"Tea sounds good," I said.

"Do you like peppermint tea?"

"Yes. Sure. Anything."

"I'm Christy. I know it's hard to remember names when you hear them all at once."

"Thanks."

She motioned to the other women on the couch. "So, again, that's Tess. And Sierra is in the chair."

My eyes went to Sierra first because of her beautiful, wild, curly blond hair. She wore a stack of gold bangles and beaded leather bracelets that shimmered and clinked together when she lifted her slender arm to wave at me. She reminded me of a mermaid.

"I love your sweater," Sierra said. "It looks hand knit. Is it?"

"I don't know. I don't think so." There was no way I was going to admit to her that I'd found it at a local junktique when I was hunting for lamps for our small apartment.

Sierra patted the underside of the simple scarf-like cocoon strapped to her front. "This is Ella Mae. She was four weeks old yesterday." Sierra folded back the tie-dyed fabric so I could see the downy head of her little one.

I hadn't realized she was cradling a newborn in her wide scarf. I smiled back but couldn't manage a comment because a lump had swelled in my throat. I blinked so I wouldn't tear up.

"Do you like honey in your tea?" Christy poured the boiling water into a white china teapot shaped like a pineapple.

"No thanks."

"I'm the same way. I like my peppermint tea unsweetened. Now, if we were having English breakfast tea," Christy confided, "I'd have both milk and sugar in it. And at least two cookies for dunking."

"At least two," Jennalyn chimed in. "Although I think we'll all need more than just two cookies tonight, by the looks of this assortment."

Christy and Jennalyn were treating me as if we were already friends. I wished my emotions hadn't gotten so elevated.

Jennalyn reached across the counter to uncover the plate of cookies I'd brought.

"Oh!"

I couldn't tell if Jennalyn's exclamation was one of surprise and delight when she saw my contribution, or if she was appalled. I stayed fixed on her expression as she examined the thumbprint cookies. They each had a chocolate kiss in the middle, popping up like an elf's cap. At least that's what Audra said they looked like when she helped me pick them out at the grocery-store bakery that afternoon. That's why my daughter had taken it upon herself to meticulously cover each kiss with green frosting and add a tiny red candy dot on top.

"How clever." Jennalyn, the artist, understood my daughter's attempt right away. "Christmas elf caps. These are adorable!"

I noticed that Christy was observing the lopsided cookies the way I had, with polite skepticism.

"Hey!" Sierra called from the couch. Her sleeping baby stirred, and she lowered her voice. "I vote that you guys bring the cookies over here and share the bounty."

"Great idea." Jennalyn went to the coffee table and cleared her artistically arranged decorations, looping the expensive-looking table runner over the back of a kitchen chair and carefully transferring the nativity set.

Tess stood to help transfer the cookies to the coffee table, and I was surprised at how tall she was. She carried herself as if she had runway experience. As she gracefully reached for the plates of cookies on the counter, I felt short compared to her.

I also realized I was the only one in this group who had short hair. Problem hair, as my mother used to call it. My baby-fine strands never grew up nor had they managed to grow out. My light brown, wavy hair fell to just below chin level. Most of the time I felt like I looked as if I'd gotten caught in a springtime shower without an umbrella. I think that's why I always noticed other women's hair. My four sisters-in-law had often said they envied my flat stomach and shapely legs. For me, I admired other women's hair.

I watched Tess out of the corner of my eye and wondered what it would be like to have thick, dark hair like hers. She wore it folded into a loose braid that hung down her back and then fell to the side when she bent to put the first few plates within easy reach for Sierra.

Tess caught my gaze and smiled. I smiled back. Her pale blue eyes stood out in a mesmerizing way against her toasty brown skin. She was stunning in an exotic, complicated way.

I took a seat next to Christy on one of the leather sofas. As the other women chatted, I drew in a slow breath. Christy was kind and a little shy. Jennalyn was outgoing and hospitable. Sierra was the free spirit in the group who had no trouble speaking her mind.

Tess would be the mystery. That was fine with me. After being the only introvert around Trevor's big clan for all the years we had lived in North Carolina, I found it nice not to be the only quiet woman at a party.

"Emily, how did you come up with the idea for the elf-cap cookies?" Sierra asked.

"It was my daughter's idea. She decorated them."

"Clever girl. How old is she?" Sierra asked.

"Ten. Well, almost eleven."

"What's her name?"

"Audra."

"What a pretty name." Tess spoke for the first time. Her voice had a warm, lilting tone. "Audra," she repeated as if my daughter were a storybook character.

Sierra helped herself to a second cookie. "Do you have only one child?"

My stomach tightened. I don't think Sierra intended for the word *only* to stand out in her question, but it did.

"Yes. Just one." I put the cup of peppermint tea to my lips and hoped the subject would change. My heart was racing again.

"Ella Mae is our first," Sierra said. "Jordan would love to have a dozen. I wouldn't mind that. I came from a big family, so I'm hoping we have lots more. Babies are amazing, aren't they? Such a gift."

I nodded and took another sip of tea.

"Do you think you guys will have more?" Sierra asked.

A circus of emotions ran through me, doubling the uncertainty I had felt on the doorstep earlier. My hand wobbled as I held the teacup to my lips. I swallowed before making a noncommittal sort of "Mmm" sound in answer to Sierra's question.

"Does anyone else want tea?" Christy lifted the pineapple teapot. "I think there's enough for one more cup."

"Sure," Sierra said. "I'll have some. It's decaf, right? Unless, Tess? Do you want the last cup?"

"I'll make another pot." Christy rose from the couch.

I used the opportunity to quietly excuse myself and retreat to the powder room. As soon as I closed the door behind me, I let out a long, slow breath.

Why is this so difficult? These women are nice. What is wrong with me?

Putting my clammy hands in the sink, I let the cool water run over my wrists, grounding me, calming me. In the mirror, my solemn brown eyes seemed to be evaluating my reflection the way I'd evaluated all the other women. It had been easy for me to find something I liked in each of them. Why couldn't I show myself the same kindness?

I'm not ready to have these kinds of conversations. Not with these women. Not with anyone. I need more time. I can't do this.

I folded the guest towel and adjusted it on the countertop.

I need to leave. Now.

Chapter 2

I returned to the great room and saw Jennalyn standing next to the kitchen counter. My plan was to discreetly tell her I wasn't feeling well, which was true. I sidled up next to her, ready to make a quiet excuse and equally quiet exit.

Jennalyn looked up. "Perfect timing! We're ready to open the gifts."

I hung back. "Well, actually, I—"

"Don't worry. You didn't miss the instructions," Jennalyn said. "I was about to explain how the favorite-things gift exchange works. Here." She placed a basketful of gifts into my arms and pointed at the coffee table.

I found a spot for them next to a plate of cookies and hesitated before sheepishly lowering myself onto the sofa.

I'll stay for the exchange. Then I'll slip out. No drama.

I noticed that my teacup had been refilled, so I reached for it and held it like a prop, grateful to have something to look at other than the women in this close circle.

"It's simple," Jennalyn began. "Everyone takes a few minutes to talk about what she brought and why it's a favorite item for her."

"We have to stand up and say something?" Christy echoed my discomfort.

"You don't have to stand. But you do have to explain why you chose what you brought. Then we all get one of the gifts to open, since everyone brought four of the same thing. Does that make sense?"

"Yep," Sierra said. "Should I go first?"

"Yes, please do."

"My favorite thing is shopping in funky thrift stores."

She and Jennalyn started talking at the same time and laughing about a shared moment they had recently while shopping at a local thrift store. They had found a vintage dresser that Sierra had turned into a changing table for Ella Mae with the assistance of Jennalyn's painting skills.

Their enthusiasm for "repurposing treasures" made me feel less self-conscious about where my sweater had come from. I also realized they called them thrift shops and not junktiques.

"I didn't have time to wrap them, so here." Sierra opened a zippered fabric pouch she had pulled from her diaper bag and displayed an assortment of at least a dozen bracelets on the coffee table. "I thought everybody could pick the one she wanted."

I waited until the others had made their selections before settling on a lime-green, plastic bangle. Since I don't wear a lot of jewelry and always feel like bracelets get in the way, I made my choice based on what I thought Audra might like.

"Thanks, Sierra." Tess gave her wrist a shimmy. "I really like this one."

"Good! I'm glad. Why don't you go next, Tess?"

Tess handed out her gifts in small drawstring pouches. Sierra immediately knew what it was.

"Is this the same fragrance you brought over with the diffuser a couple of days before Ella Mae was born?"

"Yes." Tess's buttery voice sounded confident. "No surprise, is it? One of my favorite things is fragrant oils. These are roll-on tubes of my latest favorite combination. The base is cedarwood and lavender, so it's earthy and calming. You might also pick up the faint hint of frankincense."

"What does frankincense smell like?" Christy untwisted the top of hers and rolled it on her wrist. I followed her lead, as she held her arm up to her nose and closed her eyes, drawing in the deep amber fragrance. "I love this."

"Me too," Sierra agreed. "What did you call this one? You had a name for it the other day."

"Slippers." Tess grinned, her gaze resting on me.

I smiled back. For the first time that evening, I felt relaxed. I rolled the scent on my other wrist.

"Slippers! Perfect name!" Sierra drew in another deep sniff. "Doesn't it make you want to put on your slippers and cozy up with a good book? Hey, you know what? We should start a book club."

"I've wanted to do that for a while," Jennalyn said. "I also want to do a banner word for next year the way Christy does."

"A banner word?" Sierra repeated.

"It's something I've been doing for a while," Christy explained. "I journal a lot, so I try to take some time before the start of a new year, and I simply ask God for a word. Then I write down whatever is impressed on my thoughts. I've found that the word becomes a sort of theme for the year."

"That's cool. Why don't we all do that for this new year?" Sierra glanced around the group. "Next time we get together, we can share what our word is for the year and discuss the book we all read."

"Great idea, but hold that thought until we finish the gift exchange," Jennalyn said.

Christy went next. She had made aprons for each of us. Darling aprons with long ties in the back and cute, mismatched pockets and a ruffle across the bib top. Sierra was elated and gave Christy a "you shouldn't have" look, saying that she knew how much Christy sold her aprons for in the local boutiques, and they didn't sell for five dollars.

"I used scraps on these. Don't worry. They didn't cost me more than five dollars." Christy went on to explain why aprons had become one of her favorite things. "I found that I really like wearing an apron when I'm in the kitchen. It brings back good memories of my grandmother; she used to always wear homemade aprons. I feel like I'm bringing a little of my midwestern heritage into my home." Her expression turned wistful. "I especially feel that way since my grandmother passed away last year."

"This is so sweet, Christy. Thank you," Jennalyn said. "I love mine."

"So do I," I echoed, feeling confident enough to speak up.

Tess held hers up, commenting on the colorful fabric and slipping her hand into the broad pocket. "This is officially now one of my favorite things."

"I'm so glad you like them." Christy looked slightly embarrassed by the praise.

All eyes were on me. I cleared my throat, as if I were about to make a speech. I had been so caught up in the other gifts, I hadn't thought about what to say. What came out was awkward. "I guess my favorite thing is sugar." I laughed, but no one else did.

"Because, well, here." I handed out the tissue-wrapped gifts. They were adorned with a springy ball of ribbons, hand-curled with care by Audra. "What I just said will make sense when you open them."

Sierra had hers torn open first. "Yum! Hot chocolate and a little packet of shortbread cookies. I love shortbread cookies. My mom used to send this kind to me when I lived in Brazil."

"Nice," Christy said. "A cozy moment waiting to happen. Thanks, Emily."

I nodded, still trying to take in that Sierra said she had lived in Brazil.

"Great choice on the cookies, by the way," Christy said. "This kind is perfect for dipping in hot cocoa."

"I agree," Sierra said.

I appreciated the way the others were so affirming, even though my contribution wasn't very personal. I decided to add a final thought in case it would help explain why I had come up with the idea.

"A few years ago I started a tradition with our daughter. After the tree is decorated, we turn off all the other lights and sit on the couch with our cocoa and cookies and listen to Christmas music."

"I love that," Sierra said. "I want to start traditions like that with Ella Mae. Although, I'll have to eat her cookies for her this year."

A twitter of laughter rolled comfortably over the group, and Jennalyn reached for her basket of gifts. I leaned back, glad to have the spotlight off me. Jennalyn rested the basket on her knees since most of her lap was otherwise occupied. She handed out four small, flat rectangular gifts. Our names were written with a flourish on the outside of the paper wrapping.

"As most of you know, one of my favorite things is creating handmade cards—"

"I love, love, love the beautiful invitations you made for this party," Sierra interrupted. "They were so cute."

"Thank you." Jennalyn shifted. It seemed she either was uncomfortable with the compliment or was getting kicked in the ribs from the inside.

"So one of my other favorite things is finding verses in the Bible that apply to whatever is going on in my life. Go ahead. You can open them."

Sierra held up her gift before opening it. "I get it! Brown paper packages tied up with string. Very clever."

The gifts were indeed wrapped in brown paper and tied with red string. Jennalyn looked pleased that Sierra had noticed.

We unwrapped the gifts in unison. The hand-lettered cards had a Scripture verse on them:

We confidently and joyfully
look forward to actually
becoming
all that God has had in mind for us to be.
—*Romans 5:2*

I glanced around and saw that we all had received the same verse, but the artwork was different on each of our cards. Mine had watercolored peonies painted in the top right corner. I love peonies. Jennalyn couldn't have known that; the coincidence touched me deeply. I felt as if I had received a little love note.

"The reason I chose that verse," Jennalyn said, "is because, as Christy knows, I've been coming back to it a lot over the last few months."

Christy nodded the way a best friend agrees with someone she knows by heart.

"We're all in process, right?" Jennalyn added. "We're becoming all that God created us to be. I've been trying to remember that instead of getting discouraged because things aren't going exactly the way I'd like them to. I need to relax and be confident and joyful, like this verse says."

Jennalyn's voice wobbled as she spoke, and for the first time that evening, I wondered if perhaps I wasn't the only woman in the room who was going through a private struggle.

"I love this verse," Sierra said. "It's perfect. None of us has arrived. We're all in the process of 'becoming.'"

I watched the women nod as if pondering what "becoming" meant to them.

"Anyone else notice a theme with our gifts?" Tess asked. "We can roll on our Slippers fragrance, put on our aprons to make our cocoa, and then curl up to enjoy our shortbread cookies . . ."

"While wearing our cute bracelets," Christy added, giving her bangled wrist a twist in the air.

"And memorizing our new verse for the year." Tess waved Jennalyn's card.

The others laughed comfortably, and I smiled. It felt good, like a sense of accomplishment. I'd made it this far through the night. I'd been included and accepted.

Yet deep inside, I still felt spurts of nervousness. I wanted to leave. I needed to leave.

The conversations twirled around the circle. Tess had started up a discussion with Sierra about fragrant oil combinations, and Jennalyn and Christy were discussing book options for the proposed book club.

Quietly gathering my gifts, I tucked them into my shoulder bag. Before I could stand up and make a smooth exit, Christy leaned over and said, "I liked your gift."

"Good. I'm glad."

Jennalyn had pushed herself up and moved into the kitchen, carrying a cookie on a napkin. Tess joined her, and Sierra adjusted herself to nurse Ella Mae, who was making the tiniest kitten-like pleas.

"You inspired me to start a new tradition with Hana this year," Christy said to me. "Now that she's six, she's very excited about Christmas. We're planning to get our tree tomorrow."

"You have a six-year-old daughter?" I asked.

"Yes. And a three-year-old son." Christy grinned and in the cutest voice added, "I also have a pretty great husband."

"I have one of those too." I grinned back at her.

Then, as if something pinched me on the inside, I felt compelled to add, "A pretty great husband, I mean. Not a—"

"Do you guys mind if Tess selects the first book for our book club?" Jennalyn's voice rose above the smaller conversations. "She has one she really likes and said she can text us the title."

"Sounds good," Christy said.

Sierra nodded.

I didn't make any kind of gesture of agreement or disagreement. Instead, I reached for my phone in my shoulder bag, acting as if I needed to check an incoming message. No updates were on my phone. Only an internal message from my bossy insecurities telling me to pack it up and get out of there. Leave on a high note. Mission accomplished.

My instincts knew that with a group like this, it was only a matter of time before the conversation turned again to talk of children, babies, and pregnancies. With the discussion would come questions. Questions I wasn't ready to answer, regardless of how kind and inviting all these women were.

"Wonderful!" Jennalyn said. "Tess will pick the book, and we'll meet here the second week of January if that works for everyone."

Christy laughed and raised her eyebrows at Jennalyn.

"What?" Jennalyn glanced at her chest as if making sure she hadn't left a trail of powdered sugar from the half-eaten cookie in her hand. "What did I miss?"

"Don't you think you might be a little busy around the second week of January?" Christy dipped her chin toward Jennalyn's belly.

"Oh! Right." Jennalyn smiled.

"Why don't we decide when to meet after all of us get through Christmas?" Christy suggested. "We can start reading the book now, but we don't have to set a date."

"Okay. Sounds good to me," Jennalyn said. A quiet pause followed. It seemed we had all turned our focus to Jennalyn's pronounced side view as she stood by the kitchen counter.

She must have sensed the object of our collective gaze because she patted her middle and said, "I honestly think this little wiggle bunny will come sooner than January 4, though. I can't imagine going all the way to my due date. Mostly I can't picture my poor body getting any bigger than it already is."

"That's exactly what I thought during my last month," Sierra said. "And you guys know how huge I got!"

Jennalyn looked at the half-eaten cookie she was still holding. We all watched as she pressed the pedal on the trash bin and held out the cookie as if she were going to drop it in the trash.

"I'm not saying that you're huge," Sierra said quickly. "You're nowhere near as big as I was."

Jennalyn grinned, dangling her cookie.

"You probably won't get much bigger," Christy said.

"Maybe a tiny bit," Sierra said bluntly.

"But not much," Tess offered.

"Eat the cookie!" Sierra spouted.

Friendly laughter circled the room.

"Are those your new favorites?" Christy asked. "I can make them again for your baby shower. Because, if you're right about an earlier due date, our next gathering will be a baby shower and not a book club."

I stood up. Not like a rocket but more like a blow-up snowman lawn decoration, wobbling from side to side.

"I'm convinced you're having a boy," Sierra said. "I know that's what Joel wants."

Reaching for my shoulder bag, I felt my throat tightening as I said calmly, "I need to get going. Thanks for everything. It was nice meeting all of you."

The replies came in a tumble of voices. Couldn't I stay a little longer? Did I want to be part of the book club? We hadn't shared contact information yet. Did I really have to go?

My heart was pounding so rapidly I didn't think I would be able to hold it together. Especially if everyone was going to sit there and talk about planning a baby shower.

Jennalyn followed me as a chorus of friendly "byes" and "see you laters" echoed in the background. She gave me a side hug at the door and smiled as if my exit weren't awkward at all. "I'm so glad you came."

Instead of answering by saying, "Me too," which would have been normal, I blinked quickly and said, "Thank you."

Jennalyn rested her hand on my arm, delaying my exit. "I should probably explain why everyone was making such a big deal about the baby shower."

"You don't have to."

"I want to. Because, you see, my husband, Joel, and I opted not to know if we're having a boy or a girl. Eden is a daddy's girl, for sure. But my husband comes from a big Italian family. When we announced we were expecting again, they put so much pressure on us that this one needed to be a boy. I just couldn't take it."

I placed my hand on top of hers, wishing I could make the words that were shouting in my head come through my lips in a generous act of solidarity. *Oh, Jennalyn. I understand! Big families, pressure, expectations. Yes, yes! I know exactly what that's like.*

But I just stood there, mute.

"So Joel and I decided everyone would just have to wait and find out at the same time, when the baby is born. Boy or girl, it shouldn't matter. Whenever he or she arrives, I'm hoping for nothing but love and acceptance all the way around."

My heart, like a spring-loaded mechanism, pushed my arms to encircle her in a spontaneous squishing and bumping hug.

"You get it, don't you?" Jennalyn asked softly when I pulled back.

I nodded, swallowing my surging emotions. The tears I had been holding back all night began to free-fall.

"We should go to coffee sometime." Jennalyn placed her words precisely, like a verbal welcome mat. I knew she was inviting me to tell her my story. To share with her why I felt so connected to her experience.

My head nodded, telling her yes, I agreed. We should go to coffee sometime.

But I knew I couldn't do that. I wouldn't. We moved to California to start a new story—not to gather sympathy or retell all the events that led us to this place in an effort to reboot our marriage and family.

"Good night, Emily." Jennalyn smiled calmly.

At that moment I was pretty sure I wouldn't see Jennalyn, Sierra, Tess, or Christy ever again.

Chapter 3

Trevor turned the volume down on the TV when I entered our apartment. "How was the party?" His handsome face looked hopeful. He had taken out his contacts and was wearing his glasses the way he usually did when he was almost ready to go to bed. Everything about his posture said he had been waiting up, anxious for the report.

"It was . . ."

Trevor moved his legs so I could sit on the other end of the couch. He kept his gaze fixed on me. I'm sure he could tell that I had been crying.

"You okay?" he asked.

I nodded. My emotions had leveled out while I took my time driving home. I took a mental step back and now could see that these women, as sweet and interesting as they were, just weren't a good match. It wasn't them. It was me. I needed to find some moms who had children closer to Audra's age. Moms who were done having babies. Women who lived in apartments, not luxurious two-story homes with gourmet kitchens and powder rooms that smelled like pecan pie.

"So? Tell me about it," Trevor said. "How many women were there?"

"Only four."

"Were they nice?"

"Very nice."

"Are you glad you went?"

I nodded, hoping my composed smile would convince him.

"Do you think you'll get together with any of them again?"

"No." I shook my head. "I don't think so."

He looked surprised as well as concerned.

"How was everything here tonight?" I was ready to move on to the next subject, but he wasn't.

"What about the gift exchange?" he asked. "How did that turn out?"

"It was different than I thought it would be, but it was good. Do you want to see what I got?"

"Sure." He shifted his position and seemed to look a little less concerned.

I showed him the apron, the peony card with the verse, and the roll-on fragrance. Holding up the bracelet, I said, "I think Audra might like this."

"I'm sure she will." Trevor read the verse on Jennalyn's card, put it down, and leaned back. The slightly concerned look had returned and was pulling at the corners of his mouth.

"I know that look," I said. "What happened while I was gone?"

"You can see right through me, can't you?"

"Yes." I smiled at this wonderful man who had stepped into my life when I was eighteen and changed everything. I loved him so much. "I have Trevor X-Ray Vision, you know. Tell me what happened."

Trevor adjusted his glasses. "My dad called."

"Oh?"

"He said there's going to be an opening at the Cadillac dealership in January."

"Manager position?"

Trevor nodded. "My dad said if we wanted to move back, he would hold the position for me." He paused, waiting for me to reply.

"What did you tell him?" I was trying hard to appear calm. Inwardly I could hear the circus animals pawing at their locks, threatening to break out of their cages for the second time that night and run wild through my emotions.

"I told him that you and I would talk about it, of course. And we would pray about it." He tilted his chin down, checking my expression over the top of his glasses. "Are you okay talking about this?"

I gave him an exasperated look. I didn't have a choice now that he had uncorked the touchy subject. Ignoring his question, I asked, "Did you remind your dad that our plan was to give the dealership here a full year before deciding if it was a success or failure?"

"Yes. I told him that three months isn't long enough for us to tell if this was a good decision for us."

"What did he say about that?"

"He said he knows how things have been at the dealership here and that it might be wise if we saw the writing on the wall and did what was best for our family."

"Best for which family? Ours? Or theirs?" My fingers had started rubbing the soft fabric of the ties on the apron still resting in my lap. I found a strange comfort in the soothing touch, which was a vivid contrast to what was happening inside me.

Trevor reached for the remote control, turned off the TV, and gave me his complete attention.

"I think he meant both families. With theirs, of course, it always includes what's good for the extended family business."

"What do you think is best for *us*?" I asked. "For our family."

He drew in a slow breath. "I don't know."

We sat together in silence for a moment before Trevor said, "Audra likes it here. She's made friends at school."

"Do you like it here?" I asked.

"It's . . . I don't know. I'd like it a lot more if we had our finances figured out."

This was a familiar, unresolved topic, and I really wished we weren't having this conversation right now.

"What about you?" Trevor asked. "Do you like it here? I know it's been hard to really connect with anyone or make friends. I thought your party tonight would have been a step in the right direction. I guess it didn't turn out that way."

My skin started to feel prickly. "I don't think we should make any decisions about moving based on my"—I swallowed—"lack of social skills."

Trevor looked alarmed by my comment. "Oh, sweetheart, come here. You aren't lackin' anything. Don't say stuff like that. We knew it would be hard to start fresh and try to fit in. You tried your best tonight. I'm sure you did. If those women weren't welcoming or didn't turn out to be your kind of friends, that's not your fault."

I pulled away from his attempt to draw me into a bear hug.

"Trevor, the women tonight were wonderful. It wasn't them. It was me. I'm not ready to be part of another circle of strong, confident, capable, wealthy women, like your family."

"Hey, c'mere." Trevor reached for me again. I moved closer this time and rested my head on his shoulder.

"Breathe," he murmured, stroking my hair. "It's okay."

"I'm okay," I said quickly. "Don't worry." I let myself relax against him. His affirming touch calmed me.

"Trevor, I think that just because I haven't adjusted yet, that's not a reason we should move back."

"I know."

"I think you, and me, and Audra too—we all need to have as many reasons to leave California as we had for coming."

"You're right," Trevor agreed. "That's wise. Why don't we give ourselves a couple of days to pray about it? We can work on a list of reasons to stay and reasons to leave and then sit down and talk again."

"I agree."

He leaned down and kissed the top of my head. "You ready to go to bed?"

Twenty minutes later we were curled up close in our queen-sized bed, like we usually do on the nights when we go to bed at the same time. Trevor fell asleep right away after murmuring a prayer for wisdom and asking God to help us to make the right decision. His breath ruffled over me, and his steady breathing played the lullaby my heart had memorized long ago. The cadence always brought me comfort.

I continued to pray. Silently, I asked God for strength and courage. That had been my ongoing request for several years now. Inch by inch, I felt that God had been changing me. But I wanted big changes to happen. I wanted to move past the lingering trauma that had been part of the catalyst prompting us to move across country.

I thought about how we had decided to set up our lives in a place where we knew no one because we thought that's what we were supposed to do.

Were we wrong?

The job that was waiting here for Trevor had promised so much. His own used-car lot. In his name, all profit going to him. No commissions or fluctuating income based on sales the way it had been in North Carolina.

So far, though, the "gold mine" his uncle had turned over to him had delivered very little.

In the darkness, I thought about the women I had met that night. They all seemed content. Stable. What did their husbands do for a living? Had any of them gone through really difficult times?

Then I thought about Trevor's tightly knit family. If we returned, I couldn't help but believe that everything would go back to the way it was. Trevor would go back to the way he was around them, always the baby in the family.

How would I do being around the Winslow women again? Would I be immersed in their continual flow of well-intended advice? Would Trevor and I find a way to speak up for ourselves this time?

I wiggled out from under Trevor's arm without disturbing him and rolled to my side of the bed. Pulling the comforter up to my chin, I knew I didn't want to move back to Asheville. I didn't want to be grafted back into that huge family tree and live under my in-laws' roof. We had moved away so we could figure out how to be our own little family.

We both needed to try harder to make it work here. Especially me. I could find a different job. One that paid more. I'd look for ways to save on expenses.

I thought of all the kind and familiar faces we had left behind in North Carolina. I could imagine our next video call with them and how we would undoubtedly receive lots of sympathetic expressions and strings of "bless your hearts" if we told them we were staying here.

The mental image caused my determined reasons for staying in California to line up like children on a field trip to a bread factory, eagerly sniffing the goodness in the air even before they entered. There was goodness for us inside this plan to stay and give it our all for a year. I just knew it.

The next morning we fell into our always-rushed routine. Trevor left with kisses and smiles for his "two best girls" as I hastily made Audra's lunch.

"Did you get this at your party?" Audra asked from her perch at the kitchen counter. She was holding Jennalyn's card.

"Yes, I did. Isn't it pretty? The bracelet there is for you, if you would like it."

Audra tried it on and twisted her slender arm in the air. "I don't think it goes with my outfit."

"Keep eating. We need to leave in five minutes." I left my fashion-conscious ten-year-old with a forkful of scrambled eggs in her hand and hurried to finish getting ready for work. I had to make the bed first. I knew my obsession was silly, but as a child I wasn't allowed to leave the house in the morning until the bed was made in a tidy manner. The routine, along with far too many similar housekeeping requirements, was deeply embedded in me.

I thought about my idiosyncrasies after I dropped my cheerful little blond cherub off at school. She had adjusted so well to our move. Why was I still struggling? Was it me? Was I too set in my ways? Did I need to change?

The word *change* resonated inside me like the radiating vibrations that can be felt ever so slightly after the ringing of a large bell.

We changed everything else about our lives. *What about me? Have I changed?*

I pulled into the parking lot at Peggy's Pies and drove to the employee parking area in the back. With the engine off but my hands still gripping the steering wheel, I wondered if *change* had been my banner word for the past year, the way the women had talked about at Jennalyn's. Everything had changed. Well, almost everything.

If change was the theme for this year, what would be my word for the year ahead?

I brushed off the thought and got out of the car. Something didn't feel right about asking God to give me a word, or anything else for that matter. I had asked God for so much over the past four years. Based on the way things were right now, it seemed clear that His answers to me had been no every time. He hadn't given me anything I had asked for. Why would He give me something as capricious as a word?

I decided that I was not artistic or poetic like the women I had met last night. I came from "practical stock," as my mother had often said. All that had been expected of me as a child was that I work hard, be tidy, and do as I was told.

Am I stuck in that mind-set?

I thought about how I had followed those rules and navigated my way out of the house when I was eighteen. That was the deadline set for me by my mother. Finish high school, find a job, and move out. Strangely, my brother had remained under her roof and received her full financial support until he was twenty-seven.

But that didn't matter. Not now.

The good thing was that Trevor had come into my life, and I found that the foundation of being diligent and reliable had served me well as a young wife. I kept a clean house, provided nutritious meals on a slim budget, and felt like Trevor and I were doing a good job as parents.

Those qualities didn't alter that I fell short in every way possible whenever I was measured against my four indomitable sisters-in-law. They had been my primary source of friendship and family for more than a decade. They defined me. My role with them was the same as the one I had fallen into last night. I was the quiet observer. Included, but still the extra person in the room.

"Emily?" My manager, Mr. Sanchez, had a desperate look on his perspiring face as he held the door open. The familiar scent of french fry oil and burned toast came rushing out, as it always did whenever the door was opened. "Would you be willing to pick up some more hours this month?" he asked.

"Possibly."

"I wrote down the hours and put the note on your locker. Could you tell me before you leave today?"

"I don't know. I need to coordinate my schedule with my family's."

I went into the back, pulled the sticky note from my locker and spun the dial on my combination lock. Once my purse and sweater were placed inside, I skimmed the long list of open dates on the note. It appeared that one of the other hostesses had quit or been fired. I wondered which one. Hostesses seemed to come and go every few weeks at Peggy's. My work ethic was probably what kept me showing up each weekday to walk for miles on the hard linoleum floor, clean a mound of sticky menus, and repeat the soup of the day a hundred times, all for minimum wage and zero respect or shared tips from the waitresses.

With the list in my pocket, I walked out to the chipped wooden podium by the front door that served as the hostess station. Mr. Sanchez was seating an elderly couple. I began my usual routine of cleaning the plastic cover of the seating chart. Then I sharpened the grease pencil, cleaned up the toothpick holder, and filled the bowl of wrapped peppermint candies.

Mr. Sanchez handed me some menus. No one else was waiting to be seated, so he lifted his eyebrows as if awaiting my answer on the additional hours.

"I won't be able to tell you until tomorrow. I do know that our daughter will be home from school over Christmas break."

Mr. Sanchez growled. It was what he did. Often. I had gotten used to it. He walked away, and I noticed that some of the foam snowflakes hanging over the front windows were looking pretty shabby. The snow-flakes, along with the other dusty and dated Christmas decorations that had gone up the day after Thanksgiving, were barely holding on.

I looked in the box of supplies I had brought to work my third week. The plastic bin fit on the lowest shelf of the hostess station. Fortunately, the scissors and tape were still there. During the usual slow-down hour be-tween 10:30 and 11:30, I would see if I could shore up some of the silly decorations.

It seemed out of place to have snowflakes and snowmen as window decorations in a locale where it never snowed.

Another elderly couple entered, arm in arm and both using canes. I smiled at the regulars. "Good morning, Mr. and Mrs. Thompson. Your favorite table is taken. Would you like to wait or go to your second-favorite table?"

Mr. Thompson motioned with his chin jerking up and down, as if he were too out of breath to talk and they'd better keep moving because, if they stopped to sit on the waiting bench now, it would be all over. I took slow steps and led them to their second-favorite table near the front window. Pulling out Mrs. Thompson's chair first, I kept an eye on Mr. Thompson to make sure he managed his chair all right with the help of his cane.

Once they were settled, with their cutlery positioned where they liked it and the menus opened for them, Mrs. Thompson placed her cool hand on mine. "You are a gem, Emily."

I gave her a side squeeze hug the way I always did. She patted the top of my hand as she always did. Mr. Thompson gave me an appreciative grin. The day felt a little brighter, as it always did once I had had my pat from Mrs. Thompson and my smile from her supportive husband.

Peggy's Pies was located next to Ivy Glen, a large retirement home that specialized in independent living. The "escapees," as one of the waitresses affectionately called them, found Peggy's Pies to be an easy morning walk away. It had become the place for them to obtain their second cup of morning coffee. Meals were provided for residents at Ivy Glen, but we were told they rarely included the items found on the menu at Peggy's Pies. Items such as corn chowder, triple chocolate milkshakes, and bagels with cream cheese and apple butter.

I seated the next guests, three ladies all wearing Christmas sweaters and chattering merrily. As I passed the Thompsons' table, Mrs. Thompson reached out her hand to stop me. "You didn't tell us the soup, dear."

"It's split pea today, Mrs. Thompson."

She bobbed her head slowly as if contemplating the soup. I knew she wouldn't order it. They never ordered soup. No one did at eight o'clock in the morning. But she always wanted to know what it was that day.

The Thompsons always ordered the same thing: two cups of tea, very hot with an extra tea bag each, and a bowl of individual creamers. They always asked if the waitress might bring a basket of "table biscuits," as Mrs. Thompson called the packets of saltines that came with soup orders.

We had a new waitress last week. She was assigned the Thompsons' usual table so I tried to tip her off about their order. The tea water had to be boiling hot, or they would insist on a fresh pot. They used every one of the creamers, so it was good to make sure the bowl was filled. They weren't to be charged for the crackers because they rarely ate any of them. Mrs. Thompson seemed to view the saltines as a necessary part of the table accoutrements, along with the salt, pepper, and sugar packets.

I explained to the waitress how they would spend one hour and twenty minutes enjoying their tea while looking out the window and rarely saying a word to each other. They always paid by leaving the exact cash on the table and including a quarter as their tip.

I watched the Thompsons place their order with one of the longtime waitresses that morning and wondered if Trevor and I might one day become like them, sipping tea by the window.

The question was, would we be looking out a window in California or in North Carolina?

Throughout the day, I thought about how sure I had felt last night that we needed to stay in California. When my shift ended, I was still thinking about it.

As I waited in the carpool line to pick up Audra from school, a sweet memory settled on me. It was the moment that changed everything for us six months ago. Trevor and I were cuddled up in bed. He was wrapping a lock of my fine hair around his finger.

"There's so much more to you," Trevor had said.

"More what?" I remembered not being sure I wanted to know his answer if he was alluding to weight gain or the complicated emotional journey I had been on.

Trevor said nothing about weight or emotions. He told me I was strong and intuitive, graceful and wise. He said I was a locked treasure chest of undiscovered gems and that one day I would find the key to unlock that chest. When I did, all the wealth that had been hidden inside me would be given a chance to shine.

The unrehearsed sonnet tumbled from his heart and poured over me. He didn't usually say deep and poetic things. I felt Trevor's words settle on me in an empowering way. They nested in my hair like a crown and dangled from my ears like diamonds. I felt adorned. I also felt safe. He made me believe I had value and was capable of more than I had ever let myself dare to believe. Without trying to, he made me want a new beginning.

That was the night I told Trevor, "Okay."

I remembered the way he had drawn back, studying my expression in the dim light.

"Are you saying yes?" Trevor asked.

"Yes."

That was all I needed to say. He knew I was finally agreeing to his idea, his plan that had been brewing for many months. Trevor believed that moving away from his family would be a good thing for us. But every time he had brought it up, I had said no. My list of reasons was logical and held weight with him. The risks were too great.

So, for many long weeks, Trevor was the one saying okay to me. He waited patiently until I at last, unexpectedly, caught the vision and said yes.

Now here we were, three months into the risky move and both a little terrified. We had little money. No friends. No mystical key that opened a treasure chest of glimmering potential for either of us.

Maybe we should grab the lifeline my father-in-law is throwing us. Maybe we should leave now and go back before we embarrass ourselves even more.

Chapter 4

That evening when Trevor came home, he stepped into the kitchen and gave me a very nice kiss. I was wearing my new apron and felt cute.

"You must have had a good day," I said cheerfully. "Did you sell a lot of cars?"

"No, not today. Slow day. How was your day?"

My husband is good looking. I'm not the only one who thinks that. He has always had more of a blond surfer boy look to him than a North Carolina mountain boy look. His pale gray eyes searched mine as I told him about Mr. Sanchez asking me to work more hours this month.

"How many hours?"

I pulled the list from my pocket and watched his expression as he glanced at the calendar on the refrigerator and then back at the list. "What did you tell him?"

"That I would talk with you about it. I was excited because I know we could use the money."

"I don't want you overdoing it, though. And what about when Audra is home over Christmas break?"

Audra piped up from her bedroom. "What are you saying about me?"

Trevor shook his head. Our small apartment drove him crazy. The home we had owned for six years in Asheville was so spacious that if you were upstairs, you couldn't hear a thing going on downstairs. That is, unless you were in the master bedroom and the TV in the room directly below was turned up especially loud. We lived quite differently in that house, each of us burrowed away in our own enclave.

Audra joined us in the kitchen and planted herself on the barstool. "What about Christmas break? Are we going somewhere?"

She looked so much like her dad. Fair-skinned, blond hair, light blue-gray eyes, and the same sort of smirky expression with creases in both corners of her lips when she knew she was being adorable.

"I'm trying to decide if I should take on more hours at work this month."

She looked disappointed at the news. "Well, if you do, and you have to send me someplace, I'll go to one of my friends' houses while you're working. I don't mind."

"Audra, I don't think you'll need to—"

Trevor stopped me. "Which friend's house would you like to go to?"

"Moira. She has a pool and a hot tub. All the girls in my class go to her house."

"Moira? I don't think I've heard you talk about her before," Trevor said.

"She's fancy."

Trevor and I exchanged knowing grins. "Fancy" was what Audra's friends in Asheville had called her and all the Winslow family because of the obvious wealth as well as the proper way things were done. Audra knew "fancy" girls when she met them.

"Audra, do you miss North Carolina?" Trevor asked.

"No." She paused. "Well, yes. But no. I like it here. I miss all my cousins and Gramma and Grampa. I wish they could come here for Christmas. They would have to stay in a hotel, but if Hailey wanted to stay with us, she could sleep in my bed, and I would sleep on the floor."

Audra continued creating her imaginary Christmas Day with all the mighty Winslows coming to California. Her affection for the cousins she had grown up with was endearing. When she was younger, she and Hailey would continually make up stories about kangaroos and special trees that grew pear-flavored popsicles in the winter and hot chili peppers in the summer. Hailey would spin the tale; Audra would illustrate. I kept every single picture.

"So, Audra," Trevor said slowly. "What if we could go back to Asheville in time for Christmas?"

I stopped what I was doing. My back was turned to both of them, and I didn't turn around.

Trevor, what are you doing? Don't ask her that.

"Do you mean to visit or to live there again?"

Trevor hesitated. I gave him a side glance that he chose to ignore.

"Either. Both. I'm curious. That's all."

I was so mad at him. This was not the way for us to make a decision about moving back to North Carolina! Especially when we had agreed to wait and pray and then talk about it in a few days. Baiting our impressionable daughter to tip the decision scales was not okay.

"I would like to have Christmas here," Audra said. "And also have Christmas there! If we had a time machine, we could do that. Or if we had our own private jet. We could have Christmas Eve service at our old church with candles and the singing. I could sleep under the tree by the fire with Hailey at Gramma's, but then I would wake up here on Christmas morning under our tree, and we would open presents and all go to the beach."

Our daughter's imagination seemed to provide a buffer that kept Trevor's questioning from becoming traumatic.

"Dinner's ready." I tried to sound as if my emotions hadn't just stumbled off a roller coaster.

As Audra was talking, Trevor had pulled out plates and poured glasses of water for us from the filtered pitcher in the refrigerator. He seemed as calm as ever, moving the subject on to ask Audra about school that day.

We fell into our dinnertime routine, dishing up cafeteria-style from the kitchen counter and then taking our usual spots on the couch so we could watch TV as we ate. I calmed down.

When we first moved into our apartment, we took our plates outside to the round patio table. We all seemed to like the way we had grown closer as a family during our intimate mealtimes. I was still enjoying the change from setting the table for a dozen or more places each evening at Trevor's parents' home. His family would be stunned to know how we ate now.

That night we watched another episode in a series on outer space that Audra had gotten into. The universe's vastness astounded all three of us, but Audra seemed especially curious about the stars and planets. She wanted to know how far away heaven was, and the discussion turned to an intricately spiritual one with Trevor looking up verses in his Bible and me checking out the cross-references on my phone.

It turned out to be a good night. A fun, spontaneous family night full of learning new things and being overwhelmed by the magnitude of the galaxy and the vastness of God's power. I found it comforting to think of all the things that could go wrong but hadn't. A giant rogue meteor had not entered Earth's atmosphere and returned us to the Ice Age.

Once Audra was in bed, at the risk of initiating a relational ice age between Trevor and me, I confronted him in a low voice. "Why did you bait

Audra? I thought we were going to wait before talking with each other about our decision to move, let alone mentioning the possibility to her."

He looked surprised that I was upset. "I wasn't baiting her. I wanted her opinion."

"Why? Is it because you've already formed your decision?"

"No, not really."

"Then why did you bring it up with her?"

Trevor rubbed the back of his neck. "Look," he said, trying to appear upbeat. "My dad called again today. He said he went ahead and slotted me for the manager position at the Cadillac dealership. If we move right away, I'll be able to pick up all the year-end bonuses. You know what that would mean for us. Our financial situation would change immediately."

I didn't blink.

"My brother said he would cover our flight. He said he has enough air miles, and everyone there wants us to come home for Christmas."

I felt my shoulders slump and my torso pull in as if I had been sucker punched. "What did you tell your dad and your brother and everyone else?"

I realized then that the reason he had come home looking so happy was because of the family phone call, not because he had sold a car that day.

"I told them you and I were still thinking and praying about it."

"Are we?"

He looked surprised again at my combative tone. "Yes. We are. I'm gathering information. That's all. From my dad, my brother, Audra." He paused. "What about you? What do you think?"

"I'm still praying about it."

Trevor nodded. "Okay. So am I. We shouldn't feel pressured or rushed to decide."

"No, we shouldn't."

I went to bed alone that night. Trevor wanted to watch a movie he had recorded, so I curled up with my pillow and squeezed my eyes shut, contemplating the delicate balance of the cosmos. I wanted to believe in all the things we had talked about with Audra, like how God cares for us, protecting and providing in ways we'll never know. I wanted to believe that a big meteor of another catastrophic life change had burned up before entering the atmosphere of our marriage.

Perhaps that more expansive view of the world gave me the courage to tell Mr. Sanchez the next morning that if he wanted me to work more hours, he would have to pay me more.

"You're asking for a raise?"

"Yes." I handed him the list with the dates circled when I was willing to work. The dates I didn't want to work were crossed off. He looked it over and growled.

"I'm not saying yet that I can commit to all these dates. But if I do, I would need to know that you've raised my hourly wage."

Before I left work that day, we had reached a compromise. I had agreed to one of the crossed off dates, and he had promised an hourly rate increase. He needed my final answer by noon the next day, and I promised him I would have it to him by then.

I felt victorious. It reminded me of something Trevor's mom used to quote whenever one of her daughters or granddaughters did something noteworthy. It was a verse she liked from Proverbs 31:18, "She senses that her gain is good."

I felt that day as if my gain had been good. Certainly Trevor would agree. Would it be enough to tip the decision scales toward our staying? I didn't know. But at least I could show Trevor that I could do something more to contribute financially.

When I picked up Audra from school, she chattered like a bird on a sunny morning. Her teacher had selected her to pass out the art supplies that day. For her, that was the highest possible honor. She told me how her friends had taught her a silly dance move at recess, and she would show it to me when we got home. Best of all, the spelling test had been postponed till Monday. Audra's happiness over the little things in her day made me smile.

"Your gain is good," I told her.

She leaned back and looked out the passenger window. "My life is good!" Turning to me, she added, "I hope we don't have to move."

I nodded but didn't share any of my thoughts with her. I refused to use Audra to create a wedge between Trevor and me.

We stopped at the grocery store, and I let Audra pick one item that wasn't on my stringent list. She chose her favorite ice cream and was still chattering about it merrily when we arrived home. She and I were carrying the bags down the long walkway that led to our apartment when I heard someone call out my name.

I turned to see Christy standing in front of the manager's apartment holding a little boy. "Emily, I thought that was you. Do you live here?"

My embarrassment probably showed on my face as I nodded. I felt like I was admitting to the whole world that I wasn't fancy anymore. I didn't fit with Jennalyn and her sweet but undoubtedly upscale friends. And now my secret was out.

Christy came toward me, introducing her son, Cole, who wiggled out of her arms and went up to Audra as if he already knew her. He stood in front of her, looking up with the cutest expression.

"Hi!" Audra put down her shopping bag and picked him up. "I'm Audra."

"We all loved your elf-cap cookies," Christy said. "I'm going to make some with my kids for Christmas."

Audra beamed.

"I'm surprised that I haven't run into you here sooner," Christy said. "My parents manage this apartment complex."

"Your dad is Mr. Miller?" I asked.

Christy nodded.

"I had no idea. He's been a huge help to us. We had problems with our garbage disposal when we first moved in, and he had it fixed the same day. He also took care of everything when our refrigerator broke and we had to get it replaced."

"Sounds like my dad. He can fix anything." Christy's smile made it clear that she was a proud daughter. "Which unit are you in?"

"The one at the end. I think it's the smallest unit. But it has a nice patio in the back." I felt less intimidated and decided I felt that way because of Christy. She wasn't ashamed that her parents lived here. Why should I be?

"We were so grateful when my dad took this position," Christy said. "These apartments are really nice. I know they're older, but the bedrooms are large compared to most apartments, especially in this area."

Christy motioned to a large hibiscus bush we were standing beside. "My dad has thrown himself into the landscaping, as you may have noticed."

"I have noticed. He's turned this walkway into a garden. It feels so quiet and calm when we come home. I guess I didn't realize that it wasn't always this way."

"It wasn't terrible when my parents moved in. But it was nothing like this."

The two grocery bags I was holding were starting to feel heavy. I knew the polite thing would be to invite Christy to come inside and offer her something to drink. To my relief, though, she put her arms out for Cole and said she needed to be on her way.

"My husband teaches a Bible study for teens every Friday night. I need to rush home because I said I would make cookies for them tonight. I used to do it all the time before we had two kids." She made a cute scrunched-up-nose face. "I'm not as quick as I used to be when it comes to baking cookies for fifty starving high schoolers. Plus, I have to pick up my daughter from my aunt's house, so I better scoot."

"I won't keep you. Good to see you."

"You too. I'm really glad you came the other night. I look forward to getting together again in January." Christy balanced Cole on her hip and told him to wave as she picked up the pace and hurried to the parking area.

"What's in January?" Audra asked as I unlocked our front door.

I avoided answering and asked her to open the sliding door to let some fresh air in. I was still set on my decision not to insert myself into the tight-knit group. Running into Christy hadn't changed that.

As I unpacked the groceries, I thought I might try connecting with one of Audra's friends' moms. Or maybe I could spend some time with just Christy, if she wanted to get together sometime. That is, if Trevor and I agreed we were sticking it out in Costa Mesa.

My phone buzzed. It was a text from Jennalyn saying I had left my cookie plate at her house. She asked for my address, saying she was running errands and would be glad to drop it off.

I stood frozen in the kitchen for a few moments, contemplating my reply. Why was it such a big deal not to let anyone come into my home? I surveyed our garage-sale sofa, thrift-store coffee table, and plain, off-white walls that held only two pictures, both of our family. I had put no effort into turning this place into a home.

Why was that? Did I believe from the beginning this was only going to be temporary? Did I ever think we would stay for a whole year?

I put on my apron and started to make dinner. We had been hit with a lot of harsh realities when we moved to Southern California. Trevor had stepped into a mess at the used-car company on Beach Boulevard in Huntington Beach. His uncle had offered to turn the business over to him for a dollar when he found out Trevor was secretly thinking about extracting himself from the Winslow dealership empire. He told Trevor that if he came to California, he could achieve on his own what Trevor's father had achieved long ago in Asheville.

That was appealing bait to my husband because the Winslow family business in North Carolina encompassed five dealerships. Trevor's decade of experience there had been in selling trucks, not in managing a used-car lot. To his credit, my smart husband dove in. He cleaned up the books, made necessary staff changes, and improved the overall appearance of the lot with new signs and a regular supply of colorful helium balloons on all the cars, which had been Audra's idea.

Trevor was far from turning the tide, though. Everyone in his family, sitting in their leather massage office chairs back in Asheville, apparently knew it.

Was I being unrealistic in thinking we should stay here? Was it even possible? How bad were things at the dealership? What if Trevor wasn't telling me everything?

Feelings of hopelessness fell on me. I recognized the dark, fearful emotions as being the same ones that had capsized me a year and a half ago. They began to press in on me, squeezing the breath from my chest.

No. No. Don't start thinking those things. Breathe. Breathe.

"Mom?"

I blinked and tried to focus on Audra as she scooted back into the kitchen.

"Mom, when are we going to get our Christmas tree? Can we go tomorrow?"

"Maybe."

"Can Daddy take the day off tomorrow?"

"It's Saturday. That's a busy day for him." I was having a hard time catching my breath.

Audra made one of her faces that communicated her doubt. "I thought it was never busy for him. Not like at Grampa's car place. Whenever I go to work with Daddy, nobody comes in."

I took slow breaths in through my nose, telling myself nothing was wrong. Everything would be okay.

"Mom, could you and I go now and get a tree if Daddy can't do it? I saw a tree place by the gas station. You and I could have it all set up before Daddy even gets home tonight. That would be fun, wouldn't it?"

Audra came closer and reached for my hand. I read in her eyes a streak of fear. She must have recognized my frozen posture and was afraid that I was about to have another panic attack.

I rolled my shoulders back, stood up straight, and put a smile on my lips that had begun to feel tingly. I hated that my daughter knew the signs.

"What do you think, Mom?" Her voice was animated, and she seemed intent on distracting me. "Could we get a tree? That would be fun, wouldn't it? We don't have to buy a big one or an expensive one. They could tie it to the roof of the car for us."

She waited for an answer while I worked hard to shift mental gears. She seemed to have reverted to a less confident version of herself.

"Please?" Audra squeezed my hand again.

Gazing down into my daughter's clear, worried eyes, I saw hope in its truest and purest form. Childlike hope. She was my daughter. My only child. It was Christmastime. I had it within my power to grant her wish. To give her a sweet memory. To start new memories and a new tradition for us in California, regardless of how long we stayed.

My smile came slowly. I didn't take my eyes off her sweet face.

"Let's do it," I said with steady words.

"Really?" Her expression lit up. "Really, really? Truly, truly?"

"Yes. Come on. Let's go buy a Christmas tree."

Audra squealed and twirled in a circle. It was her signature happy dance that first emerged when she was a toddler. I was glad she hadn't grown out of it.

"Can we tell Daddy?"

"I thought you wanted to surprise him."

"I think we should tell him, and maybe he wants to help us pick it out. Or if he can't, at least he knows we didn't leave him out on purpose."

I reached for my phone and saw that Jennalyn's message about my plate was still on my screen. I quickly typed, **Could I come pick it up tomorrow?**

Then I sent Trevor a text, explaining our spur-of-the-moment plan as best I could. He came back right away with, **I'll meet you there.**

Audra did another happy dance. "Can we have our cocoa and cookies tonight after the tree is decorated? Just you and me? With the lights off and everything?"

"Absolutely." I was thrilled that she remembered. I reached for my purse, feeling steady. Everything was fine.

Audra slipped her hand into mine as we headed down the lovely garden walkway past all the other single-story apartments. I wondered how many more times she would want to hold my hand like this. She was maturing quickly in other ways. I needed to make this Christmas one to remember.

Chapter 5

When Trevor left for work on Saturday morning, he took Audra with him for the day. She had loved every moment of our Friday afternoon tree hunt at the nearby gas-station lot.

So did I.

We had pizza for dinner while we decorated the slender tree to the sounds of all our favorite Christmas carols. Trevor sang out on "Joy to the World" at the top of his lungs. Audra and I joined in, trying to match his verve. He looked happy, and that chin-up look of his filled something in me that had been running low. I think it was my supply of hope. Hope that we would have enough money by the end of the month. Hope that we were doing what was best for Audra and for us. Hope that we could stay in California. I liked just being us and starting our own traditions.

Audra and I followed up with the promised cuddle time on the sofa with our cocoa and shortbread cookies while Trevor went to bed early for the first time in a long time. We squinted our eyes until they were only slivers. That way we could watch the tiny white lights turn into falling snowflakes or dancing angels. We talked about stars and the first Christmas. At Audra's request I looked up the verses in Luke about how the angels sang.

"Tomorrow I'm going to make cutout angels," she said when I tucked her into bed. "Lots and lots of angels."

I didn't want to deny her the project, but the truth was, over the past few weeks, Audra's creative craft skills had already provided our apartment with all the homemade decorations we needed. The next morning she must have realized we had few places left to affix a row of singing angels.

Undaunted, Audra convinced her pushover father that his office was in need of her handmade angels, snowflakes, red and green paper chains, and, of course, a Christmas tree. She already had calculated how he could buy the tree on the way to work and where it would go in front of the big window. She looked so happy when she skipped out the door with her bin of art supplies.

Trevor gave me a look before he left. I thought it was because we had come to what I thought was a mutual decision that morning about my taking on additional hours at work. He was probably realizing that Audra would accompany him at work lots more in the weeks ahead.

Though maybe the look was because he thought I was the one trying to tip the balance in favor of a decision to stick it out here. Why else would I be agreeing to things that would make Christmas so memorable in our home and at his office?

What he didn't realize was that going to work with him and decorating his office were all Audra's idea. This was her joy. Certainly he would see that today when she started cutting out her paper angels and snowflakes at his desk. Trevor would understand why I always supported Audra's creativity; it gave her a sense of well-being. Especially after all the disruption we had put her through this year.

I had the morning to myself, so I made a cup of coffee and sat on the couch, admiring the pretty tree. When we had moved, I had packed only the ornaments that had sentimental value. They all fit in a medium-sized plastic bin along with my prized nativity set that my grandmother gave me when I was seven. She said it had been a gift to her when she was young and that it came from Italy. I believed her because the word *Italia* was stamped on the bottom of each of the figurines. Years later, my mother said it wasn't true.

"Your grandmother bought that at a yard sale." My mother's voice can carry such an edge when she is determined to make a point. "She was always putting on airs. You know that she came from nothing, like the rest of us. I don't know why she wanted you to believe her life was more important or more interesting than it really was."

Trevor once said that "withholding approval" was my mother's superpower.

"If she was a Marvel comic character, she would assault people on the street by telling them everything they were doing wrong and then disappear into the crowd," he said.

I disagreed with him when we were first married. I told him he was being disrespectful. My deep-rooted instinct was to defend my mother and explain to him again how difficult her life had been after my dad passed away and how she had to raise my brother and me on food stamps.

Trevor liked to point out how well off my mom was now and that she had no reason to always try to level any kind of happiness whenever it looked like it might pop up. Because she still was choosing to withhold approval, Trevor chose to limit our relationship with her as a family. He didn't like the way my mother corrected Audra or how critical she was of me.

As for what my mother thought of Trevor, it goes without saying. That he and I married when I was barely twenty and lived in his parents' huge house the first two years did and will always evoke a disapproving shake of her head. I avoided telling her that we had moved back in with his parents after our finances were dismantled. That was the beginning of the great distancing between my mother and me. I had relegated her to a need-to-know status, and I knew she resented it. Trevor said it was okay to set boundaries and self-protect.

I felt like a little girl who still wanted a mother. A nurturing, involved, kind, and loving mother who wanted to see me flourish.

Staring at the Christmas tree, my vision blurred. My rising tears kept the lights from turning into dancing angels or fluttering snowflakes. Instead, the dots of once-bright hope looked like they were melting into the branches. I wondered if I had swung too far the other way once I became a mother. Was I too affirming and quick to indulge Audra's whims? My daughter was free to create and dream in ways I never had been encouraged to do as a child.

I blinked until the tree came back into focus. My phone was buzzing on the counter. I picked up the cell phone and saw that I had missed a call from Jennalyn while I was pondering motherhood. Her voice mail said she was heading out to do some Christmas shopping because her mother-in-law had come by and taken Eden for the day. Jennalyn said she would leave my cookie plate in a bag by the front door in case I could pick it up.

I texted back with a simple, **Okay. Thanks.** It would be easy to swing by her house and then do a little Christmas shopping of my own for Audra and Trevor. My new schedule had me working every Saturday till the end of December, so this was my best chance to try to find nice gifts for the two people who mattered most to me.

I tidied up the apartment, made sure all the doors and windows were locked, and sent a text to Trevor to let him know that I was going to run errands.

I was just about to leave when I heard a knock on the door. Peeking through the spyhole, I saw that it was Mrs. Miller, Christy's mom.

I opened the door but kept the screen closed. "Good morning."

"I'm sorry to bother you, Emily. My husband wanted me to ask if you would mind if he planted some cuttings along your back fence."

I didn't know Mrs. Miller's first name, but now that I knew Christy, I almost felt as if I should know it because then I'd call her "Miss" and add whatever her first name was. That's how Trevor had been raised to speak to family, friends, and neighbors. The familiarity couched in politeness was something I liked.

"I'm sure it's fine," I said.

"He likes to have me ask the tenants first." Mrs. Miller's hair was salt-and-pepper gray and never seemed to be arranged in a particular style. It covered her ears and framed her face with natural waves that appeared to all be going in different directions. She was shorter and much rounder than Christy. The similarity I now saw between them was in their nose and lips. They had the same sort of quiet smile.

"I met your daughter," I said.

"Oh?"

"Christy," I said, not sure how many daughters she had. "I met her at a party at Jennalyn's."

"I'm so glad you did." Peering past me into the apartment, she smiled. "And I see you have your tree up. How nice."

"Yes. Audra talked us into buying one last night."

"It's just the right size, isn't it?"

I felt rude not opening the screen door, so I invited her to step inside to have a better view.

"It's lovely." Mrs. Miller came closer and admired several of my favorite ornaments and a few of Audra's handmade snowflakes. "Your tree reminds me of the ones we used to cut from the woods when our children were little. Christy may have told you that we lived on a farm."

"No. But I remember her saying she had a grandmother from the Midwest who inspired her apron making."

"That was my mother." She smiled and leaned in to take a closer look at an angel ornament made of feathers.

"How long ago did you move to California?" I asked.

"Quite some time ago. Christy was in high school. Our son was about your daughter's age."

"Was it a big adjustment for them?"

"Yes and no." She seemed to be trying to remember.

The back-and-forth meter of our conversation felt offbeat, as it often can when two introverts are trying to make an everyday sort of exchange sound comfortable and normal.

"What prompted you to move here?" I wasn't sure why the question popped out of my mouth, except that I was curious.

"My sister and her husband live here. In Newport Beach." Mrs. Miller paused as if her answer to me wasn't exactly the reason for their move but she was trying to decide how much she should say.

Turning to me with an expression of uncomplicated honesty, she said, "We had financial difficulties for quite a few years when we were on the farm. Our solution was borrowing against the mortgage. The expenses got ahead of us. In the end, we had no choice but to sell everything."

I stood still, eyes wide and unblinking. Her explanation for their move mirrored the reason for our move. *We had to sell everything* were words I hadn't yet spoken aloud because of the weight of shame I felt. Mrs. Miller seemed free from such a weight.

I heard my wavering voice confess, "That's what happened to us too."

Her expression softened. "It's a painful blow, isn't it?"

I nodded. Never did I expect I would meet anyone in this corner of the world who could understand what Trevor and I had gone through. Mrs. Miller not only understood, but she also was on the other side of it all.

"Trevor and I got in over our heads with medical bills." I knew I didn't have to explain the details to her. Just saying the words made me feel as if something big was breaking up inside. I wanted the truth to keep smashing the stigma so that the bits would get smaller and float away.

I leaned against the side of the couch, feeling a tremor of nerves, and opened up even further. "The medical expenses were for in vitro treatments."

At first she seemed unfamiliar with what I was saying. Then her eyebrows rose behind her glasses and she concluded, "Was that in order to get pregnant with your daughter?"

"No, actually, we wanted another baby. We still do. Audra came easily. Unplanned. She was born three days before our one-year wedding anniversary. We thought it would be just as easy the second time. But . . ." I gave a little shrug since the conclusion of my last sentence was obvious. I didn't want to say anything else. I'd probably said too much. I couldn't believe the way it had all gushed out.

What I appreciated most about our halting yet surprisingly easy conversation was that she didn't reply with any of the "bless your heart" comments that had become so familiar to me over the years from all the well-meaning moms, grandmas, and aunts in my life. She didn't make a single comment about how I was still young enough to have lots of babies or that Trevor and I should simply relax and it would happen naturally.

Mrs. Miller looked into my eyes but didn't say anything. Her quietness on the topic was comforting.

I can't explain why, but I decided to keep talking. Not because the silence needed to be filled, but because I felt free to speak about the deep pain.

I didn't feel defensive with Christy's mom, nor did I feel embarrassed. I felt at home. Mrs. Miller had stepped into my corner of the world. I could say whatever I wanted. I wanted to get it out.

"The doctors called it secondary infertility. I didn't even know such a thing existed. We tried everything. The expenses kept adding up."

She nodded her understanding.

"The treatments cost tens of thousands of dollars. Everyone in Trevor's family wanted to help, but my husband can't stand to be in debt to anyone for anything."

"You have a fine husband. Trevor is always the first tenant to drop off the rent check at the first of the month." Mrs. Miller added, "Norman and I appreciate that."

"That's how my husband is. And that's why Trevor couldn't take the pressure he felt from the rising debt. I was feeling anxious all the time. It wasn't good for either of us. Then we received a final report that our numbers were too low and that, basically, nothing was left for us to try. It just wasn't going to happen."

I took a deep breath, wondering how much more I wanted to say. I tried a few more sentences.

"We tried to accept it and talk about other options, but by then we had no equity left in our house. We already had borrowed more than we ever wanted to from my in-laws. They kept saying it would all be worth it when the baby came. Hopefully, a boy baby, they said. But that didn't happen. I didn't realize how much the long process had been affecting me but then . . ."

I stopped. I didn't want to say any more. Mrs. Miller didn't need to know any additional details. I simply said, "It was too much for all of us. So when Trevor's uncle offered him a business opportunity here, we sold everything and moved across country."

"Do you have family in the area?"

"No. Trevor had an uncle close by. But he moved after we arrived."

Mrs. Miller reached for my hand. She gave it a warm squeeze and let go.

I was glad she pulled away with the same swiftness as when she had reached out with her expression of sympathy. If she had wanted to hold on to my hand or say a lot of things about how I needed to be strong or trust God more or if she had started quoting any of the verses I had heard so many times about how all things work together for good or how God has plans to prosper me or that I should learn to be content with what I have, I would have dearly regretted sharing with her all that I did.

As it was, I had no regrets. When she pulled away, I could still feel the warmth from her brief touch. Her gesture was a bit of heartfelt cheer from one woman who had survived starting over to another one who was in the midst of the restoration process.

Mrs. Miller said she needed to be on her way but that her door was always open if I wanted to stop by. I appreciated that. We were standing at the screen door when she added, "It's the little, familiar things that help in times of transition, isn't it? Like putting your Christmas tree up so you can enjoy it."

I nodded. Last night had been one of the best evenings the three of us had experienced since we had moved. The happy feelings still encircled us that morning when we stood together and admired our handiwork in the daylight.

"When our family first moved from Wisconsin," Mrs. Miller said, "we lived in a small rental house in Escondido. That's in north San Diego County. I don't know how well you know the area."

"Not well at all."

"Well, I remember feeling quite low when we first saw the house. My dreams of our children being raised on a farm were gone. We didn't know anyone in Escondido. I had to find a job for the first time in my life. Everything had changed."

I knew exactly what she was talking about. I wanted to reach over and give her hand a quick squeeze, but I didn't.

"The house had a front porch. Not a big one. But it had a porch, which isn't common in this area. A plant had grown in an arch over the steps up to the front door. I didn't know what the plant was when we moved in, and I thought it was dead. I had never seen anything like it in Wisconsin. But do you know, my husband brought it back to health."

She smiled. "It was night-blooming jasmine, and it brought me so much happiness all the years we lived there. The fragrance became my favorite. I was glad when it blossomed every spring. You could smell the sweetness each time the front door was opened."

"Is that the plant with the tiny white flowers?"

She nodded.

"Isn't that the big bushy plant that grows over the entry into this apartment complex?"

"Yes, it is."

"I always wondered what that was. It's so fragrant. When we moved here at the end of August, it was full of blooms."

"Well, when we moved into this apartment complex a few years ago, Norman brought cuttings from the plant at our home in Escondido. He knew how much I liked opening the door and smelling the jasmine."

"That is so sweet. I mean, the jasmine is sweet, but it's so sweet that your husband did that. And now everyone else who lives here gets to enjoy it too."

Mrs. Miller looked down as if she was unsure of what she wanted to say next. Christy definitely had inherited traces of her mother's shy mannerisms.

"Emily"—she looked up at me—"you and Trevor brought a lot with you to California."

I motioned behind me at our sparsely adorned apartment. "Actually, we hardly brought anything. We acquired all the furniture here."

"I'm not talking about furniture. I mean you brought a lot in here." She patted her heart.

I felt a lump swelling in my throat.

"Plant what you love, Emily. Plant the sweet things in your new life here. They will grow." She studied my response, as if she were uncertain whether she had said too much.

I felt like I might cry. She didn't know that Trevor and I were sitting on a teeter-totter of indecision about whether we would cancel our one-year lease and return to the safety net that waited for us on the East Coast.

As she walked away, I found my voice and called after her, "Thank you, Mrs. Miller!"

She turned, offering a wave and a gentle smile.

Instead of reaching for my purse and dashing out to my car, I closed the door and returned to the couch. For at least twenty minutes I sat there, staring at the Christmas tree. The lights seemed to be twinkling a little brighter. Fluttering angels and floating snowflakes.

Plant the sweet things.

I wasn't sure what those sweet things were. Spending time with Trevor and Audra came to mind. I loved being with them. I liked my job. I didn't love it. But I liked feeling that some of the daily guests were happy to see me and that my welcoming smile was a bright spot in their day. I liked our apartment more and more. It was cozy, and even though we couldn't have a private conversation and Trevor hated that part, I liked the way the three of us had grown so much closer as a family in our smaller living space.

I stood and unplugged the Christmas tree lights. It seemed pointless to think about planting anything. Not while the question as to whether we should return to North Carolina still hung over us. And especially not when my gut told me that Trevor was leaning toward returning.

For now, for today, I could buy Christmas gifts for my husband and daughter, and that was how I wanted to spend the rest of the morning. Regardless of where we were on Christmas Day, this was my chance to find something meaningful for the two of them, and I was determined to seize the moment.

Chapter 6

The sky had clouded over, and the air felt much cooler than usual when I stepped outside. As I walked past one of the apartments, I could hear muffled Christmas music and the words, "It's beginning to look a lot like Christmas."

Yes, it is.

Passing under the arched trellis of the wintering jasmine, I made sure I didn't pause long enough to give space to melancholy thoughts about whether I would live here long enough to see the sweet thing blossom again.

Instead, I strode to the apartment parking area with my chin up. I climbed into my car, a white compact that came from the used-car lot. I didn't pay attention to the make or model when Trevor brought it home. All that mattered was that it was reliable and the interior was in good condition.

While I waited at a stoplight, a smattering of raindrops flung themselves at the windshield. I had to remember how to adjust the speed on the windshield wipers since I rarely used them in the continual California sunshine.

That's when a different trail of melancholy thoughts settled on me. My previous car had been a Lexus with heated leather seats that felt like melted butter on cold mornings. Trevor liked that my luxurious sedan had every upgrade and add-on available for that model. The color was a special-ordered pearlized cream. She was a honey to drive. I admit I had adopted a car-snob attitude when I waited in the carpool line in North Carolina at the private school Audra attended.

The light changed in front of me, and I snapped out of the memory. Those days were over and that attitude was long gone. I was humbled but grateful now to simply have my own car and to manage to maneuver through the constant traffic.

Two blocks later I hit another red light. The congestion around 17th Street in Costa Mesa was ridiculous. I fiddled with the radio, trying to find some Christmas music. My thoughts were hopping all over the place. I wondered if I had done the right thing by sharing our experiences with Mrs. Miller. Trevor didn't like it when our personal details were known outside his family.

I hope he won't be upset that I told Mrs. Miller so much.

I turned down Jennalyn's street and parked in her driveway since I knew I would only be there a few moments. The raindrops fell in a fine spray as I trotted up to the front door. Her lovely home looked just as charming in the misty morning light as it had when I first saw it lit up at night.

My cookie plate was not waiting by the door as Jennalyn had said it would be. It had been a couple of hours since she had texted me. I wondered if she had forgotten. Maybe she hadn't left to go run her errands yet.

I hesitated to ring the doorbell but then decided it would be easier and faster than coming back this way after I went shopping. Besides, I didn't plan to linger if she invited me inside.

No one came to the door. I decided Jennalyn must have forgotten to put out the plate. I stayed under the protective eaves and tapped a text, letting her know I would stop by another time. As I was typing, I thought I heard someone calling out from inside. I rang the bell again, and the voice grew louder. I couldn't tell what the person inside was saying. I tried the doorbell one more time and waited with my ear next to the door.

It sounded like Jennalyn's voice crying out.

I tried the door handle and found it was unlocked. Inching the door open, I called out, "Jennalyn, are you here?"

"Yes! In the kitchen."

I made my way quickly to the kitchen and saw Jennalyn lying on the floor, her back propped against the dishwasher.

"What happened? Are you okay?"

"Careful!" She leaned her head back and took in a big breath, squeezing her eyes closed.

I grabbed a kitchen towel from the counter and threw it over the small puddle I had almost stepped in. Kneeling by her side, I tried to assess the situation. "Did you fall? Jennalyn?"

"Haahaahaa . . ." She relaxed her shoulders and looked at me, tears glistening in her eyes. Her expression left no doubt as to what was happening. I felt a rush of adrenaline.

"Where's your phone? I'll call your husband."

She nodded and then pointed to her foot. "My ankle . . . I fell."

Her feet were bare, and her loose pants were hiked up. I could see that her left ankle was swollen and was turning black and blue. She must have slipped and twisted her ankle as well as having her water break, which started what seemed to be active labor.

I rummaged through her purse on the marble countertop but didn't find her phone. "Is it in another room?"

Jennalyn started crying. "I don't know." She caught her breath and in choked words said, "I was looking for it and then . . ." Her eyes squeezed closed again, and she grimaced as her body seemed to be on automatic pilot.

Gathering my wits, I said, "Okay. I can call him on my phone. Or do you think you need to get to the hospital first? I can make the call on the way."

She shook her head back and forth, but I didn't know which part she was saying no to—my calling her husband or my taking her to the hospital.

"My car is in the driveway," I tried to sound calm and practical. "Let's get you into my car. I really think you should go to the hospital."

"Yes." She extended an arm to me so I could help her to stand.

"Okay, let's try it this way." As she leaned forward, I saw that just enough room was between Jennalyn and the cupboards for me to get behind her and loop my arms under her armpits. That seemed like the best way to help her straighten her posture and use her unaffected foot for leverage.

"Okay, here we go." I pulled up.

She rose only a few inches before a loud wail streamed from her open mouth. "No, no, no!"

I lowered her as gently as I could, and she breathed in quick gasps. Clearly she was in intense pain and not only because of the contractions. With sympathetic shock, I suddenly felt nauseous. Then everything inside me went calm.

"Jennalyn, listen. This is what I think we should do. I'm going to call an ambulance. Then I'll get ahold of your husband. What is his name again?"

"Joel."

"Right. Joel. Okay. You just stay as comfortable as you possibly can." I pulled out my phone and dialed 911.

Jennalyn's eyes were squeezed closed, and her lips were smashed together as if she was trying not to scream or cry out in terror.

My heart was pounding in my throat when the dispatcher answered my call. As calmly as I could, I stated, "My friend is in labor. She's fallen and hurt her ankle. We need an ambulance." I gave the dispatcher Jennalyn's street address and said they should come inside to the kitchen at the back of the house.

I hung up and dashed over to the sofa for some throw pillows before making any more calls. Propping one of the pillows under her head, I asked if that helped or would two pillows be better.

She didn't answer.

"Jennalyn? Jennalyn! Can you hear me?" I knelt beside her and placed the palm of my hand on her clammy forehead.

She seemed so focused on the overwhelming contraction that she had blocked out everything else. I sat beside her on the floor.

"It's okay," I said as calmly as I could. "Breathe. The paramedics are on their way. I'm right here for you."

Her eyes remained closed. She breathed out slowly through her open mouth.

"Okay, good. You're doing really well." I reached for another kitchen towel that was hanging from the handle of the nearby stove and used it to dab her forehead. "It's going to be okay. You're doing great, Jennalyn. You really are. You're going to be fine."

Tears streamed down my cheeks. I didn't know if anything I was saying was true. What was true was that I was terrified. I had no medical training. I get queasy at the sight of blood. Audra's loose, wiggly teeth were enough to make me squeamish.

I didn't want Jennalyn to pick up on anything I was feeling. With a trembling hand, I pulled her hair back from the side of her face where a handful of strands had stuck. With the dish towel, I stroked her forehead again and tried to think of what to do next. The moment felt surreal, as if I had stepped into a movie and somehow had a supporting actor role although I didn't know my lines.

Another contraction came over her like a wave. She reached for my hand and squeezed it so tightly I nearly cried out in pain. The wave receded, and she released her grip. I shook my hand to restore the feeling.

She must have noticed because in barely a whisper she said, "Sorry."

"Shh. Don't talk. There is absolutely nothing to be sorry about. You're doing well, Jennalyn. Just breathe. It's going to be okay."

I glanced at the clock on the microwave and tried to guess what time it was when I arrived. My mind was racing. The contractions seemed frighteningly close. She was wearing loose pants. Should I try to pull them off? How long would it take the ambulance to arrive? I wished I had parked on the street instead of the driveway so the ambulance could pull right in. Had I given them the right address? Where was my phone? I'd just had it. Should I find it so I could call Joel? Or was it more important for me to stay next to her since she seemed so unstable?

Where was that ambulance?!

Jennalyn's chin dipped, and her shoulders curled in. I knew that another contraction was about to overtake her. I offered her my hand once again, and she gripped it firmly. My mind kept racing as I spoke a string of what I hoped were comforting words. I had never been a birth coach. Trevor been mine, and I remembered how much his calm, assuring statements had kept me centered during labor.

"You're doing a great job. Really great."

In the distance I heard the wail of the ambulance and breathed deeply along with Jennalyn as her contraction receded. "They're here!"

She released her choke hold on my hand.

"You're doing so good. Hang in there. The paramedics will be here, and they'll know what to do next."

Two male paramedics entered the kitchen as another contraction seemed to be rising. They were on the floor beside me in a flash, assessing the situation and opening the box of medical gear. I could barely catch a deep enough breath to answer their questions about how she had fallen and how close the contractions were.

"Her name is Jennalyn," I added, slowly pulling out of my cramped position on the floor and rising to my feet.

One of the men cradled her head with his large hand resting on the pillow. He leaned in close. "Jennalyn, I'm Martin, and this is Ben. We're going to help you."

Her eyes fluttered halfway open for only a moment. Her skin seemed terribly pale.

My thoughts were jumping all over the place. All the calm I had experienced earlier was all used up, and I was back to a high anxiety level, even though the medical professionals were right there.

I stood back as Martin placed his hand on her midriff and then on her side. Ben was examining her ankle. "Does this hurt?"

Jennalyn let out a yelp and then moaned softly. Another all-encompassing contraction took possession of her frame.

The intensity was evident. The two medics exchanged glances. Martin leaned in close again. "Jennalyn, we need to cut off your clothes so we can see what's happening with your baby. Keep breathing. Yes, good. Just like that."

Ben went to work with a large pair of scissors. Martin looked up at me and pointed at the floor beside Jennalyn. "I need you to sit right here. Yes, like that."

I got into position.

Martin moved the pillow from under Jennalyn's head. While supporting her back, he said to me, "Now put your legs out straight on either side of her. Scoot in closer. Closer. There. Like you're on a toboggan together. That's it. Good."

"Jennalyn, you can lean against . . ." He looked at me. "What's your name?"

"Emily."

"You can lean back on Emily. Yes, just like that. Very good. We're going to check—"

"She's crowned," Ben announced before Martin could finish his sentence. Martin gave me a nod as if he assumed I knew what to do next. And maybe in some ancient, intrinsic, womanly way, I did.

Jennalyn's shivering upper body rested against me. I wrapped my arms around her, keeping her steady. She grabbed the sides of my legs and followed Ben's brusque commands. I whispered words of comfort over her and prayed silently.

"I'm with you. I'm here." Those two short lines were the ones Trevor had repeated when I was in labor with Audra. I remembered how much it had helped to hear that and be reminded that I wasn't alone.

"Almost there. Stay the course." Ben's firm voice sounded more like a military command than anything a doula would say. He told her how to breathe, and I followed his instructions as well.

As Jennalyn's frame became rigid, I remained steady. As she released her grip on my legs, I stayed upright. My body supported her completely. I could feel through her back the tightening of her every muscle.

We were in sync for three agonizing contractions, and then Ben barked the command to "Push!"

I couldn't believe the strength Jennalyn summoned after she had seemed so close to fainting. The first all-out push was followed by only a short breather before she was told to push again. And then again.

Three heroic pushes, and the baby was out!

"It's a boy."

"A boy?" Jennalyn repeated.

"Yes! You have a boy." My voice cracked and I started sobbing. I couldn't help it. Wiping my tears with the back of my hand, I repeated the declaration the rest of her family had been so anxious to know: "You have a boy."

Ben and Martin continued their careful flurry of motions. A moment later the awaited and welcome sound of the baby's first cry echoed around us.

"You did it." My arms were still wrapped around Jennalyn. I pressed the side of my head against hers. "Well done, little mama." I went from crying to laughing quietly. It was all so miraculous. So messy and immediate and real.

I didn't watch what happened next. I was more focused on Jennalyn as one of the paramedics must have tied the umbilical cord while the other grabbed a throw blanket off the couch. Martin pulled a garbage bag from under the sink. We remained in our snow-sledding position. Jennalyn's whole body was quivering. The little hero, briefly washed off in the kitchen sink and now wrapped in the big throw blanket, was placed in Jennalyn's arms.

"Oh, look at you. You're perfect. Hello." Her voice was weak. "Ow," she murmured as Martin pressed on her stomach, coaxing the final step to be completed. "Ow."

Ben had moved on to her black-and-blue ankle, which was now very swollen. He wrapped it as Jennalyn continued to wince and her infant began to cry.

Martin had risen to his feet and was reporting to his dispatcher that they would take Jennalyn to Hoag Memorial Hospital.

"What can I do?" I asked. The question was intended for Martin, but Jennalyn answered in a thin voice.

"Can you call Joel?"

"Yes, of course." I began to pull back so I could stand up.

Martin placed a hand on my shoulder. "Don't move yet. Wait till we get the stretcher."

During the few minutes it took for them to position the equipment and lift Jennalyn onto the stretcher, I had a chance to take a long look at her little miracle.

"He's beautiful," I whispered. "I'm so happy for you."

Jennalyn leaned her head on my shoulder. "Oh, Emily, you came at just the right moment. I can't believe what you did for me. I will never be able to thank you enough."

"Shh. Don't use up your strength."

"We're going to need your help to get you on the stretcher," Ben said. "Emily, can you scoot back? More. Okay, now support her back with your hands. No, that's not going to work. It's too tight in here. You'll need to move out all the way."

I tried to make my exit with the least amount of jolting to Jennalyn. It was a bumpy endeavor.

"Here," Jennalyn said once I was on my feet. "Take him."

I reached for her son with trembling arms. My eyes filled with tears as I whispered, "Welcome to the world, little one."

Martin and Ben expertly transferred Jennalyn to the gurney. I placed the bundled-up baby boy into Jennalyn's arms and watched her stroke his cheek and study his little face.

Impulsively, I leaned over and kissed Jennalyn on the side of her head, my lips barely brushing a nest of her matted hair. "You did it. Well done. I'm so happy for you."

She stretched her neck, trying to hold my gaze as they wheeled her out. Her strength had dissolved. Her lips mouthed an inaudible response. I couldn't tell what she was trying to say.

It didn't matter. My heart heard her.

I knew.

Chapter 7

The next couple of days following the unconventional and early arrival of Alexander Gideon Marino were filled with extra hours of work, long conversations, and strings of group text messages between Christy, Tess, Sierra, Jennalyn, and me. I could barely keep up with all the comments.

The best news in the conversations was that the six pound, four ounce, seventeen-and-a-half-inch cutie had spent only one night in the hospital with his mommy. Both were home and adjusting well. Clearly, he had been ready to make his grand entrance in spite of what the charts, dates, and measurements had determined.

The other good news was that Jennalyn's twisted ankle wasn't broken. She had a bad sprain. The doctor outfitted her with a walking boot and told her sometimes a sprain could take longer to heal than a break if it's not taken care of.

Jennalyn's husband, Joel, was the head chef at an upscale restaurant in Corona del Mar named the Blue Ginger. He took the week off after the surprise arrival of Alex. His mother, GiGi, spent her waking hours with Joel and Jennalyn, making meals and endlessly rocking baby Alex so that Jennalyn could sleep.

That's great, Sierra had texted in response to Jennalyn's assurance that all the bases were covered. But isn't there something we can do?

Tess had replied, Do you need anything? I can buy groceries. Text me a list.

Christy asked, Do you want me to take Eden for a day or two?

I was thinking about what I could add to the offers when Jennalyn replied to all of us saying, Thank you, but I don't need anything. She went on to tell us that her house had never been cleaner, nor had she ever had such a full refrigerator. She insisted that Eden wanted to stay home with the new baby and that GiGi was giving her lots of attention.

My tail-end offer was sincere. Please let me know if I can do anything at all!

Jennalyn's reply was, Emily, you already helped in the most important way possible.

Her words made me smile. What we had experienced together had been extraordinary. The closeness I felt with Jennalyn and the other women through all this was surprising.

Trevor was patient with my continual retelling of the amazing event whenever Audra wasn't listening in. I honestly think he was a little irritated every time I talked about it, even though I tried not to be too graphic or share any personal details about this woman he had never met.

On Monday night, as soon as Audra had gone to bed, Trevor came into the kitchen where I was emptying the dishwasher.

"Hey." His expression was serious.

"Everything okay?"

He lowered his voice. "I didn't want to tell you earlier, but my dad called this afternoon. He wanted us to know that they have been praying for us and they're hoping we can come to a decision by tomorrow."

"Tomorrow?"

He nodded and pointed to the patio, indicating that we should have this conversation outside if we wanted to be somewhat certain that Audra wouldn't hear us.

I put on a sweater and took a seat at the patio table. He closed the patio door and started with his voice low and thin. "I've been looking at all the angles, Emily, and I gotta say, it makes sense for us to pack up and head out as soon as Audra goes on Christmas break."

I hadn't expected Trevor to be so direct and decisive. Pulling my sweater close and folding my arms in front of me, I opened my mouth and then closed it. I didn't know what to say.

He buried his fingers in his thick hair and rested his head in his hands with both elbows planted on the patio table. "I don't know what else to do."

A wave of matter-of-fact clarity came over me the way it had when I was with Jennalyn and knew I couldn't give in to the discomfort and emotion of the moment but needed to think clearly. "Let me ask some questions, okay?"

"Go ahead." He released his seemingly weighted head and looked at me.

"At one point back in October, I think, you said a guy contacted you and said he wanted to buy the car lot. If I remember, you told him you couldn't because of the understanding you had with your uncle."

"That's right."

"What if you called your uncle, explained how things have gone for you, and see if he would be okay with your selling the business now?"

"I've thought about that. But if I sold it, what would I do? Why would we stay here? I still would need a job."

"Maybe you could take the profit and start a small dealership." I knew there was much more involved in obtaining a dealership. As soon as I tossed out the idea, I regretted it.

"It's not that simple."

"I know. Never mind."

"Besides, if I did sell, I would want to make sure Uncle Glen was paid whatever he believed would be due to him since our arrangement would have changed. After that, I don't think there would be enough of a profit for me to start much of anything."

We sat in silence for a few minutes. My mind was still logically spinning through the options.

"Let me toss out some scenarios," I said. "These are possibilities, not plans, okay?"

He nodded. I suggested all kinds of ideas. He spiked every one of them back over the net. For a few minutes I felt like we were playing verbal volleyball with grenades. Thankfully, neither of us pulled the pins; it was nothing more than catch and release until Trevor made the final toss.

"We can't make it work here financially," he said. "That's the bottom line."

"I know."

"So you agree that we should move back? Leave on the nineteenth?" Trevor pushed back his chair and stood. I recognized the move. If we were at the car dealership and I were a customer, his standing would mean that he was about to stretch out his hand to me and say, "Do we have a deal?"

After a moment I decided that I should answer with the truth. "No."

"No?"

I shook my head. "I don't think we should leave. Not yet."

"Why?" He looked stunned.

"I don't know. I just think there's more for us here."

"More what?" Trevor asked.

"I don't know. I just think we're not done here yet."

Trevor gripped the back of the patio chair and stared at me. "I can't believe you're saying this."

"We agreed that we were going to stick it out for a full year. That's what we said when we made the decision to come to California."

He clenched his jaw. He looked lost.

"Do you remember when we told your parents that we had decided to move here?"

"Of course."

"Your mother said she thought we were trying to run away from our problems instead of facing them."

"I remember."

"We both disagreed with her. You even said that we weren't running away but rather running toward our future. Both you and I had prayed about it a lot. We agreed this was the right thing to do."

"That's because I thought I could turn the car lot around and it would become a decent source of income." Trevor's arms were folded across his chest. "We've already been over this. It's not profitable."

"I know. But my point is, we weren't afraid to come," I said. "We were in agreement about what to do, and we looked your mom and dad in the eye and told them we were not letting fear make the decision for us."

"Right. I remember. I was there."

I understood his irritation, but I needed to finish my thought. I leaned across the table, hoping my intuition was right. "I think if we left now, we would be letting fear make the decision for us."

Trevor started pacing. "Maybe we should be afraid."

He reminded me that his parents were anxious for an answer.

"I know they are. But it still needs to be our decision." I knew it was close to blasphemy to ever speak against my in-laws, but I went ahead and said what was becoming clear to me. "As kind and caring as your parents are, I think they're pushing their opinion too hard. It seems like you're worried about upsetting them."

Trevor stopped pacing. He stared at my unflinching expression and then sat down, crossed his arms, and appeared to be deep in thought. I couldn't tell if my insight had helped or harmed.

A few moments later, he looked up at me. "I know we said we would give it a year, but we can't wait that long. We'll wait until January 1. That's when we'll make our final decision. We'll stay through Christmas, since year-end should bring in the most sales. I'll give it my all, and we'll see what happens. By New Year's Eve we'll know. We'll decide then."

Trevor watched my expression closely. "Do you agree with that plan?"

"Yes."

"Good." Deciding not to decide yet seemed to take the unbearable burden off him. At least for the moment.

"What are you going to tell your parents?"

"I'm going to tell them that we decided together to stay through the end of December. That's what is best for our family at this time." He sounded as if he was practicing a speech.

"How do you feel about everything?" It was one of those questions I should have learned by now not to ask. My husband didn't know what to do with "feel" questions. Of course this wouldn't feel good to him. He liked to have all the numbers, all the logic, lined up and fitted in place like a bunch of cogs so that when the handle was turned, all the wheels would move together.

To my surprise, he had an answer. "I feel like there's something else. Something I'm missing."

"What do you think it is?" I asked.

"I don't know."

Trevor stood and kissed me on the top of my head. He was done. He needed to go inside and put his mind on other things. I lingered at the patio table a little longer, thinking and praying.

For the first time, I noticed that some scrawny bushes had been planted along the back fence. They must be the cuttings Mrs. Miller said her husband was going to put in. I went over to look at them more closely in the dim glow of the patio light. I had no idea what the shrubs were or what they might grow into.

Leaning my head back, I looked up and felt a raindrop on my forehead and then another on my chin. "Melted snowflakes" Audra had called them when it rained earlier that day.

If I could prolong any of the years of our daughter's life so far, this would be the one. Her journey from nine to ten had been a difficult year. I hoped we wouldn't end up repeating the same uprooting and transplanting pattern as she moved from age ten to eleven.

At least we have a few more weeks to decide.

I was determined to make this Christmas a good one for all of us.

The "melted snowflakes" continued to fall all the next day. Work was slow because many of the regulars preferred not to venture outside on such a day. But we were busy enough for me to stay my entire shift. I picked up Audra and decided that instead of going home, we should stop by to see Trevor. I thought I could use the excuse that I wanted to see the Christmas decorations she had worked so hard to create. What I really wanted to know was whether he had given his parents the update and how they had reacted.

Trevor was busy when I arrived. He looked happy. Excited, even. I guessed he must be in the middle of closing a deal with the client who was seated at his desk. The other salesman, Carlos, also had a client at his desk. He looked up and told Audra that he loved her decorations.

"What about the tree? Do you like the tree?" Audra asked Carlos.

"The tree is the best of all." He turned back to his client and said something in Spanish, pointing at the tree and then at Audra. They smiled and nodded at her.

We slipped out and drove home the long way, with the Pacific Ocean on our right. The winter sky had faded to a pale gray-blue color and the low, thin clouds were stretched out along the horizon like lumpy, lazy cats napping on a windowsill.

"We're going to the beach on Christmas Day, aren't we?" Audra was fixed on the view out the passenger's window as I slowly made our way south on Pacific Coast Highway.

"I'm not sure what our plans are yet."

"I asked Daddy, and he said he couldn't say." Audra thought a moment. "Usually when he says he can't say, it's because the answer is yes but he's trying to keep it a surprise."

"Is that so?"

"Most of the time."

"A more important question is, what do you want for dinner tonight? Chicken and vegetable soup? Or chicken and vegetable soup?" I had played this game with Audra since she was little. She seemed to still enjoy the chance to offer her opinion even when there was no real decision for her to make.

She rested her index finger on her chin. "I think we should have . . ."

"Yes? Yes? What is your final answer?"

"I think we should have *vegetable* and chicken soup!"

"Okay, then! Vegetable and chicken soup it is."

"With extra noodles."

"Extra noodles?"

"Yes. And for dessert we should have seven-layer fudge brownie cake with double chocolate frosting, whipped cream, and raspberries on top."

"Oh my!"

"Or we could have . . ." Audra's imagination needed her artist's notepad so she could fully express her idea of the perfect dessert with her colored pencils. She thought another moment and seemed to come up empty.

With a drop of reality taking her voice down a notch, she asked, "What do you think we should have?"

"I was thinking maybe we could have apple slices," I said.

"Dipped in peanut butter?"

"Sure. Why not?"

Audra gave an exaggerated sigh. "I was really hoping for cinnamon bonbon coconut strudel."

I chuckled and glanced over at her. Apparently her imagination hadn't switched all the way back to the reality of what our meals were usually like.

"How scrumptious! I've never even heard of cinnamon bonbon coconut strudel."

"That's because I haven't opened my bakery yet. When I have a bakery one day, the best, most favorite thing everyone will buy will be my famous cinnamon bonbon coconut strudel. It will win the gold star for the best new recipe in the galaxy."

"In the galaxy. Wow! I can't wait until you open your bakery."

"First I have to become a famous artist. Then I'll become a baker."

"You know what? We should do some baking. We could make Christmas cookies."

"Mom, are you serious about baking cookies?" Audra was looking at me with a tentative smile, and her eyes opened wide.

I glanced back at the road. "Yes. Why not? I think it would be fun. First time for everything. I'm not saying they'll be like Gramma's cookies or pies or anything else she bakes. But we can try."

Audra clasped her hands together as if it was the only way she could express her joy while confined by the seat belt. "My Christmas wish is coming true!"

I thought she was being especially dramatic but didn't comment. It was good to see my daughter so content.

That night, after Trevor put her to bed and closed her door, he came out to the living room. "Did you know that the kids in Audra's class wrote their Christmas wishes on cutout ornaments and taped them on a board at school?"

"No."

"Do you know what our daughter's wish was?"

"I'm afraid to ask."

"She wants to bake cookies with you."

"Seriously?"

"That's what she just told me," Trevor said. "Then she told me you promised her on the way home that you were going to bake with her on Saturday."

"I did promise her we would bake on Saturday."

"I thought you had to work this Saturday."

"Oh yeah. I forgot. Well, we can do it in the evening."

Trevor gave me a side glance that seemed to say, "We'll see how that goes."

"Do you think she'll be okay hanging out with you again at work?" I asked.

"She was fine last time. Although, she got glitter all over my desk and I made her clean it up. She didn't like that very much." Trevor sat down next to me on the couch and looked at the house renovation show I was watching.

I expected him to say what he had said a few weeks ago when I was watching an episode of this show. He thought I was torturing myself with all the images of big luxury homes while I was confined to a small apartment. I didn't have a reply for him last time. If he said anything tonight, I would tell him that renovation shows were my version of Audra's cinnamon bonbon coconut strudel. A girl's gotta dream.

He didn't comment on the show, though. Instead, he said, "I told my dad today that we're going to wait it out here until January." He kept looking at the TV.

"What did he say?"

"Not a whole lot. I don't think that was what he was expecting."

Trevor reached over and put his hand on my leg. "I've set a new year-end goal. It's not nearly as ambitious as my initial sales goals for this year. But if I hit my goal amount, well, it'll be a good thing."

The commercial came on, so I did what I usually do and put the volume on mute. Trevor turned to me and gave me an affectionate kiss. I knew that he had come home stoked about selling two cars that day. The message in his kiss and in his expression was more than happiness over selling two cars, though.

I smiled at him and kissed him back, a warm, inviting, deep kiss.

Trevor reached for the remote control. He set my program to record, turned off the TV, and without a word, took me by the hand.

I willingly and eagerly let him lead me to our bedroom. Or, as he had dubbed it ever since we moved to Southern California, the Real Happiest Place on Earth.

Chapter 8

The next weeks were dotted with some happy moments here and there in the flow of our family routine. I was working nearly forty hours a week and didn't have much free time.

Sierra texted a week before Christmas asking if Audra and I wanted to come over and make cookies with her and her mother-in-law. I found out via our back-and-forth text messages that Sierra and Jordan had moved to the nearby city of Irvine shortly before their baby girl was born. To my surprise, they lived with Jordan's parents. Knowing that made me think I wouldn't mind telling Sierra that we had lived with Trevor's parents.

Thanks for the baking invite, I texted back. **I'm working extra hours, so I can't join you. Thanks for thinking of Audra and me.**

Sierra's reply was, **We'll have to do something next year.** She included a laughing emoji face in case I didn't catch the "next year" reference.

The reality was that the chance of my doing something with Sierra or any of the other women from the party next year was still a big unknown. I didn't want to think about Trevor's January 1 deadline.

I did think about Jennalyn, though. All the time. I felt a longing to invite myself over to her house so I could hold baby Alex and rock him and see how he looked now that he was almost two weeks into his little life.

But I held back. I didn't go see Jennalyn or baby Alex. I think I was trying to protect myself from getting too close.

Then I received an invitation from Christy. I don't know why, but I found myself saying yes to Christy after saying no to Sierra. The invitation was to spend Christmas afternoon with her extended family at her aunt and uncle's beachfront home in Newport.

After the depressing Thanksgiving Day Trevor, Audra, and I had with our dried-out turkey dinner and failed board game, the idea of being part of a big gathering on Christmas sounded good. Trevor and Audra agreed it would feel more like a holiday if other people were around, the way it had always been at my in-laws' grand house.

Three days before Christmas, Mrs. Miller came to our front door with a small loaf of bread gift wrapped for us. Audra was beside me when I opened the door. "Did you like our cookies?"

"Yes, very much."

"Did Mr. Miller like them?"

"Yes, he did."

I appreciated that Mrs. Miller was always kind to Audra. The cookies had turned out pretty good. Not great, but we had fun with the mixing, baking, and general mess making. We made double batches of two different recipes: sugar cookie candy canes and, of course, more elf-cap cookies since Audra said they were her "signature cookie" now. We baked enough to take a plate around to everyone in our small apartment complex. That was Audra's idea, and it turned out to be a good one because we finally met all our neighbors.

Mrs. Miller handed me a small card. "I wrote down my sister's address," she said. "I wasn't sure if Christy had given you Bob and Marti's contact information yet."

I didn't tell her that Christy already had texted all the details to me so I didn't need the card. I found it endearing that she had written it out for me.

"We'll see you on Christmas Day, then." Mrs. Miller thanked Audra again for the cookies and went on her way. Audra politely waited until she was down the path before closing the door. Trevor had instilled in her that small gesture of courtesy. He said she should never appear to be closing a door on someone. She also wasn't allowed to go to her room and slam her door, as several of her cousins did whenever they didn't get their way.

"I think it's banana bread." Audra sniffed the wrapped loaf. "Can we have some tonight when you and I watch our movie?"

We had a quiet evening, just the two of us, because Trevor had a customer who couldn't come in until seven. Audra curled up next to me on the couch and made appreciative "mmm" sounds as she nibbled on her slice of banana bread that I'd warmed up. We were halfway through the feel-good, cozy Christmas movie when Audra said, "I miss our family."

"Our family?" I pulled back and tried to read her expression.

"Our bigger family. I wish I could see my cousins for Christmas. And Gramma. I miss her a lot."

"Why don't we call her in the morning?"

"Did you send her the card I made?"

"Yes, I did."

"And all the paper ornaments I made for everyone?"

"Yes. I mailed the package last week. They should have all your beautiful ornaments and pictures by now."

Audra sighed. It was the first time since we had moved that she had expressed such a direct sadness about not being with Trevor's family. It didn't help that the movie was about a family reuniting at Christmas. But by the time she went to bed, the cloud seemed to have lifted. She was chattering about how she was going to make a sandcastle on Christmas Day and how she wanted me to take lots of pictures to send to her cousins.

Two days later, a knock sounded on our door at a few minutes after eight o'clock. A delivery man left a big box on our doorstep. Trevor hauled it inside, and Audra unpacked the abundance of beautifully wrapped gifts.

"They're all from Gramma and Grampa!" Audra placed each gift under our tree. "Look how many presents we have now!" She planted herself at the foot of the tree, arranging each gift so that the tag was easy to see. She then counted all the ones with her name on them.

"Do you think I could open just one now? Maybe this little one?"

"We're going to wait until Christmas morning," Trevor told her. He pulled a glass from the cupboard and searched the inside of the refrigerator for something that apparently wasn't there.

"What are you looking for?" I asked.

"I thought we had some juice."

"We do. Second shelf."

"I don't see it."

"It's in the back. On the right."

"Oh. Got it."

Trevor had seemed anxious and distracted the past few days. He hadn't reported on how the late-night customer meeting had gone or how his year-end sales goal was looking, and I hadn't asked.

"Daddy?" Audra tried using her charms to persuade her father. "I'm not asking to open all the presents or even most of the presents. Just this little tiny one. Please?"

"No, Audra."

"Mom?"

"I think we should stick to the plan, just like Dad said."

Audra sighed dramatically, as if she were going to faint underneath the tree from sheer suspense in the presence of all the gifts.

"Audra." Trevor gave her a stern look.

"You'll be glad you waited," I added. "We have candlelight service at church tonight, and then we'll open all the gifts tomorrow morning. After that, we'll go to Bob and Marti's at eleven."

"Bob and Marti's," Trevor repeated. "You say their names as if you already know them."

"I'm guessing they're a lot like Mr. and Mrs. Miller."

"Except they live in a beachfront house." Trevor chomped into a slice of toast. "Audra, when we meet these people, you call them Mr. Bob and Miss Marti, do you understand?"

"Yes, Daddy."

Trevor nodded to Audra and looked at me. "Are you sure we should still do this? Spend Christmas Day with people we don't know?"

"I thought you wanted to go."

He shrugged.

"We can cancel, if we need to. Although I did say that I would bring a salad. I already bought everything to make it. I kind of feel like we should follow through since they're expecting us."

"I just don't want to get stuck there," Trevor said. "Let's agree now that if any one of us decides they're ready to leave, we all leave right then. Okay?"

"Okay." I could tell he was uncomfortable already, which was unusual since he was by nature so outgoing and social. At least he was around his relatives. He didn't know any of the people who would be at this Christmas brunch except for our apartment managers, Mr. and Mrs. Miller.

"We can't leave too soon." Audra popped up and trotted into the kitchen. "We have to stay long enough so that I can make a sandcastle. Remember? It's my Christmas wish."

Trevor gave Audra an impatient look. "I thought your Christmas wish was to make cookies with your mom? Didn't you already do that?"

"That was my first Christmas wish. I have three wishes, and the second one is to make a sandcastle on Christmas Day." She drank the rest of her apple juice she had left on the counter. "And I want to take lots of pictures of the sandcastle to send to my cousins."

"Is that your third wish?" Trevor seemed to be warming to her unintentional charm.

"No, that's still part of the second wish."

"Okay. So what's your third Christmas wish?"

"I can't tell you."

Trevor put on a mock expression of shock, and I was glad to hear the way his voice was playful. "Why not? You told me the other two."

"I was just kidding. I'll tell you." Audra's glee was evident in her smile and shining eyes. "But I think you already know, Daddy, because I told you before."

"Let's pretend that you didn't tell me yet," he said.

Audra leaned closer. With her hand shielding the side of her mouth, she whispered something in his ear.

Trevor glanced at me. His slight wincing expression made me think that Audra must have wished for something that was impossible for him to deliver.

A vivid memory of Trevor's gift disaster on her fifth birthday came to mind. I wondered if he was thinking about it too. Audra had wished for a pink unicorn. Trevor trolled the internet until he found just the right stuffed unicorn and wrapped it inside a huge box, thinking it would be fun for her to open and hunt for the toy.

The gift took center stage at the extended family birthday party. Audra could barely contain herself as she opened the large box. She combed through the mound of crumpled tissue paper until she found only the small plush toy unicorn at the bottom.

She threw the unicorn across the room and let out a wail as urgently as if she had been cut and was bleeding. It was the worst meltdown she had ever had. Between her piercing screams she cried out, "I meant a real one, Daddy! A real one!"

The relatives picked up on what was happening and laughed heartily, which embarrassed and infuriated Audra even more. She stomped out of the room and, for the first and last time, slammed the bathroom door.

Mortified, Trevor and I went to her and had what my mother-in-law later called a "come to Jesus" meeting. Our stern scolding revealed to Trevor and me that her reaction didn't come from acting out as a spoiled and only child. Her whimsical mind truly believed that somewhere in this wild world, unicorns were real, and if anyone could make her wish come true, her daddy could. Now, here we were, with a ten-year-old who was still making wishes.

I sent Audra to go brush her teeth and put on her sweater before she went to work with Trevor. As soon as she was in the bathroom and I could hear the water running in the sink, I turned to Trevor.

"Another pink unicorn?" I asked quietly.

"She wants to sleep under the Christmas tree with her cousins like she did last year."

I could tell that Audra's wish had taken Trevor into a dark hole.

"Do you wish we were in Asheville right now?" I knew that was a dangerous question and wasn't sure why I ventured to put it out there.

He didn't answer. I wished I hadn't asked. I studied his expression as he scrolled through his phone. He seemed to be putting on a brave face, as if he could hide his fears from Audra and me. I hoped he could at least be upbeat enough to make it through Christmas. He and I would have our own "come to Jesus" meeting on January 1. Until then, I didn't want to be the only one who was trying hard to hold it all together.

"We can do lots of video calls with the cousins," I suggested.

"Sure." He didn't look up.

"That reminds me," I added quickly. "I told Audra she could call your mom this morning."

"Okay."

I glanced at the clock. "I need to leave for work. Could you set her up on a call when you go to the office?"

Trevor nodded and swallowed his last bite of toast. "Audra!" he called out. "Put a wiggle in it."

As I drove to Peggy's Pies, I thought back on when I was going through the years of my deepest, darkest stretches while dealing with infertility. Trevor had often said that he wished he could carry the pain for both of us during that time so that he could take the disappointment and burden off me.

A revealing thought came to me as I sat at a stoplight.

Having a second baby was my pink unicorn.

I had believed with such childlike hope that it could happen. Everyone told me it would happen. All those years. All those steps. All that waiting.

Then, when it didn't happen and we were told it couldn't, I was crushed. Emotionally set adrift. The move to California, along with the routine of work and home, had turned into a new harbor for me. More and more I was feeling anchored here.

I pulled into the parking lot at work and thought of how Trevor seemed to be the one set adrift now. He was far from the familiar bowlines his extended family had always provided. Had his uncle's used-car lot been Trevor's pink unicorn? Was he realizing that the gift handed to him wasn't what he had envisioned, and now he was feeling overwhelmed by the disappointment?

As much as I wanted to take on the burden for Trevor, I was beginning to see that this was his journey. I could stay in the boat with him, so to speak. But I could not take control of the rudder or convince him of the way he should chart his course.

My heart felt heavy for Trevor as I walked into work ten minutes early that morning and saw that we already had people waiting to be seated. Lots of our regulars had family visiting, and the tables were full. We had to open the back room and push tables together to accommodate a party of eleven followed by another party of eight.

The rush never let up. By lunch we were short of everything but guests. One of the servers quit on the spot and walked out at noon. It was the worst day ever. No one, especially not Mr. Sanchez, had a pinch of Christmas spirit to show to the customers crammed into the small waiting area.

I teared up twice but quickly blinked away the evidence so that the rude and disgruntled out-of-town guests wouldn't see. One man loudly belittled his elderly mother for choosing to have lunch on Christmas Eve in such a dive. He refused to eat at Peggy's Pies and held the door open so that his mortified mother could make her way out on her walker.

I recognized the woman but didn't know her name. She looked as if she had had her hair done and was wearing a bright red Christmas sweater with a pretty silver pin in the shape of a wreath attached to her left shoulder, as if the pin were a special badge of honor. If she was treated that way by her son, she did deserve a badge of honor.

I wondered if Trevor's parents felt embarrassed or belittled because we didn't return to North Carolina before Christmas. I hoped they didn't. They had been so good to us, to me.

I decided that I would make sure to talk to my mother-in-law soon and tell her how much I appreciated her. I tried to calculate if I could squeeze in a call that afternoon, even with the time difference.

I was supposed to get off at 2:30 but ended up having to stay until 3:00, when the restaurant was scheduled to close and stay closed on Christmas Day. Hopefully the general attitude of all the employees would be better when we returned on December 26. I was more than ready to return to my schedule of fewer hours and slower shifts.

"You forgot something," Mr. Sanchez called after me as I was heading for the door. He held up an envelope and for a moment I had a sudden Christmas wish. Not unlike my dreamy daughter's wishes, I hoped the envelope was a check. A Christmas bonus check that Mr. Sanchez had decided to bless all the employees with.

Mr. Sanchez handed me the envelope, and I recognized it as the Christmas card I hadn't yet opened from Mrs. Thompson. She had handed it to me the day before when I seated them at their favorite table. I had tucked the envelope under the seating chart, forgetting to take it with me at the end of my shift that day.

"Thank you." I took the card from my exhausted-looking boss and wished I had asked Audra to create a card for him so I could at least offer him a tiny bit of cheer.

"Merry Christmas," I said.

He growled.

I was at the door when I heard him call out, "Merry Christmas to you too, Emily. *Feliz Navidad.* And thank you."

I took his rare thank-you as his version of a Christmas bonus and was grateful enough.

Traffic on the way home was heavy, and drivers seemed even more impatient than usual. I placed a call to my mother-in-law's cell phone. It went to voice mail, so I left a short Merry Christmas greeting, told her I loved her and that we were doing okay but that we were all going to miss being with everyone tomorrow.

I turned on the radio, hoping for Christmas carols to lift my spirits. Instead, the station was playing an inspirational message. The polished voice of the speaker was saying how this was the moment in history on which all of eternity hinged—Christmas, the arrival of Emmanuel, which literally means, "God with us."

I realized that aside from family, friends, and goodwill to men, I barely had given any thought to what this holy day represented. The voice on the radio continued by telling the ancient story again with a sense of urgency.

"Do we understand, fully understand, the gift that has been given to us?" the preacher asked.

I turned up the volume.

"God is with us. We are not alone. He is right there, with you, wherever you are at this very moment. He came to us on that first Christmas. Think of it! God, the sovereign ruler over all the universe, came to us. Why? Because He loves us. He wants us. He is with us. Right now. He is with you. Whatever you are going through, He is with you."

I felt each staccato phrase tap against my heart. I wanted to believe that everything was going to be okay. I wanted Trevor to feel anchored and to know that God was with us.

Now I was the one with a Christmas wish. Only one. I wished for Trevor to be at peace.

Chapter 9

*M*y mother-in-law outdid herself with her gift giving for us that Christmas. She said she had held off sending her box until she was certain that we wouldn't be returning to Asheville. When we started unwrapping gifts on Christmas morning, I was pretty sure she had loaded the box with even more gifts once she found out we would be "alone" for Christmas.

Trevor appreciated the four board games she sent with his name on all of them. Audra apparently had told Gramma about the board game fail at Thanksgiving. I had picked up two at a thrift store, but when we got them out after dinner, both were missing key pieces. Now we had four games to choose from.

The best gift was the art set my mother-in-law sent for Audra. The colored pencils, paints, brushes, and other essential components came in a large leather case that had Audra's initials engraved in the corner. I knew Audra would use it and take good care of it. She loved the gift and couldn't wait to call and tell Gramma so.

Trevor set us all up on a video call to the clan that was gathered at my in-laws' house. The noise and merry chaos that appeared in snatches every time the phone was passed off to someone else was so familiar.

"I love the art set, Gramma. Thank you so, so, so, so, so, so much."

"You're welcome, darlin'." With a tease in her voice, she added, "I'm so, so, so, so glad you like it. Are you having a nice Christmas there in California?"

Audra chattered about the cookies we had made and delivered to the neighbors, the decorations she had created for the dealership, and how we were going to the beach that afternoon to make a sandcastle.

I caught the surprised look on my mother-in-law's face as I peered over Audra's shoulder. She continued to appear caught off guard when Audra added that we were having a big Christmas lunch with the "nice man and lady who own our apartment."

"I don't think they own the complex," Trevor corrected her. "They're the managers."

His mother appeared as if she hadn't heard him correctly. "Did you say you're having Christmas lunch with your apartment manager?"

"Yes. At the beach," Trevor added. "Well, at a beach house of one of their relatives."

I could tell this was difficult for Trevor. In thirty-four years, he never had missed the Winslow family Christmas Day of bedlam and joy. The faces on the video call seemed to all draw in closer as if trying to read my husband's expression. I thought about my Christmas wish for him, that he would be at peace. My wish turned into a prayer.

"I hope it's a fun day for you," one of his sisters said. "We all wish you were here with us. I hope you made the right decision."

My mother-in-law slid in and with a smile said, "Won't that be an adventure for you, Audra! Christmas at the beach. Be sure to send us lots of pictures of your sandcastle."

"I will, Gramma." Audra came closer to Trevor's phone. "Gramma, I decided to have two Christmas wishes this year. Making sandcastles is my second wish."

"What was your first wish?"

"Baking cookies with my mom since we couldn't bake pies with you."

Gramma Winslow appeared sweetly surprised. The creases were beginning to deepen across Trevor's forehead. I knew that was a sure sign that he was holding in what he was feeling. Both he and I had forgotten about Audra's wish to sleep under the tree last night. Our plan to have her call her cousin Hailey was also forgotten. It seemed she had let it go too. I hoped Trevor would be able to do the same.

"I received your voicemail yesterday, Emily," my mother-in-law told me. "Thank you for calling. I miss all of you very much."

She was tearing up, and so was I. We said our goodbyes, and Audra took her new gifts to her bedroom. Trevor and I sat close on the couch, and I rested my head on his shoulder.

"At least nobody asked about the business," Trevor said. I slipped my arm through his and cuddled closer. "I appreciate that."

"Did you tell your father about the goal you set for this month?"

"No." Trevor leaned his head back. I adjusted my position so that I could stretch my fingers into his thick hair and massage his scalp. This had always been one of his favorite ways to relax. My touch seemed to be working because he took a deep breath and let it out slowly. On the tail of his breath was a whispered, "I'm sorry."

"For what?"

"For bringing you here and putting you through all this."

"Trevor, this was our decision, remember? We both wanted this. I'm not complaining."

"I know. You never complain."

"I wouldn't say never." I reminded him of the way I had moaned excessively the day before about work and the rude customers and how I hated that we ended up being late to the Christmas Eve service and had to sit in the back.

"Okay. Almost never." He pulled away and turned to look at me. "Are you happy?"

I didn't expect his question. Nor did I overthink my answer.

"Mostly." I knew I probably shouldn't ask him the same, but I did. "Are you?"

Trevor's gaze was fixed on mine. Audra was returning to the living room, so we knew she was likely to insert herself into our conversation. His answer was, "Not yet."

I couldn't tell whether his reply was intended to be a subtle romantic invitation. His expression didn't have the usual focused and sincere look I had come to recognize when he was eager for us to "get alone and close the door," as he called it. The "not yet" seemed to relate more to his year-end goals at the dealership.

What if he reaches his goal? What will that mean? That we're staying? Or that we'll have enough to fund our trek back to all that is familiar to my husband? And what if he doesn't reach his goal? Will we have to borrow money from his parents so we can move back?

"We should call your mom," Trevor said suddenly.

"Oh, okay." I went over to the counter and unplugged my phone. I had missed three text messages. All of them were from Trevor's extended family and included photos of the kids opening gifts. One was of Trevor's dad standing by the fireplace on Christmas Eve reading the Christmas story from the book of Luke the way he did every year. The nostalgia got to me as I scrolled through all the photos. I showed them to Audra and Trevor with some hesitation.

"I like this one." Audra pointed to a close-up of Hailey holding a big box of European chocolates, the traditional gift sent to the Winslow family every year from one of the luxury car manufacturers. "I remember those candies. They were shaped like seashells."

I was grateful Trevor didn't ask Audra what else she remembered and turn the rest of our morning into a painfully sentimental voyage on the sea of Christmas Past. Instead, he told her to get dressed so we could get going and find real seashells for our Christmas Present.

We pulled up in front of the beach house at exactly eleven o'clock and exchanged glances. The house wasn't like the many cottage-style houses in that part of Newport Beach. This two-story structure was twice the size of the other bungalows and reminded me of an Italian villa more than a beach house.

"What do you know about these people?" Trevor asked.

"Not much."

"I think they must be fancy," Audra said. "Much fancier than Mr. and Mrs. Miller."

Trevor drove up and down the narrow streets looking for a parking spot. He finally decided to circle back to the house, drop us off, and then go find a place.

"I don't mind walking back with you," I said. "Then we can all go in together."

"Why? You have stuff to carry. Let me drop you off."

His tone made me think that if I pressed my choice, we would end up arguing, and I didn't want that. The truth was, I was nervous. As nervous as I had been before going to Jennalyn's party. It would be so much easier to ring the doorbell if Trevor was beside me. He always knew what to say and how to start conversations with strangers.

I also had a slight fear that he might go back to our apartment and text me saying that he would pick up Audra and me when we were ready to leave. He had never done anything like that before, so I knew my fear was irrational.

If Audra hadn't been with us and if she hadn't been jabbering about how much she couldn't wait to see Christy's little boy, Cole, I think I could have easily told Trevor we should cancel and go home. It would be so much less stressful for us to spend the day alone, with a constant stream of Christmas movies and the last of our Christmas cookies. We could take Audra to the beach later that day, make a sandcastle, and watch the sun set. A plan like that was much less risky.

With my palms sweating, I got out of the car in front of the impressive home and walked with Audra up to the front door. She rang the bell, and the door swung open almost immediately.

"Merry Christmas!" A nice-looking older man smiled and motioned for us to come inside. His dark hair was graying at the temples, giving him a stately but well-groomed appearance. There was no mistaking that his smile was genuine.

He leaned down to Audra's level. "Did you bring doughnuts?"

Audra shook her head, taking his comment seriously. "Mrs. Miller told us to bring a salad."

He snapped his fingers in an "oh too bad" fashion. With a jovial smile that made his eyes crinkle in the corners, he said, "A man can dream, right?"

Audra caught on to his teasing. "I brought my new art set. I could draw a picture of a doughnut for you."

He laughed and looked up at me. "I'm Bob. You must be Emily. And don't tell me . . ." He returned to eye level with Audra. "You must be Audra."

My suddenly confident daughter lifted her chin. "Princess Audra, if you please, Mr. Bob."

I was stunned. Trevor said she had been cheeky with some of the customers the days she had gone to the dealership with him. I was ready to apologize and say something about how she must have been watching too many Disney movies.

Bob didn't miss a beat. He raised an eyebrow. "Princess Audra, is it?"

With a precocious smile Audra said, "Well, a girl can dream, can't she?"

Bob burst into the best sort of laughter. He gave a playful bow and bid us welcome to his "humble abode." With a glance at me, he said, "You are going to be just fine here."

His unusual comment fell on me like a blessing. I felt calmed and included in his home and with his family. I considered taking Audra aside and instructing her not to be so flippant. But I knew that might spoil her outgoing enthusiasm for the day. Perhaps I needed to relax more with her and accept that her personality was developing to be more like her father's and less like mine.

Bob took the salad bowl from me and led the way into the great room where a dozen people were gathered. He made a quick introduction of a cluster of five guests who, he explained, were all connected to his real estate business. They seemed to be in their own discussion and simply gave me a polite nod.

A formal dining table was pushed up against the floor-to-ceiling windows that looked out on the long stretch of golden sand leading to the water. The table was covered with an assortment of platters and bowls of delicious-looking food. Running down the center were beautifully placed silver and white Christmas decorations. The image was stunning. The way the sunlight shone made the whole room seem to sparkle.

"Hi, Emily." The soft voice beside me in the swirl of people, music, and conversations was Christy's. "I'm glad you came." She gave me a hug, and I returned the same.

"Is your husband with you? I wanted to introduce him to Todd, my husband."

"He's trying to find a parking place."

"We rode our bikes here for that very reason. It's tough to find a spot."

I looked across the room and saw that Audra had found her way to her favorite little blond three-year-old, Cole. Sitting next to Cole was an adult version of Christy's toddler. There was no doubt that he was Cole's daddy. The funny thing was that Todd reminded me of a Winslow with his square jaw, blond hair, and clear blue eyes. I was sure that if Todd and Trevor stood next to each other, I wouldn't be the only one who would see the resemblance.

That is, if Trevor finds his way here.

"Have you met my aunt yet?" Christy asked.

"No."

I scanned the room and smiled at Mr. and Mrs. Miller who were seated beside each other on the leather love seat next to the stunning Christmas tree. A middle-aged woman with short hair and glasses stood in front of them sipping from what looked like the same crystal stemware my mother-in-law had. "Is that your aunt?"

Christy glanced over her shoulder. "Yes and no. That's my husband's aunt. Aunt Linda. My aunt Marti must be in the kitchen. I'd like you to meet her. She's . . ." Christy started walking, so I followed her back through the entryway.

"My aunt is . . ."

We walked past the wide staircase and into a large kitchen that appeared to be recently remodeled because everything looked state of the art. No one was in the kitchen.

Christy seemed to still be at a loss as to what she wanted to tell me about her aunt Marti. She led the way back to the entry just as the doorbell rang. Christy opened the door, and I felt a wave of relief to see Trevor standing there.

"Hello, I'm Christy." She welcomed him inside.

"Trevor." He pointed at me. "I'm the guy who follows this girl wherever she goes." His gaze then went above our heads to the grand staircase behind us.

Christy and I turned to watch a petite woman with stylish, short dark hair come down the stairs with a regal, floating-on-air appearance. Her outfit of long pants and a top with butterfly sleeves shimmered as she approached us. Even her dainty shoes gave off a golden slipper sort of glow.

I glanced at Christy. She seemed to be watching my expression. I hoped my calm look and slight nod let her know she didn't need to explain anything about relatives to me. I understood how it could be with the ones who had a lot of money. I was just glad that Audra hadn't been with us. I'm sure she would have spouted something awe-inspired and slightly embarrassing at the sight of such a dramatic entrance.

Marti approached us with warm politeness and shook our hands. I noticed her diamond rings and perfectly manicured nails. I couldn't stop looking at her. Marti was Mrs. Miller's sister, and yet she was in every way the opposite of Christy's mother.

"So glad you could join us," Marti said. "Please. Enjoy the buffet. Merry Christmas."

Trevor seemed as taken aback as I was. Not only with the theatrical gestures Marti was making but also with the outgoing demeanor of Christy's uncle Bob and the extravagant details found all over their home. Trevor and I had both worn jeans, thinking we were going to a beach house and spending the afternoon sitting in the sand with Audra.

Fortunately, I had learned how to fit in with our well-to-do Winslow clan, so that helped me forget that we were underdressed or that my wooden salad bowl didn't match any of the upscale serving dishes on the buffet table. Trevor struck up a conversation with the real estate group, but the conversation didn't go very far once my husband revealed that we were renting and not sure how much longer we would live in the area.

Christy brought her husband over to the buffet table as we were dishing up and introduced us. Trevor and Todd started talking about cars. I felt uncomfortable with the way things so far had turned into a meet and greet for potential business deals.

I made my way over to the empty sofa when Christy went to fetch something for her aunt from the kitchen. I watched as Trevor and Todd held their plates, standing and talking but not eating; Todd must have suggested that they sit down because the two of them went outside to the adjoining patio and sat at the table. They seemed caught up in an animated conversation that I guessed was about carburetors and hubcaps. I could see them through the window and felt grateful that at least they seemed to have hit it off. I just hoped Trevor wasn't trying to turn this into a sales pitch.

I found lots to chat about with Christy's mom and felt more relaxed than I had expected. What surprised me was that a short time later Trevor came inside and said he and Todd were going to ride bikes down to Todd's house. He wanted to know if it was all right to leave Audra and me for about an hour.

"Sure. Why are you going to his house?" I asked.

"He has a restored VW van. I've gotta see it."

"Is he thinking of selling it?" I asked cautiously.

"Don't know. Doesn't matter. I want to check it out. I'll be back."

He looked happy. I wasn't going to say or do anything that might mess with that look on his face. A few minutes later I noticed the two of them out the window. They were on beach cruisers that had child bike trailers attached to the back. I hadn't expected to see my husband on a bike, grinning like a little kid, today.

Christy and her parents were on a video call to her brother and his wife. Marti and Linda were both chiming in about the weather, the food, the gifts. I picked up that Christy's brother and his wife were in Oregon visiting her family. From the many voices that came through the phone, it seemed similar to how Trevor's family had sounded when we called them that morning. I noticed that Mrs. Miller had put on a resolute expression and was saying all the right things to her son and his wife with slightly exaggerated cheerfulness.

She reminded me of Trevor's mom. I thought of how every mother must have the same Christmas wish—that she could be with all her children for the holidays.

Almost every mother.

I hadn't called my mom and my brother when Trevor had suggested it that morning. We had gotten sidetracked and then hurried out the door. After reaching for my purse beside the sofa, I pulled out my phone and saw that my brother had sent a text.

Merry Christmas! Enjoy that California sunshine.

That was all. It was fine. At least he thought of me, and I appreciated that.

My mother was spending Christmas with him and his family in Albuquerque, the way she always did. I knew I should call but decided I would wait until Trevor and Audra could be on the call with me.

After all these years, I really should stop feeling sorry for myself. The truth is, I would feel more uncomfortable with them than I do here with people I've never met before.

I returned to the buffet table and scooped up a second helping of the delicious stuffing Christy's uncle had made. I took a seat on a chair tucked to the side of the tree. I was slightly hidden yet able to watch all the movement in the living room and beyond. Todd and Christy's six-year-old daughter, Hana, had taken to Audra, and my little girl had taken on the big sister role to both Hana and Cole with pleasure. She was seated cross-legged under the tree reading new storybooks to them when the doorbell rang.

"Oh, good!" Marti exclaimed. "Jennalyn and Joel have arrived with their little ones. I was hoping they would make it."

My heart skipped a beat. I didn't know they were coming.

If I had made a second Christmas wish like my daughter did, this would be it. The chance to hold baby Alex. Perhaps it would be for the last time.

appy noises echoed through the house as Hana and Cole jumped up to greet Jennalyn's toddler, Eden. The three of them joined hands and came trotting back to Audra under the tree, ready for more stories.

Jennalyn hobbled toward me in her walking boot. I stood quickly to greet her. She hugged me for a long time before pulling back and introducing me to her husband. Joel hugged me and kissed me soundly on the cheek.

"You are famous to everyone at the Blue Ginger and to everyone in our family. Even my relatives in Italy know about you." Joel's voice was loud and cheerful. His personality matched his voice.

"Every time we tell the story," Joel told me, "your role grows grander. You're now the angel who arrived at just the right moment and gave my poor wife the strength she needed to bring our son into the world." He reached for me again and hugged me. "Thank you, Emily. Thank you."

My response was to smile. Only smile. I couldn't find words equal to his. The experience still felt so vivid and close to the surface that the memory brought tears to my eyes.

Jennalyn smiled at me. "I still don't know what would have happened if you hadn't come when you did."

Alex released a wail from the baby carrier Joel had placed on the floor next to the couch.

"Do you want to hold him?" Jennalyn asked.

I nodded vigorously but was still too choked up to say anything. I had been longing for this moment ever since I had held him only minutes after he was born.

Joel unfastened the straps in the baby carrier and proudly lifted his son. He placed Alex in my arms and then stepped back, asking if he could take a picture. "I need a photo of our angel."

I didn't like being called an angel. But I did like holding baby Alex and studying his tiny features. He was adorable. His cheeks had filled out, and he had already started to lose some of his newborn hair.

"I'm in love," I whispered to Jennalyn.

"Isn't he sweet?" She brushed the back of her fingers across his cheek. "He's done so well. He doesn't sleep more than about four hours at a time yet. But once he puts on a few more pounds, I'm sure he'll go a little longer between feedings."

Todd's aunt Linda stepped closer and gazed at Alex with an unexpected tenderness. She looked at me. "So you're the one who replaced me."

I knew that an older woman had resigned from being the hostess right before I was hired at Peggy's Pies. But Linda didn't at all seem like the sort of woman who would work as a hostess.

Christy had come closer too. She must have read the confusion in my expression because she said, "Aunt Linda is our ob-gyn. She delivered Hana and Cole."

"And I would have been there for the arrival of this little guy." Linda gently touched her finger to his nose. "That is, if he hadn't been in such a hurry to get out and see the big world."

"Well, it was getting a little crowded in there," Jennalyn said with a chuckle.

Focusing on me, Linda said, "I'm glad you were there, Emily. From what Jennalyn told me, it sounds like you're a natural birthing coach. A future midwife, perhaps."

"I didn't really do anything," I stammered. "I didn't know what to do. The paramedics arrived in time for the birth."

"They did their part," Linda said. "But what you did was equally important. Don't underestimate the nurturing power of what you did. You were right there with her, physically and emotionally. By entering the process along with Jennalyn in such a tangible, nurturing way, she was able to draw from your strength."

"That's true," Jennalyn agreed.

"It's primal," Linda said. "Women nurturing women in a very present, physical way has been the foundation of midwifery since the beginning of time. When you add the deeper level of emotional support the way you did, Emily, it makes everyone else's technical role much easier."

Linda added one more thought, as if she were leading a private workshop with the cluster of women in the room. "Don't you see? The paramedics were able to focus on the baby because you focused on the mother. It's a practice that's returned to Western culture over the last few decades, and I, for one, am glad to see the trend. Not every woman can do what you did, Emily."

"All I know," Jennalyn said, "is that I would never want to have another baby without that same kind of support and comfort. You have no idea what it meant to me, Emily."

I felt a surge of emotion coming to the surface and tried very hard not to cry.

"Jennalyn, are you thinking of another baby already?" Linda's voice had a teasing upbeat to it.

Jennalyn looked as if the thought horrified her. "One at a time, please."

We laughed, and Alex's eyes fluttered at the soft burst of noise. The women around me murmured sweet words of comfort to him as I held him and slowly rocked from side to side.

I hadn't told Trevor or anyone, but since Alex's birth I had dreams, vivid ones, about giving birth. I was the one feeling the contractions first-hand, not through Jennalyn's back. I was the one crying out and panting for breath. My subconscious seemed to be reliving the extraordinary, tense moment over and over. I was grateful for this beautiful moment with a circle of women when all was calm and I could hold him.

Out of the corner of my eye, I saw Audra watching me. The little ones had toddled off, and only Hana remained at Audra's side, smoothing the long hair on the new doll she was holding. I met Audra's gaze and smiled at her. She turned to Hana and whispered something that Hana appeared to be only slightly interested in.

I wondered what Audra told Hana. More importantly, I wondered what her keen listening skills had gathered about Alex's birth and my in-volvement in the dramatic event. She undoubtedly knew more than what I had told her.

I wondered what Trevor had told her or what she may have overheard when she was with him at the car lot. Did she know we were closing in on our January decision deadline?

I settled in one of the comfortable chairs and looked down at Alex sleeping peacefully in my arms. The Christmas music had been rolling around us all day and now moved on to a pretty instrumental arrangement of "Away in a Manger." Hana walked over to me with Audra beside her. They both leaned in for a closer look at Alex.

In the sweetest little voice, Hana softly sang to him along with the music. *"The stars in the sky look down where He lay. The little Lord Jesus, asleep on the hay."*

I wasn't the only one in the room who caught the innocent serenade. It lasted only a few moments before Hana went over to her grandma and climbed up on Mrs. Miller's lap. Christy and I exchanged the kind of smile shared by two moms who find delight in their little girls.

Hana's spontaneous song had stirred in me the deeper thoughts I had pondered yesterday on the way home from work. All the threads attached to the true story of the first Christmas wove themselves together in my mind. I felt part of it all.

The loss of all hope, a birth in the midst of uncomfortable circumstances, a sleeping baby—all these threads had wrapped themselves around my life this year. I felt connected to the ageless promise that had been fulfilled in such a tangible, human way with the birth of our Savior. It astounded me that even little children still sing of that moment in history on which all eternity hinges, as the radio preacher had said.

Emmanuel, God is with us.

Alex was squirming so I adjusted his position. I felt as if my heart had just filled up with hope. Not necessarily hope that we would have another baby. Or hope that we would get a grip on our finances or that we would make the right decision in January. Those ominous, ongoing issues were just part of what I was starting to feel hopeful about.

Mostly I found that I had hope because I believed more than I ever had that God was really with me. He was with us through everything. He was right there, close and engaged, whispering the encouragement I needed and letting me draw my strength from Him.

"I'm ready to defend my championship," Bob announced, breaking into the bubble of my thoughts. He sat beside me and spread out a board game on the coffee table. Looking around, he asked, "Where did Todd and Trevor go?"

"They went to our house," Christy said. "They'll be back soon."

"Then for the first round, it's you and me, Norman." Bob motioned for Christy's dad to come sit on the couch next to him. "Who is clever enough and brave enough to dare to challenge these two mighty men who sit before you?"

"Me!" Hana raised her hand and scurried over to her grampa, crawling up on his lap.

Mr. Miller took his granddaughter's adorableness in stride. Clearly she was smitten with her grampa, and the admiration was mutual. I was used to seeing Mr. Miller in overalls trimming bushes or uncurling a garden hose to wash down the walkway at the apartment complex. This was a side of the big, quiet man I hadn't seen before.

"May I play?" Audra asked.

"I thought you'd never ask, Princess Audra," Bob said. "Anyone else on your team?"

Audra looked at me only for a moment. Her gaze moved on to Mrs. Miller. Apparently my child, who picks up on everything, had managed to figure out something I hadn't yet. She had found out that Mrs. Miller's first name was Margaret. With all the sweet manners her daddy had taught her, Audra went over to Christy's mom. "Miss Margaret, would you please be on my team?"

The game began. I found a chair near the window and kept a greedy clutch on Alex. The real estate agents had all gone, so the group felt cozier to me. Jennalyn had settled on the love seat with Joel, who was holding out a forkful of food and convincing her to try it. They made a cute couple.

The room seemed to hum with Christmas music and the happy sound of children laughing. Eden came bounding into the living room. Seeing her mother's lap unoccupied, she scrambled to take what had once been her rightful place on the throne. Jennalyn whispered in her ear, and Eden grinned and nodded.

If Norman Rockwell had been able to peer decades into the future and paint what the ideal, God-loving modern family and friends would look like celebrating Christmas, this would be it. The scene I was observing would have filled his canvas with all the right expressions, lighting, and visible evidence of warmth between the people gathered together.

I tried to figure out why this afternoon felt different from the many Christmases I had spent with Trevor's family. It came down to the way that everyone in this room seemed to be comfortable. Comfortable in who they were and how everyone was dressed, comfortable with the kinds of food and the amount of food they ate, and comfortable with each other, old and young. I felt included. I felt comfortable.

When was the last time I felt like I belonged in a group this large?

Before I could scroll through a lifetime of memories to come up with an answer, I saw Trevor and Todd waving as they cruised past the windows and disappeared around the side of the house with the bikes.

Trevor came in still wearing the cool new sunglasses I'd given him for Christmas. He scanned the room for Audra, and when he saw her entrenched in the game, he went over to the buffet table. With a handful of carrot sticks in his fist, he strode across the room to me and with a wild grin said, "You wouldn't believe Todd's car. Classic. I mean, baby, it's a gem."

"Does he want to sell it?" I asked.

Trevor chomped into another carrot and shook his head. "No. He never should sell it. I'm tellin' you, if I had the patience to fix one up the way he did, I'd make it happen in a heartbeat."

I noticed that Trevor's faint accent had returned. That told me he was comfortable too.

"Guess what else this Daddy of the Year did?" Trevor asked.

"I can't imagine." I kept my voice low, hoping Trevor would catch on that I was holding a sleeping baby.

His enthusiasm got the best of him. "We brought back sand toys. To build a castle for you-know-who so she can have her second Christmas wish."

Audra looked up. She turned to us with her eyes opened wide.

"I think we need to have our daughter's hearing checked," Trevor said. "She's tuned in way too strong. Any chance we can get a doctor to lower her hearing? Just a tiny bit?"

Audra politely excused herself from the game and came over to us with her hands behind her back and an irresistible grin on her face.

"Yes?" Trevor teased, waiting for Audra to speak her mind.

She rocked back and forth from her heels to her toes, not saying a word.

"May I help you with something, miss?" Trevor asked.

"I heard you say 'wish.' It's one of my favorite words, you know, so I always hear it. Even if I'm asleep."

"I don't doubt that for one moment," Trevor said. "What would you say to the idea of making a sandcastle?"

Audra didn't need to be asked twice. As soon as the final moves had been completed on the board game and Uncle Bob had maintained his championship position, everyone got ready to hit the beach.

"I'll catch up with you," I said.

"This is a family project," Trevor said.

"Daddy." Audra took his hand. "She's holding a baby."

"I can see that." Trevor leaned in and took a good look at Alex. "Hi, little guy. Aren't you handsome! You know, I heard a lot about you. I mean, a whole lot."

Joel laughed from where he was seated next to Jennalyn. "You and I will have to swap stories sometime." He stood and came over to introduce himself to Trevor.

The two of them started talking, and soon Todd came in with a big blanket under his arm.

"Anyone want to go out on the beach and build sandcastles?"

"Me!" Hana raised her hand. I was beginning to notice that raising her hand was one of her favorite things to do, just as it had been for Audra.

Within a surprisingly short time, the entire group made a grand exodus out to the beach. Jennalyn stayed at the house so she could nurse Alex and because she said she honestly didn't feel up for the trek through the sand. Christy stayed with her, and they invited me to stay too. I knew I couldn't miss the sandcastle building.

"This was Audra's wish," I explained. "Her Christmas wish."

They both nodded their heads, fully understanding what it was like to have a daughter who gets an idea in her head and doesn't let it go.

The air was warmer than when we had arrived at eleven. The wind had chased away the haze, and the sky was spectacularly clear and blue.

"I'm so glad we came outside," Marti exclaimed as we tromped through the sand in our bare feet. She had changed into a pair of ivory linen pants and a long sweater over what looked like a silk top. I noticed all the particulars because, to me, the outfit she had changed into looked just as expensive and nice as the butterfly top she was wearing when she first greeted us.

Trevor and Todd led the charge across the wide beach down to the shoreline since we needed water to make the sand stick together. Christy's dad was carrying the bag of sand toys over his shoulder. He looked like an able Saint Nick replacement. All he needed was a white beard, a red coat, and a Santa hat.

Bob opened up the two beach chairs he had lugged through the sand.

Marti seated herself gracefully, and Mrs. Miller lowered herself into the other. Todd spread out the big beach blanket as everyone discussed what kind of sandcastle should be built.

Audra looked like she was in heaven. Sandcastles at the beach, plus an audience! She couldn't have dreamed anything better.

Soon the adults decided that with all the kids and the three competitive fathers, this should be a contest. The lineup was Trevor and Audra on Team Winslow; Joel and Eden on Team Marino; and Todd, Hana, and Cole on Team Spencer. Bob would be the referee, and Mr. Miller would keep Cole entertained if he started doing more destroying than building, or if he tried to run into the ocean, which he already had attempted twice.

My role was official photographer. I took my job seriously, capturing dozens and dozens of shots from all angles. Hana looked at me every time I came near to their castle and struck a cheesy grin with her eyes closed. Every time. She was so cute. Wide smile, not moving a muscle, and always with her eyes squinting closed.

Audra looked up at me when she and Trevor were nearing completion of their fortress, complete with a ring of broken shell fragments around the base and a bulbous bit of seaweed affixed to the top as a creative rendition of a flag.

"Take a picture now." She leaned close to Trevor and brushed her wind-tossed hair out of her eyes using the back of her sandy hand.

I turned my phone both directions and took six shots. "Looking good, Team Winslow."

"Can you send that to Gramma and Hailey and everybody right now?"

I selected the best shot and started to write a text to go with it.

"Send it to them and tell them we're having the Best. Christmas. Ever," Audra shouted.

I peered at Trevor. His hair was going every which way. He had sand on his face. His jeans were soaked up to the knees. He smiled up at me, and all I could think was that he looked like a man who, for one blissful afternoon, didn't have a care in the world.

"Okay," I said, not taking my eyes off my handsome husband. "That's what my text will say." Then I did it. I typed, **Audra said to tell you, we are having the best Christmas ever.**

My thumb hesitated, poised over the Send button.

I couldn't do it. No mother wants to hear from her son's wife that their first Christmas without her is their Best. Christmas. Ever. I deleted the words and sent the photos of my husband and daughter smiling wildly. No caption needed.

Chapter 11

We stayed on the beach until after sunset and came home sandy but happy, with a lot of leftovers that Bob insisted we take. I made turkey sandwiches while Trevor told Audra to shower and wash away the bits of the beach she had brought in with her. As soon as she closed the door, he motioned for me to help him to pull something from the closet. He pointed to the box with the three deflated air mattresses we had slept on when we had first moved into the apartment.

"Find as many blankets and pillows as you can," he told me.

As quickly as I could, I gathered bedding and collected all our throw pillows. Trevor had Audra's mattress inflated and positioned just right under the tree. We exchanged giddy expressions as I made the bed look like a pillow-festooned slumber party waiting to happen.

"Quick. Turn out the lights," Trevor whispered.

Audra emerged in her pajamas and stopped short the moment she saw the setup—a princess lounge beneath the twinkling Christmas lights. She ran to us squealing and wrapped her arms around Trevor and then gave me an equally exuberant squeeze.

"This really is the best Christmas ever!"

I loved watching Trevor's happy expression as much as I enjoyed the way Audra cozied herself into her nest of pillows and blankets and didn't stop smiling.

We ate our sandwiches together under the tree and talked in low voices as if this were a sacred ceremony. In some ways, it was. Maybe it would become another one of our new traditions.

At Audra's insistence, Trevor and I pulled the blankets off our bed and joined her on separate air mattresses. I can't say that we managed to snuggle down for a "long winter's nap" the way Audra did. It was a rough night for the two of us but well worth it.

I was behind all the next morning. I was three minutes late to work, which was the first time I was tardy. Mr. Sanchez acted as if my job were on the line. The day went quickly, and when I arrived home, the house was a mess. All my Christmas cheer was siphoned as I remade our beds, deflated the mattresses, and vacuumed. Trevor had taken Audra with him to work. The two of them didn't return home until after seven, but Trevor had sold a car while Carlos had sold two. It was enough to keep him still feeling the Christmas cheer.

A good night's sleep back in our own bed helped. But I was late to work again. My rhythm was off since I wasn't taking Audra to school. Mr. Sanchez growled. I apologized. The scent of burned toast filled the diner. It was a normal day.

The next day was a repeat except I was on time, and the first guests I seated were Mr. and Mrs. Thompson. I hadn't seen them since before Christmas. She had a smile for me and asked if I had a nice holiday.

"Yes, it was wonderful. How was yours?" I steadied the chair for her and gave her my usual shoulder hug.

"We had a quiet day." She straightened the cutlery at her place by the window. "Our dining room served us a lovely ham dinner."

"That sounds nice. The soup today is turkey noodle, by the way."

Instead of pondering the soup-of-the-day announcement as she usually did, she reached over and touched my arm. "Emily, did you like your Christmas card?" Her expression reminded me of an expectant child.

At first I didn't know what she was referring to. Then I remembered the card Mr. Sanchez handed me when I was leaving on Christmas Eve.

"You know what? I put your card in my purse, and I am embarrassed to tell you that I think it's still there. I haven't opened it yet."

"Oh." She looked terribly disappointed. Mr. Thompson appeared concerned, as if my negligence might dampen his sweet wife's disposition.

"I promise I will open it right after I get off work today."

She seemed satisfied that her kindness wouldn't be ignored. As she opened her menu, I returned to the hostess station, making a mental note to find her card and thank her for it the next time I saw her.

However, I forgot to look for her card.

The next morning Christy had invited Audra to spend the day at their house, so with the scramble of Audra getting all her art supplies together and Trevor herding her out the door, I was late to work for the third time that week. Mr. Growls took me aside and gave me a warning. I felt terrible. The whole day was bumpy.

Thankfully, Audra had a great day. She titled herself a "junior babysitter" and said that Christy had invited her to come again the next day. Christy confirmed in a text that Audra had been a huge help with Hana and Cole. She said Audra was welcome to come anytime.

Trevor was quiet and moody. I didn't ask how things were at work. Neither of us had much to say to each other. It felt oppressive knowing we were nearing the decision deadline after we had such an uplifting time with our new friends. Why hadn't we connected with them like this in August when we moved in? Not that it would have changed our financial position.

I loved being a family. Just our own little family and spending the day celebrating with new friends. The impression that God was with us had been so pronounced over Christmas. Why did I feel now as if I were floating in a murky river?

On Monday morning I arrived at work a full ten minutes early. As soon as I walked in the door, I remembered that I still hadn't opened the card from Mrs. Thompson. I was pretty sure it was in the bottom of my oversized purse along with all kinds of coupons, receipts, and other junk I needed to clean out.

Fortunately, the Thompsons didn't come in that day, so I didn't have to apologize again. Even so, I went back to my locker on my break and scrounged through my messy purse in search of their card. It wasn't there. All I could hope was that when I saw them sometime next week, Mrs. Thompson would have forgotten about it.

That evening as Audra watched TV, I emptied my purse on the counter and performed a long overdue purge.

"I need a smaller purse," I muttered to myself.

Audra replied without taking her eyes off the TV. "You can use the gift card Gramma gave you."

That child hears everything!

I returned only the necessary items to my shoulder bag and tossed everything else. Continuing with a round of cleaning and organizing in the kitchen and bathroom, I set my sights on the withering Christmas tree. It looked sad beneath the weight of the decorations. That's when I realized it had every right to be weary; tonight was New Year's Eve.

Without announcing my intentions to Audra, I pulled the Christmas box out of the closet and took some ornaments off the tree.

"Do we have to take it down already?" Audra jumped up and stood between me and the tree as if she were an extreme conservationist and I was threatening some sort of endangered species.

"It's time." My tone was firm. I kept focused on my task and invited her to help me.

She did so reluctantly, without saying anything. Once all the ornaments were tucked back in the box and the nativity set was safely wrapped and stored, I gathered up the edges of the skirt beneath the tree. It was a white flat sheet that I had arranged around the base. Audra had come up with the idea, saying that it would look like snow.

The problem was that the crumpled sheet was now full of dry pine needles tucked in every fold and crevice. I had Audra open the sliding door so that I could wad up the sheet and take it outside. As I was giving the sheet a good shake, something floated to the ground.

It was Mrs. Thompson's Christmas card.

"Audra, do you know how this card ended up here?"

"I found it in your purse. I put it under the tree so you would see it. I didn't open it."

"You shouldn't go through other people's purses either."

"Dad told me to look for a coupon for pizza. I knew you usually throw them in your purse."

"Okay. Well, next time ask before you go through my things."

I put the card on the patio table and finished shaking out the sheet, deciding I would wait to haul the tree out of the house until Trevor could help me in the morning. The final round of vacuuming would have to wait until then. I threw the sheet into our compact washing machine located in a closet by the front door. It was noisy, but it worked, and I didn't have to go to a laundromat, so I was thankful.

"Bedtime," I told Audra.

She sounded like a teenager when she gave me an exaggerated sigh and trudged off to brush her teeth. I sighed too when I sat on the edge of her bed. As eventful and joyful as Christmas had been, this entry into the new year was the opposite.

"When will Dad be home?" I noticed she had started calling Trevor "Dad" all the time now. It seemed to be another indicator that she didn't see herself as such a little girl anymore. I was glad she still wanted us to tuck her in.

"Soon."

"Could you pray with me?" she asked.

"Of course."

"I'll go first." Audra's prayer was thoughtful. She even included Carlos from the car lot. I prayed something short and sweet, kissed her, and closed her bedroom door.

Trevor was standing in the living room.

I jumped when I saw him. "I didn't hear you come in." I spoke as low as I could so that Audra wouldn't pop out of bed and come join us. The washer was in full spin cycle, which explained his unnoticed entrance.

The creases in Trevor's forehead told me that all had not ended well this last day of the year.

Trevor pointed to the patio. I took the throw blanket off the couch with me, tossed it around my shoulders, and sat at the table. He closed the sliding door and sat down across from me.

"We didn't make the goal." He drew in a deep breath.

I sat with him in silence for a moment before offering the only encouragement I could think of. "My paycheck will be higher this month."

"It won't be enough. Rent is due tomorrow. Our car insurance is due on the fifth. The list is long. We can't keep coming up short. This was our biggest month. Eleven cars. That's good. But it's not enough. It won't be enough."

His voice sounded surprisingly steady.

I reached across the table and slid my hand under his. I felt like my hand was a little bunny coming in from the snow and hiding in the sheltering cave of my husband's constant care. No words rose up for me to offer to Trevor. Nothing I could say would change anything or fix anything.

I felt an unexpected calm. I wouldn't call it peace. Maybe it was confidence. The confidence wasn't in Trevor or in our choice to move to California. It wasn't related to the dealership. What I felt was a closeness to God. I still felt sad, but I sensed that the God of this universe was with us. He saw. He knew. He was here.

We sat silently for a few minutes, my hand sheltered under Trevor's. I waited for him to make a declaration of what was now obvious.

"What I'm going to say next might not make sense." Trevor locked his gaze on mine.

"Okay."

"I think we should stay in California and figure out what we're supposed to do."

"You do?"

He nodded. "What do you think?"

I wanted to be careful with my words. His demeanor seemed different, and I wanted to make sure I was reading him correctly. "I'd like to stay too. However, I think I'm at a place where I'm okay if we leave. But I keep thinking this is where we're supposed to be."

Trevor studied my expression.

"Do you feel like there's something more for us here too?" I asked.

Trevor nodded and shrugged at the same time. It was more of a twist than a gesture of indecision. "I don't know what it is, exactly." He shifted in his seat again. "Todd said something Christmas Day that I keep thinking about. We were talking about what it looks like to trust God and believe He is at work even when you can't see it."

"What did Todd say?"

"He was telling me how he and Christy met when they were young, and he believed he was going to marry her, but she was dating another guy. He said he kept praying and trusting and waiting even though it made more sense for him to walk away."

I liked hearing Christy and Todd's love story from her husband's point of view. Obviously, it was a good thing that Todd hung in there and waited for Christy. What I liked even more was that Trevor and Todd had connected the way they did.

"Todd challenged me to wait and trust God. He used the example of Abraham in the Old Testament and how he trusted God for what seemed impossible. Todd even prayed with me about whether we should stay."

"And?"

Trevor leaned back and let out a deep breath. He pulled his hand away from mine and folded his fingers behind his head. "I think we should stay."

"Okay," I echoed.

"What's that?" Trevor dipped his chin toward a white envelope on the table amid the seashells and bits of driftwood Audra had collected on Christmas. I had rinsed off everything and set it outside to dry.

"It's a Christmas card from one of the ladies who comes into Peggy's every week with her husband. I told you about Mr. and Mrs. Thompson."

"The couple who just drink tea."

"Yes, that's them." I reached for the card and slid my thumbnail under the flap. Pulling out the Christmas card, I noted the snowy scene and a snowman wearing a red Santa hat on the front. A piece of paper fell out when I opened the card.

Unfolding the letter-sized piece of paper on nice stationery, I read the letterhead aloud, "Wright, Connelly and Medina . . . Attorneys at Law?"

"What?" Trevor lowered his arms and leaned in. "I thought it was a Christmas card."

I skimmed the typed letter and read it again, holding my breath. It couldn't be right.

"What is it?"

I handed Trevor the letter for him to read. There was no way I could read it to him. My mouth was open, and my eyes were fixed on him, not blinking.

Trevor's expression of stunned amazement mirrored mine. He still had a voice, though.

"It says that Evelyn Thompson is giving you money."

I blinked. "I know."

He scanned it again. "He says he's her attorney, and she does this every Christmas. She selected you this year. You're supposed to go to their office and fill out some forms so they can release the check."

He looked at the card and the attorney's letter again. "It looks legitimate."

I started to breathe again. The amount listed would cover our rent for two months.

"Emily, what did you do for this woman?"

"Nothing."

"Nothing? Are you sure?"

I shrugged. "Well, I do always tell her the soup of the day."

Trevor's laugh must have roused our neighbors. My husband kept laughing, and I decided it didn't matter how loud he was. This was extraordinary. Beyond any Christmas wish I had made.

Even though we had a couple of hours before midnight, someone a few blocks over was lighting off fireworks, and all the dogs in the neighborhood were going crazy.

"Happy New Year," Trevor roared. He hopped up and pulled me from my chair, tossing the blanket on the ground.

Wrapping his arms around me, Trevor kissed me. It was one of the top five best kisses he had ever given me. I knew my lips and my heart would remember that New Year's Eve kiss for a very long time.

Chapter 12

S o you're saying that all you had to do was sign some papers at the attorney's office, and he handed you a check?" Sierra was seated next to me on the sofa at Bob and Marti's house where almost twenty women were gathered for Jennalyn's baby shower.

I nodded, glancing over my shoulder to see who else may have heard Sierra's comment.

"That's crazy!" she said.

"I know." The news had spread about the check because Trevor had been so open and enthusiastic about it. He couldn't wait to tell Todd since the gift seemed like an affirmation of our decision to stay.

Trevor's favorite part of our step-of-faith story was that we had decided to remain and trust God for our finances before we opened the card. I wanted God to receive all the credit. Well, and maybe sweet Mrs. Thompson should get a little credit too.

I just felt funny about everyone knowing.

It meant all these people also knew how desperate our financial situation was. That was probably a pride issue I needed to deal with. A few years ago, a gift like that would not have been an amount that could change our lives. Now it changed everything.

Christy's aunt Marti had decided to host a baby shower for "just us girls" and had come up with the theme of royalty when everyone was making sandcastles on Christmas, two weeks ago. The setting was as lovely as it had been on that special day.

When we arrived, each of us was presented with a ladies-in-waiting tiara. I removed mine after the first ten minutes, but Audra wore hers proudly, sitting straight and poised, taking it all in.

Jennalyn was opening her gifts, and the first one was from Marti. It was a specially knit crown for "Prince Alexander" made from gold yarn and embellished with small gems cut from felt and sewn into the cap.

Sierra's attention shifted to Alex as the cap was placed on his head. I was glad because I didn't want to keep talking with Sierra about Mrs. Thompson's gift, especially if anyone else could overhear us.

I thought maybe later I would tell Sierra about the way we thanked Mr. and Mrs. Thompson. It seemed to mean a lot to them. Audra made them a thank-you card, and Trevor came to Peggy's Pies one morning so that he could meet them and thank them personally. He invited them to come to our home for dinner whenever it was convenient for them. We hadn't set a date yet, but every morning when they came in, they said they were checking their calendar.

Jennalyn looked so happy, seated on a chair that occupied the corner where the Christmas tree had been. She wore a long indigo-blue dress. Her smooth, dark hair flowed over her shoulders, and on her head had been placed a wreath of white and pink flowers with green leaves that gave her the appearance of the most lovely, earthy, and elegant image of motherhood. She was the queen for the day, and we were her willing subjects, eager to pay homage to the gift of new life that God had blessed her with.

My daughter's inner fairy princess was enthralled with all of it. Especially the sandcastle cake, which Marti had ordered from an exclusive baker who was apparently connected to the Blue Ginger restaurant where Joel worked.

The gifts were opened with lots of oohs and aahs from Prince Alex's loyal subjects. It seemed that Jennalyn genuinely liked the blanket and stuffed lion toy that Audra and I gave her. Audra hopped up to follow some of the other women to the table where the cake was being served. I stayed where I was and watched the others cluster in small bunches, eating cake and chatting.

"I hope I didn't embarrass you earlier." Sierra slid in next to me on the couch.

"Don't worry about it."

"I did embarrass you, didn't I?"

"A little. It's okay, though."

"I'm over the top sometimes." Sierra had lowered her voice, sincerely apologetic. Her baby girl was positioned over her shoulder, and Sierra was gently patting the diaper end of Ella Mae's floral onesie. "It's so good that you guys are staying and that God is providing and everything. Jordan and I have been in a season of figuring out what's next for us, and I think I got so excited for you and Trevor because that's how I would feel if something unexpected like that happened to us."

Sierra had twisted her wild curls up into a knot soon after she arrived and positioned her tiara like a moat around the fortress of hair. Renegade strands had escaped and looked like blond streamers having their own party on top of her head. I couldn't dislike free-spirited Sierra or hold a grudge.

I turned toward her so that my body language would convey friendliness even if I still felt timid around her and a little nervous about what she might say next.

"We're grateful for how it worked out for us to move here," Sierra said. "I think I'm still adjusting, though. To everything. You know?"

"Yes, I do know." I took a risk and told her, "Trevor and I lived with his parents for almost ten months before we moved to California."

"You did? How was it for you guys?"

"Necessary." I gave a nervous laugh. "That's how it was."

"I hear you," Sierra said.

"It was mostly good," I added. "Challenging sometimes."

Sierra nodded her understanding. "I love my in-laws. I really do. They're great. And they are so sweet with Ella. But it's different. I mean, really, really different from how Jordan and I lived in Santa Barbara. He's working all the time, and we hardly see each other. I know it's hard for him because he feels like he's failed at providing for us as a family. His dad is big on the husband being the head of the home and being responsible and everything."

"He sounds a lot like my father-in-law. Trevor felt the same way. Like he had failed as a spouse."

"I mean, Jordan is responsible. His whole career up until now has been photography. It's hard to make a living in the arts. Now that he has a desk job, I feel like I'm watching him wither a little bit each day. We have thousands of photos of Ella that are incredible. But, you know. It's just hard."

"I know."

She switched the burp cloth and Ella to her other shoulder. "I can't imagine how hard it was for you guys to move all the way here from South Carolina."

"North Carolina," I quickly corrected her. It was instinct for me to do so. For some reason Trevor's family never wanted anyone to consider them as being from "the other Carolina." I didn't fully understand why it was such a big deal.

"Moving here was a big change for us and for Trevor's family," I said. "They're all very close. Trevor is the youngest of five kids."

Sierra grinned. "I was in the middle of a family of six kids. Big families are becoming a dying breed, aren't they?"

I nodded.

"What about you guys? How many kids do you want?"

I didn't reply. I was debating what I wanted to say. Our conversation had been refreshingly sincere and honest. Maybe it would be okay at this point in our growing friendship to give my standard answer of, "We'd like as many children as God blesses us with."

I didn't say anything, though, because Marti called out, "Princesses!" Standing next to Jennalyn in her chair, Marti cleared her throat. "We've come to the part of this celebration that I have been looking forward to the most. Christy, would you come here, please?"

Christy put down her cake plate and took her place beside Jennalyn's chair, next to her aunt. She reached over and slipped her hand into Jennalyn's and gave her a smile.

"We are going to bless our guest of honor," Marti declared. "As some of you know, this is a tradition of Christy's that I used to watch with fascination. They blessed their house, their children, and every woman who was honored at a birthday party or shower under their roof. I see it as a beautiful, holy moment that we get to share because we are Jennalyn's women."

Marti glanced at an index card cradled in the palm of her hand. She didn't seem nervous but rather intent on what she wanted to say. "As you know, Jennalyn's mother went on before us to the Great Celebration, as I like to call it. She wasn't here, on earth, to be with her daughter when she entered motherhood with the birth of Eden and now of Alexander."

I felt a clench in my chest. I didn't know her mother had passed away.

"This adds another layer of importance as to why we circle our Princess Jennalyn today. We want to bless her and remind her that she is not alone on the journey of motherhood. We are with her. We are here for her. We are her women."

I choked up. Marti's dramatics had seemed a bit over the top. But now I saw that what she was saying and doing came from a deep place in her heart. All the frills and the tremble in her voice were there because of her passion. It was beautiful.

Marti mentioned that if Eden hadn't been home with the sniffles, she would be part of this moment with us. Then Marti invited us to stand, sit, or kneel facing Jennalyn. Marti would read a short poem and verse, she explained. Then Christy would pray a blessing over Jennalyn and baby Alex, who was cradled in Jennalyn's arms.

Marti paused at the end of her instructions and turned to whisper something to Jennalyn and Christy. They both nodded and looked at me.

"Emily." Marti offered me an outstretched hand. "It occurred to me that you should stand with us. Would you please join us?"

I felt I had no choice.

Taking my assigned place on the other side of Jennalyn, I brushed back my flyaway hair, even though it wasn't really in my eyes. I looked down at Alex sleeping soundly in Jennalyn's arms. I kept my gaze fixed on him and tried not to think about all these women watching me.

Marti leaned in and whispered to me, "You don't need to say anything unless you would like to."

"Okay. I mean, no. I won't say anything. Thank you," I whispered back.

"That's fine." Marti's low voice was surprisingly calming while still directive. "Now, would you place your hand on Jennalyn's shoulder? Yes, like that. Very nice."

Turning to address the gathering of women who were all taking the pageantry as seriously as Marti was, she read the poem with heartfelt inflection. The last line caused her voice to quaver. I'm certain I would have cried if I were the one doing the reading. The sentiment was perfect for Jennalyn in every way.

Marti continued by reading Psalm 113 as dramatically as if she were on a theatrical stage.

"Praise the Lord!
Praise, O servants of the Lord,
 praise the name of the Lord!

Blessed be the name of the Lord
 from this time forth and for evermore!
From the rising of the sun to its setting
 the name of the Lord is to be praised!
The Lord is high above all nations,
 and his glory above the heavens!

Who is like the Lord our God,
 who is seated on high,
who looks far down
 upon the heavens and the earth?
He raises the poor from the dust,
 and lifts the needy from the ash heap,
to make them sit with princes,
 with the princes of his people.
He gives the barren woman a home,
 making her the joyous mother of children.
Praise the Lord!"

I looked over at Christy as she then placed her hand on Jennalyn's forehead. In a confident and natural manner, Christy smiled at Jennalyn and then at Alex. Her words rolled out, sounding like an unrehearsed prayer, almost like a half-sung benediction. The blessing for Jennalyn and for her newborn son was one of the most sacred, simple, and beautiful things I had ever heard spoken over a woman at a shower of any kind.

All the guests echoed an "amen" at the end. Mrs. Miller caught my gaze and smiled at me the way she had before Christmas when she told me about her jasmine bush.

I started crying. The tears felt warm as they pooled at the corner of my upturned lips. My hand moved, unplanned, to the back of Jennalyn's head. As if beckoned by some ancient, motherly, nurturing instinct, I stroked her soft hair the way I had when she was in labor. The crown of fragrant flowers that circled her head filled my senses as I drew in a deep breath.

Something sweet and eternal had been planted in all of us that day.

I don't remember much of the rest of the baby shower. There were tears, hugs, thank-yous, and kisses brushed on my cheek. Audra and I left, both of us wearing our tiaras, but neither of us speaking.

All I could think about were the many showers I had attended in the past, during which the focus had been silly and embarrassing party games. The conversations at those gatherings had been about diets—or rather "eating plans"—clothes, skin care, and, of course, cars. There was always talk of cars.

Not today. Marti had made this celebration all about Jennalyn and her baby boy.

As Audra and I walked the three blocks to where I had done a ridiculous job of parallel parking, she slipped her arm through mine. I was thinking of how none of the women with whom we had shared such an extraordinary afternoon had any idea what kind of car I drove. I didn't know what they drove either, thanks to the scattered parking.

"Mom?"

"Yes?"

"Could you and Dad bless me?"

I smiled at my fanciful wish maker. "Do you mean the way we blessed Jennalyn today?"

"No, I mean the way Miss Christy blesses Hana and Cole when they go to bed. I've heard what she says. I can tell you so that you get the words right."

"Let's ask your dad about it when he gets home."

Satisfied with my answer and probably certain that Trevor would do whatever she asked, Audra picked up the pace on the way to our car.

Trevor was in favor of the idea, especially after Audra had gone into exhaustive detail about the baby shower. She recited the blessing she had heard Christy pray over Hana and Cole. She even took Trevor's hand and placed it on her forehead so that he would know exactly how it should be done.

When bedtime came, Trevor and I stood next to Audra's bed. She had her comforter pulled up, her eyes closed, and her chin lifted with a honeyed grin, waiting for her blessing. Trevor had brought his Bible with him. He told Audra that the variation of Miss Christy's blessing was actually from Numbers 6:24–26.

She opened one eye as if to protest and say that it wasn't a Bible verse Miss Christy prayed. But Trevor already had his hand on her forehead, and when she heard the first line he read, she settled back and let him finish all the verses.

"Amen," Audra said at the end.

"Amen," Trevor and I echoed in unison.

"I wouldn't mind if you wanted to do that every night," Audra said.

Leaning over to give his princess a kiss, Trevor said, "As you wish."

I gave her a kiss and told her I loved her. Holding hands, Trevor and I exited, closing the door and heading into the living room. I was thinking that for all the moments we had fumbled as parents and for all the things we had done incorrectly or incompletely, this singular moment fell into the we-did-good category. My heart was happy.

"Do we have any laundry that needs washing?" Trevor asked.

I pulled back and gave him an incredulous look. "Why in the world would you ask such a thing?"

"Because"—he slipped his arm around my waist and pulled me close before murmuring in my ear—"when the washer is going, you can't hear other noises."

I liked the way his thoughts were heading. "You know, I think the rug by the kitchen sink is looking pretty dirty."

He gave me an amorous look. "We better do something about that."

The next morning Audra was pouring herself a bowl of cereal while Trevor and I were doing what had become our customary morning dance in the kitchen, trying to maneuver around each other in the compact space.

"What was all that noise last night?" Audra asked.

Trevor and I exchanged side glances, keeping our expressions unchanged.

"What noise, sweetheart?" I asked.

"That thumping and pound, pound, pounding sound."

Trevor lowered his chin and turned his head so Audra couldn't see his repressed smile.

"It was the rug," I said.

I shot Trevor a "don't you dare lose it" look. "I was washing the kitchen rug, and it's kind of a big rug."

Trevor started coughing and made an exit for the bathroom. I turned my back to Audra and opened the refrigerator as if I were looking for something.

"Mom!"

"Yes, Audra?"

"Don't you think you should see if Dad's okay? It sounds like he's choking."

"Trev?" I called out. "You okay?"

He cleared his throat and called back, "Yeah, I'm good."

Trevor didn't return to the kitchen. I was glad because I knew he would send looks my way, shooting them across the room like Cupid's arrows.

I pulled my smile back, cleared my throat, and shot a side glance at Audra. She was reading the side of the cereal box and seemed oblivious. Although, with this girl I knew we could never be certain.

"Mom, may we go to the beach this weekend?"

"Possibly. It's supposed to rain again toward the end of the week."

"We could go in the rain."

"Why don't we decide when we get closer to Saturday?"

"Okay." She hopped down and went to get her backpack for school.

"Audra, come back here and take your bowl to the sink, please. I am not your personal slave."

As soon as I heard myself spout that last line, I winced. I had grown up hearing that from my mother and had vowed I would never say it when I was a mom. The words had popped out so effortlessly.

"Sorry," I said, when Audra returned and picked up her bowl.

"For what?"

"For saying I'm not your slave."

Audra looked unaffected by the words. She hadn't taken them inside her heart along with a dose of shame the way I always had. "Okay," she said. She started back toward her room but then stopped and turned to me.

"I would never think you're a slave, Mom. It's like what Miss Marti said. You're a princess. Me too. That's because God is the King of kings, and we are His daughters."

I stood where I was, not moving. How did she understand that truth so clearly? She was only ten. I was thirty-one, and I still had a hard time grasping what that meant.

My daughter seemed so grown up as she meandered off to her room with her self-image glistening.

Chapter 13

*J*anuary brought more rain than any of the TV weather reporters had predicted. By the third week of on-and-off rain, the news updates escalated. News crews went on location to the Santa Ana River, and the cameras zoomed in on where the aqueduct had been compromised. Officials offered explanations about why past damage hadn't been repaired during the dry months.

We kept the TV on a lot more since we were near the potential flood zone. For two days the local news gave us safety tutorials in case of flooding and issued warnings about safe drinking water. Trevor put together an emergency kit and went over our family evacuation plan.

On the night of the next big storm, we all wore our clothes to bed and had a survival suitcase packed and waiting by the front door.

As the night wore on, Trevor and I didn't sleep much. We listened to the rain hitting the metal covering over our patio. Around two in the morning we got up and padded into the living room. Trevor turned on the dull outside light and used his flashlight to check the backyard. The cracked concrete patio was wet, but the water wasn't coming toward our back door. The narrow area along the back fence was a muddy mess, but we didn't appear to be in any danger of flooding. We returned to bed and slept fitfully for the next few hours.

Trevor was the first one up the next morning. He had the TV on with the volume low. Pointing to the screen, he said, "Only four inches. No damage from flooding."

I stared at the TV feeling an unexpected surge of anger. "The storm only brought four inches? Why did they say it was going to be so bad?"

Trevor shrugged and turned to another news channel. "Maybe there's more coming."

We fell in step with our usual Wednesday morning routine since the weather wasn't going to cause school closures. I couldn't let go of my anger. All the preparations had been expensive and disruptive. Audra had been frightened, and I felt the exhaustion that came after days of waiting and not knowing.

"You okay?" Trevor had just watched me throw away a dried-out heel of bread as if it had personally insulted me.

"They made all those announcements." I pointed a butter knife at the TV.

"No one knew for certain what the weather was going to do," he said. "The major storms have all passed. They predict light showers this afternoon. That's all. It was better for us to be prepared, don't you think?"

I let out a low grumble.

"What? You're disappointed that we aren't filling sandbags right now or driving through flooded streets to a shelter?" Trevor looked as if he wanted to laugh at me.

"No." I tried not to show the intensity of my emotions at that moment.

"That's what you sound like." He was definitely grinning now.

I looked away and kept my frustration to myself because Audra had returned to the kitchen and was ready to go.

She chattered all the way to school about how she was glad that classes hadn't been canceled and that the flood hadn't come. Today was art and music day, and she hoped the teacher would let her sit in the front this time.

"I hope so too, sweetheart. I'll see you after school." I pulled out of the carpool lane and felt the exasperation inside me simmer again.

Why am I so angry?

I remembered something my counselor had told me after I had hit my lowest point over a year ago. She said anger is one of the stages of grief, and I shouldn't be surprised if I struggled with anger as I processed the results of our infertility treatments.

"But I'm angry at the weatherman," I said aloud as I sat waiting for a light to turn green.

A row of logical thoughts lined up as if they were ready to present their case to me. It wasn't the weatherman's fault. It wasn't anyone's fault. I had heard that before.

The light changed, and I moved forward, recognizing the invisible connection. The anger I felt was kin to the conga line of hope-dashed moments I'd lived through for so many years. My life had revolved around the same process we had just gone through. Get ready. Take the necessary steps. Follow the instructions of the professionals. Then wait, never being sure of the outcome.

I pulled into the parking lot at Peggy's Pies and muttered, "I'm still mad."

The skies overhead were clear. The sun had taken its usual spot just over the top of the roof of the restaurant.

"I'm surprised you're willing to show your face this morning," I growled at the radiant orb as I trucked to the front door.

It turned out I wasn't the only one who felt grouchy that morning. The return of the sunshine meant we had a return of our regulars. Nearly all of them wanted to talk about the storm. Most of them sounded disappointed that it hadn't brought the predicted flooding.

Listening to them hushed me up. I calmed down as I repeated all morning how glad I was that everything had turned out the way it did. One of the waitresses had run out of patience with the conversation by the end of her shift. She came over to me and said, "It's like they all paid their money to see a show, and since the curtain never went up, they want their money back."

I thought about her words when I got off work and headed to Audra's school, ready to join the lineup of cars in the drop-off/pickup lane. The clouds had been gathering since noon. As I waited, the rain started. The invigorated drops touched my windshield like tap dancers.

It reminded me of a rainy January afternoon in Albuquerque, where I grew up. As a child, when it rained, I would read. I had a favorite chair by the window where I would sit and read and look at the way the raindrops hit the glass, and then I would read some more.

During the ordinary, sunny days in Albuquerque, I would have a list of chores that I would accomplish as quickly as I could and then venture over to my friend Cassie's house. Her mother let her watch TV after school, among other things. That was where I found out what was popular for girls my age. I learned songs from listening to Cassie's favorites over and over. I pictured myself in outfits like the ones in Cassie's teen magazines.

I remember always waiting, nervously, for my mother to ask what Cassie and I did at her house. I knew she wouldn't approve of the TV shows, the music, or the magazines.

Strangely, my mother never asked.

My swell of anger from that morning had dissipated. That is, until this new thought about my mother settled on me. Did she simply not care about what I was doing as long as I wasn't underfoot? Or did she trust me to monitor myself at that age? I suspected the answer was lack of interest. And that's when the anger returned.

A week after the flood-that-didn't-happen, I was home alone while Trevor was at the grocery store with Audra. I decided to call my mother. I had been thinking a lot about my childhood; maybe she and I could reminisce together. I'm not sure how I came up with that fairy-tale notion. Maybe I thought there was a first time for everything. Since I had been in a reflective mood for a week, maybe she had been, too, and we could stitch together some shared memories.

It had been more than a month—almost two—since I had talked with her.

She answered, and I did what I always did. I worked my way through the usual topics: How was the weather? Did she have a good time at my brother's over Christmas? Did she manage to avoid getting the flu?

Her replies were short and cordial, as usual. She asked how Audra was enjoying school, and if she had used the gift card my mother had sent.

"Not yet. She's trying to decide what to use the gift card for. I mailed you a thank-you card that Audra made."

"Yes, I received it."

"Oh, good. She's becoming quite a little artist."

"Yes, I noticed that."

"I don't think I was much of an artist when I was her age."

"Hmmm." It seemed my mom was trying to remember.

"I'm not sure where the creative gene came from."

She didn't reply, so I kept going with the informal thank-yous. "By the way, Trevor and I appreciated the gift card you sent us for Christmas too. I'm guessing you saw my thank-you note. It was in the same envelope as Audra's."

"Yes, I saw it. Thank you."

"We haven't used our gift card yet either. But we will. It was very generous of you. Thank you."

A pause followed where I anticipated a "You're welcome" to be inserted. My mom seemed distracted, so I threw out a question that I hoped would spark some good memories. "Do you remember the Christmas when the electricity went out and we opened our gifts by candlelight?"

"Yes."

"That was a good Christmas."

She didn't reply. Maybe that hadn't been a good Christmas for her.

"We thought our electricity might go out last week. We've had a lot of rain here. They predicted flooding."

"Yes, I heard about that."

"It didn't happen, though. Everything was okay." As soon as I realized we had circled back to the weather, I knew I had run out of things to say. A pause followed.

"Well, I just wanted to call and see how you're doing."

"I'm doing well. Thank you for checking in."

"Okay. Well . . ." I glanced at the wall where I had recently hung a framed photo of Trevor and Audra on Christmas Day. They were next to their sandcastle on the beach. The setting sun had created a radiant burst of light right behind their smiling faces and captured the moment perfectly.

Even though my mom hadn't asked, I concluded the call with, "We're all doing fine here."

"Good."

"Bye, Mom."

"Goodbye, Emily."

I went over to the sofa and stretched out, staring at the ceiling.

Why did I think anything would be different this time? What is that saying about the definition of insanity?

I sighed.

The truth is, I keep hoping that one day she will say, "I love you." That's all. Just "I love you, Emily." How can it be so difficult for a mother to say that to her own child?

I thought of how my mother was always polite. She wasn't mean. She had done admirably well after my father had passed away and she had to raise my younger brother and me alone. But my lifelong defense of my mom by explaining how difficult things had been for her was waning. The older I got, the more I realized that Trevor had been right all along. My mother's superpower was withholding approval.

Was that why I struggled to feel accepted by other people?

Don't go there. You don't need to psychoanalyze yourself right now.

I rolled off the couch quickly, as if it had been the sofa of a therapist. I didn't want to ignite any of the anger tinder that had caught fire so quickly before. I'd been in a calm place emotionally for the past few days, and I wanted to stay there.

A few days earlier I had stopped at a thrift store with Audra. One of the finds I had brought home was a small gold frame that cost only fifty cents. I pulled it out of the hall closet and carried it into the bedroom. In the back of my Bible was the card Jennalyn had given each of us at the Favorite Things party. Taking it out, I was happy to see that when I placed the card over the frame, it was just the right size.

Later, when Trevor and Audra came in with their bags of groceries, I was still in a steady mood. The bit of cleaning and organizing I had done helped me to feel like I had accomplished something useful. And I had framed the card and placed it in the center of the windowsill above the kitchen sink. Next to it was a small cleaned-out jelly jar that I had filled with broken bits of seashells Audra and I had collected on our trips to the beach when we first had moved here.

"Hey," Audra said, "that's new." She flashed a quick smile of approval at my artistic attempt. "Dad said I could watch a show on his iPad in my room as long as I use the earbuds."

"And?" Trevor prompted her.

"And if I come help you with dinner right away if you ask me to."

"Okay." I smiled at her but had a sinking feeling. Trevor must have had something to say to me that he didn't want her to hear.

As soon as Audra was in her room with the door closed and the groceries were put away, Trevor said in a calm voice, "I talked to my dad today."

I was beginning to dislike every conversation with Trevor that started with, "My dad called today."

Trevor leaned against the counter and crossed his arms. "It seems my mom and dad have reframed our decision to stay here."

"What do you mean?"

He kept his voice low. "When we talked to them on New Year's, apparently I said that you and I had decided to 'stick it out' here."

"Yes."

"They took it to mean that we were going to 'stick it out' here until the end of Audra's school year."

"Did you tell him you meant 'stay here indefinitely'?"

"No."

"Why?"

"Because my dad said he and my mom found a place for us to live so that we wouldn't have to move in with them. It's not a very big house, he said, but they put in an offer on it and thought we could lease it from them. They would carry the note."

"Trevor . . ."

"I know. I didn't expect any of this. I thought we were clear with them."

"I guess we weren't."

"My dad also said a senior sales position is open now at the Cadillac dealership. It's not the manager position he offered before, but he's going to hold it for me until the end of June."

The anger I had managed to repress earlier was now sending flames up my neck. "What did you tell him?"

"I told him I would have to call him back."

I looked away.

"Emily, don't do that."

"Do what?"

"Withdraw like that. We need to talk about this." Trevor uncrossed his arms and tried to place his hand on my shoulder.

I pulled away.

"Tell me what you're thinking," he said.

"I'm thinking that we already discussed all this." I spun around to face him; my voice was white-ember hot. "We said we were going to stay. Remember? I thought you meant we were staying indefinitely. Are you telling me now that all along you were planning to only stick it out until June? You're driving me crazy!"

He didn't reply.

I wanted to slug my husband. I couldn't remember ever wanting to hit him before. The force of rage that had so suddenly ignited inside me was frightening.

My throat was so tight, it hurt to speak, but I had to ask the question that had surfaced. "Has it been your secret plan all along to go back in June?"

"No, of course not! I don't have a secret plan." His voice rose. "I have no plan. Can't you see how difficult this is for me too?"

Well, then get a plan! This is too painful for both of us. We already went through all this indecision. I don't want to do that again. I want to feel like I'm home.

I didn't speak the words aloud because they were smoke, not flames. The fiery blast that had run through me had burned every last emotion I had left standing. Ever since New Year's Eve, my heart had been trying to move forward with hope. I had believed that this was it; living here was what was next for us. God was with us, wasn't He?

All my hopes and wishes were now ashes.

I felt the tears welling up. I didn't issue permission to any of them to tumble out. Not one drop. I wanted to stay mad, even though nothing was left for my raging thoughts to burn down.

Trevor's jaw clenched and unclenched. I watched him look over my shoulder as if there were something or someone behind me competing for his attention.

A rogue tear escaped. I refused to let any more follow. Being ignored was such a deep wound in my soul that I felt frozen in time. It was as if I had fallen into a small, dark space inside myself where all was very quiet.

Then Trevor read aloud, his gaze still fixed behind me. His voice was low and as rough as gravel. "We confidently and joyfully look forward to actually becoming all that God has had in mind for us to be."

I wished I had never bought that frame at the thrift store or inserted the card or placed it on the windowsill. Jennalyn's verse from Romans seemed to mock everything I felt at that moment.

Confidently and joyfully look forward?

How could I be confident about anything?

"I'm going to bed," I said in a thin voice. "I don't want anything to eat."

Trevor didn't stop me. I closed the bedroom door softly. There was to be no slamming of doors in our family. I knew the rules.

Flopping on the bed, I then rolled on my side and curled up like I remembered doing when I was a child and my mother would send me to my room. I always felt small and sick to my stomach when she disciplined me this way. I felt covered in shame for something I had done or not done. Once it was because I left my shoes in the wrong place. Another time I accidently broke a dish. The worst memory was when I had mistakenly closed my brother's finger in a door.

My punishment was always isolation by being sent to my room. Nothing was said. No scoldings were given. No spankings or restrictions.

The technique was efficient and effective because I always tried hard to be attentive. My goal in life as a child was to be faultless. I think that's why I responded so completely the first time I heard the gospel. The possibility of feeling the release of all that guilt was irresistible. The promise of grace, unlimited grace, drew me to God.

My head started pounding the way it always did when I tried to hold in my tears. I finally let the tears surface and flow until they soaked my pillowcase. The pounding in my head felt like a drum. Memories of our many years of infertility treatments marched in time to that beat in a circle around the bed.

I couldn't stop thinking of all the well-meaning women in Trevor's family and how I had quietly taken in their endless advice for years. I had gone to every specialist. I had tried every oil, herb, position, and food. I had read every book and followed every chart they had supplied me with. I had been a willing pupil. A diligent student.

And I had failed.

I was the only one in the clan who had failed to produce a son—another Winslow male heir to carry on the dynasty.

Rolling on my back, I wiped the last tears away and took a long breath. I folded my hands over my stomach and felt as if my barren womb were swollen with painful thoughts. I wanted to be delivered from the past, and somehow I believed that could only happen here, in this place of new beginnings.

I can't go back to North Carolina. Trevor needed to understand I couldn't go there. Not now. Not yet. Not until I found a way through this or past this.

Chapter 14

The next couple of weeks were difficult. I worked hard to organize my thoughts. Once my emotions were in a more reliable place, I told Trevor that I felt this was the place for us for now.

He didn't disagree. But he kept going back to the promise of a house and a job as tickets to stability for us. "I've come to the conclusion that you and I can make it work here or there," Trevor told me. "The only way that will happen, though, is if we agree on what's best for our family."

"What do you think is best?" I asked him.

He looked so lost when he said, "I don't know. I just don't know."

I appreciated the way he kept his parents at bay, telling them that he and I needed to keep praying and talking things through before we could respond to their offer. It felt like Trevor was sticking up for "us" and that made me feel settled enough to carry on in this stretch of limbo that we had entered once again.

I don't think his parents understood why we were taking so long to decide. They honored the boundary, though, and let us have time. They didn't call or text either of us for a couple of weeks.

Valentine's Day hit during that stretch of radio silence from the mother

ship. I tried to do something special for Trevor and decided to make banana pudding with crushed vanilla wafers on top. I knew it was his childhood favorite. I think I was trying to provide him with some comfort food
and demonstrate that while I would never be a phenomenal cook like his
mom, I could still make a few things that would brighten his day. I guess
I wanted him to believe that I was all he needed. Audra and me. We were
his family.

He came home with a bundle of red roses for me. In keeping with our
uber-frugalness, he pointed out that it was only half a dozen. Then he kissed
me, and I liked the gift of his kiss more than anything. It had been a while
since he had kissed me or offered any other expression of affection.

I pulled the roses out of the grocery-store wrapper that still had the price
sticker on it and cut the stems before placing them in a vase.

"Trevor"—I counted the roses a second time—"there are seven roses
here."

Audra, who was at the kitchen counter, said, "Maybe because it's Valentine's Day they added a bonus flower." She was laying out all the valentines
she had received at school that day and sorting them as if she were playing
some sort of matching game.

"Thank you," I said again, catching Trevor's eye. "They're beautiful."

Our family dinner was simple. At Audra's request, I had bought a heart-
shaped cookie cutter the week before. The cookie cutter had been put to
good use all day—from our heart-shaped morning toast to our dinner of
heart-shaped hamburger patties. Audra appreciated the whimsy more than
Trevor did.

He did a good job of making the family dinner special for Audra by
surprising her with a small box of chocolates and a little stuffed bunny that
was holding a sign that said, "I wuv you." Audra took the bunny to bed with
her that night and called to us to come bless her. It had become our routine.

None of the nights had felt as precious and important as the first night, but Audra seemed to glow every time.

The unresolved topic hung between Trevor and me with more urgency that night. Maybe the dinner and gifts reminded him it was a holiday and that invited melancholy feelings. Or maybe the buzzer had sounded on his internal timer, and he felt he needed to get in the game.

Trevor went into the kitchen and pulled out the bowl of what remained of the banana pudding. He pulled two spoons from the drawer. I expected him to tilt his head, indicating that we needed to talk out on the patio.

Instead, he held up a spoon for me.

"I'm full," I said. "It's all yours."

He grinned and took a big scoop. "So good," he garbled.

I smiled. Valentine's gift accomplished.

"I'm going to leave work a little early tomorrow night. Todd asked if I would help out with a group he leads for high schoolers."

"Oh?"

"He's been leading this informal group for a lot of years. It's a Bible study held in a garage. He told me at Christmas that he needed help and asked if I would be interested."

"I didn't know that."

"I told him I couldn't help because of work. Plus, I didn't know if we were going to be moving right away." As he talked, his voice sounded less heavy. "He called the other day and asked again, so I said I would help."

"That's great."

"I know. It's been a long time since I've done anything like this."

I leaned against the kitchen sink, bracing myself in case he had any other surprise information. He finished off the rest of the pudding, and with sweet banana breath, he kissed me.

I kissed him back.

Slipping my hand into his, I led my husband to the Real Happiest Place on Earth. That night we gave each other what we both really wanted for Valentine's Day.

The next night I waited up for Trevor. I was eager to hear how things had gone at the Bible study with Todd.

Christy had texted me that afternoon to say how much Todd appreciated Trevor's willingness to help out. She told me the group was called The Gathering, and they had grown to more than fifty high school students. They were packed into the garage of one of their friend's homes.

Trevor was buoyant when he came home. He reminded me of a younger version of himself, as he talked about the original worship songs Todd played on his guitar. "It was really something to see the mix of students all worshipping together like that. Reminds me of when you and I met."

It had been a long time since he had smiled at me with a look of endearment. I loved what The Gathering had done to him.

"Todd taught from the book of James," Trevor went on. "Did you know he's a Bible teacher? He teaches Old Testament at South Coast Christian Academy. He also leads mission trips for the school to Kenya every year. One of the guys was telling me about it. If I was eighteen again, I think I would have signed up right then. I didn't know any of that about him. Did you?"

"No, I didn't."

"Todd said he would like me to help out with the group as often as I can. If it's not a conflict for anything with you and Audra, I told him I would."

I felt a new sense of hope. Did this mean that Trevor was thinking we were about to step out of Limbo Land and make a final decision to stay?

"I'll help up until June, of course."

My shoulders dropped. "June?" My toes curled and uncurled, awaiting what he would say next.

"Yeah, June. They don't meet during the summer."

"Oh."

I felt more fragmented than ever when we went to bed that night. Trevor fell asleep first. I curled on my side, trying to piece together what all this meant.

If Trevor gets connected to Todd and this group of teens, will that influence his decision to stay? Or will the financial part in all this override everything in the end?

I didn't sleep well that night.

The next day I was scheduled to work for eight hours starting at seven o'clock. All I could think about during my shift was how much I wanted to go home and take a nap. Jennalyn had invited me to go to her house that night, and I wasn't sure that I wanted to go. A week ago I was eager to meet with everyone. I felt differently now that I was back in an emotional trench.

Trevor texted me as I was leaving work, saying that I didn't need to pick up Audra because he was getting off early, and the two of them would bring pizza home for dinner.

I should have taken advantage of the lull and snatched a short nap as soon as I got home. Instead, I cleaned the bathroom, which led to a hands-and-knees floor scrubbing. I have no idea why I thought that was a good idea.

By the time Trevor and Audra entered with the pizza, I was in need of a shower and had convinced myself I wouldn't go to Jennalyn's.

"You almost didn't go that first time," Trevor reminded me. "Look how glad you are that you did."

"I know. I'm just tired."

"You should go, Mom," Audra added. "I would go if I were you. You haven't seen baby Alex in a long time. If you go, you can hold him while he's still little."

"He's not even three months old yet. I'm sure he hasn't grown that much since the baby shower."

"You won't know unless you go tonight." Audra glanced at Trevor. I suspected he had told her to coax me since I already had told him I probably wouldn't go.

The pizza box was sitting on the counter unopened, and the two of them were looking at me as if they were going on a food strike if I didn't agree to head over to Jennalyn's.

"Okay, fine. I'll go."

As I showered, I used a new conditioner Audra had convinced me to buy because it was on sale. My hair seemed longer and fuller. The change gave me a boost of confidence. I left at a few minutes before five o'clock feeling lighter than I had for many days.

Standing on the welcome mat at Jennalyn's front door, I felt different than I had the other two times I had rung her doorbell. So much had changed in the way I related to these women.

Yet little had changed over the months with the uncertainty Trevor and I were experiencing. None of them knew the tug-of-war my heart had been going through. None of these women could have imagined how unstable our future was.

Is it a good idea for me to keep meeting with them? Getting closer and closer with them is only going to make it more painful if we leave.

Before I could talk myself into bolting, Sierra came up behind me with Ella Mae cozily tucked into her baby carrier that locked into the car seat.

"Emily! How are you?" She hugged me the way a longtime friend affectionately greets another.

I felt like an imposter.

Inside we found Jennalyn, Christy, and Tess at the kitchen counter where Tess was holding baby Alex. Jennalyn was tossing a colorful salad in a beautiful blue bowl with a Mediterranean design.

I stepped over to the sink to wash my hands. Turning to reach for the dish towel that hung on the handle of the oven, my thoughts flashed to an image of that dish towel, this kitchen, and the event that took place over two months ago in the same spot where I was now standing. It seemed unreal.

Alex started to cry. His wail was surprisingly strong for such a little guy.

"Here, I'll take him," Jennalyn said. "He's past his usual dinnertime."

"What can we do?" Christy asked.

"Everything is ready." Jennalyn reached for Alex and took one last look at the food on the counter. "Why don't you all grab something and take it out to the backyard?"

I joined the other women and carried a basket of warm baguettes wrapped in a linen cloth. The sight that met us was charming and inviting. I hadn't seen Jennalyn's backyard before and was taken aback by how enchanting it looked. Several mature trees dominated the space. They spread their leafy branches like an umbrella over a long table that took center stage on the grass. The mismatched chairs, simple white plates topped with salad bowls, and the awaiting glass bottles of spring water made it clear that we were anticipated. Welcomed.

I noticed half a dozen Mason jars hanging from the branches on long wires, each one cradling a votive candle. They seemed to be in readiness, too, with a promise that they would cast a warm glow on our conversation around the table once the evening twilight gave way to the hush of the night.

"It's so inviting," I said to Jennalyn, who was following me with Alex in her arms. He had stopped wailing for a moment, apparently recognizing his mother's touch.

"Nothing fancy," she said. "Since the rains stopped, I've been eager to get outside. This is the first time we've attempted a dinner, so you guys will have to help me figure out what needs improving."

Alex seemed to remember why he had been crying earlier and broke into an urgent plea for his mother's full attention.

"Everyone, find a place; make yourselves comfortable." Jennalyn already had seated herself in the chair at the end.

"Are you expecting more people?" Sierra asked.

I had noticed, as well, that the table was set for double the number of our group.

"I invited some other women, but all of them canceled. It's just us. Feel free to remove the extra plates."

Christy and Tess efficiently rearranged the place settings, which made more room for the large salad bowl, bread basket, and the small bowls of olives, almonds, and cranberries, which were toppings for the bountiful salad.

We settled in. Sierra took the bench seat that was covered with a colorful patchwork blanket. It worked out perfectly for her to keep Ella beside her in her carrier.

Christy suggested we hold hands and say a prayer before we ate. I reached for Tess's hand across the table and for Sierra's next to me.

I bowed my head and waited for one of the women to pray aloud. No one said anything. After an awkward moment, Christy prayed, "Father God, I want to thank You for each of these women and for the way You brought us together. Thank You for the beauty of this little hideaway spot. Would You bless our time together and bless our conversation? Amen. Oh! And thank You for the food."

Sierra added a finalizing "amen," and we all looked up, releasing our hands and glancing at each other.

Christy's face was rosy. "Sorry, I wasn't sure if I was supposed to pray or Jennalyn was going to."

"I wasn't paying attention." Jennalyn was adjusting her top and trying to get Alex in a better position. "Sorry."

"Do you need a pillow?" Sierra asked. "I saw your nursing pillow on the couch."

"Would you grab it? Thanks so much."

Sierra went into the house, and Christy motioned for Tess and me to help ourselves to the salad. Tess reached for the salad tongs and dug in. I met Christy's gaze across the table. "I get flustered, too, whenever I pray aloud."

"It doesn't seem right to apologize for praying," Tess said. "I'm learning from all of you. The only prayers I know are a few short rhyming ones that I memorized as a child."

"Where did you learn them?" Christy asked.

"From a nun." She handed the salad bowl to me. "I went to a Catholic school in third and fourth grade. Then it was public school after that. What about you guys?"

"Public school," Christy said.

"Me too," I said.

Sierra had returned with the pillow for Jennalyn. She also had a throw blanket. "Is it okay if I bring your blanket out here in case anyone gets chilly?"

"Sure. Thanks for the pillow." Jennalyn settled in and said, "I went to private school all the way through. What about you, Sierra?"

"Homeschool and private Christian school. Then Rancho Corona University with Christy."

Christy nodded in remembrance. "Seems like ages ago."

"It sure does." Sierra drew back the corners of the linen that covered the crusty bread. "This looks delicious."

"I have a confession." Sierra broke off a chunk of the baguette, dipped the end in one of the three dishes of olive oil and balsamic vinegar on the table, and said "Yum" as she took a bite.

"Is that your confession?" Jennalyn teased. "Yum? You're confessing that the bread is yum?"

"No. My confession is that if this was supposed to be our first book club meeting, I didn't read the book. Sorry, Tess."

"You don't have to apologize."

"Yes, I do. You picked out a book for us months ago. We were going to start a book club. I got lost along the way."

"The reason I invited everyone tonight was because I thought it would be fun to get together," Jennalyn said. "Trust me, I haven't read any books lately either."

The two moms of infants exchanged a chuckle and nod of mutual understanding.

"I thought we were getting together tonight to talk about our word for the year," Christy said.

"I hope not," Tess said. "Because I don't have anything to share on that subject."

Jennalyn raised her hand. "Before anyone else apologizes for not reading a book or coming up with a special word for the year, let me assure you, there is no agenda. I just wanted us to get together because, to be honest, I've been going a little crazy being inside with a newborn and a toddler."

"I hear you," Sierra said. "Well, minus the toddler. I can imagine your cabin-fever level during all the rain was double what mine was."

"So who were all the other people you invited?" Tess asked.

"Some women I've met over the past few months. One was a nurse who took good care of me at the hospital after Alex and I were wheeled in. Another woman I met at physical therapy last week."

"Is your ankle still bothering you?" I asked.

"It's actually my hip that's been the problem. I compensated too much when I was in the foot brace, and it threw my alignment off. I'm better now."

"I'm glad to hear that," Christy said. "I didn't realize you were having trouble."

"I didn't want to make a big deal about it."

"You can make a big deal with us." Tess looked at me and then at Christy. "And I hope you don't mind my saying this, but I'm glad it's just us tonight."

No one else added to Tess's comment, but inwardly I agreed. When we had stepped outside and I saw the table set for nearly a dozen people, I immediately felt anxious. Like Tess, I was glad it was just us.

Tess said, "I mean, I know how much you love drawing women together like this, and I'm the first to say that I've benefited from all the women you've introduced me to over the years. But this group right here—this feels good to me. Just the right number of women and the right balance of personalities."

Jennalyn looked around the table at the rest of us. "You know, I think that's a good point."

"I'm not trying to tell you who to invite and not invite to your fabulous soirees," Tess said.

"My mom always had luncheons for larger groups," Jennalyn said. "I've tried to duplicate her parties. Sometimes I think the women in the generation before us had more time to get together or needed to be in a bigger group, or something."

None of us agreed or disagreed.

Jennalyn looked stunning in the glow of the candles that now gave off their radiance above us as well as in the middle of our feast. She was comfortably seated in the head chair, nursing her son, with her long hair pulled back by a wide, folded scarf so that her face caught all the light. She looked like a modern-day Madonna and Child statue.

"One of the things I learned from my mother," Jennalyn said, "was to always make room at the table for everyone."

"It's a beautiful legacy she passed on to you," Christy said. "You are a haven maker, Jennalyn. Just like the title of the book Tess suggested we all read."

"I don't know if I'd call myself that. So many times when I've invited women to come to something at my home, they say they'll come, and then the day of the gathering, they cancel. Why do you think that is?"

"Women are afraid to commit," Tess said. "At least that's the category I usually fall into."

"I think they're afraid to be known," Christy said. "That's how I felt when you first invited me to your summer soiree years ago. I felt inadequate as a new mom, and I didn't know what to talk about."

Jennalyn grinned. "That night it turned out to be just you and me, and we found lots to talk about."

"Starting with that chocolate amaretto . . . What was that cake Joel made for us that night?"

"Oh, right. I remember that. I'm going to ask him to make another one for our next gathering."

I considered sharing that I almost had canceled the night of the Favorite Things party and considered doing so again tonight. But I didn't say anything. Maybe I was one of the women she was talking about who was afraid to be known.

Was that because I thought no one would want to spend time with me if they found out we might be moving? Or was it that I didn't want to open up and talk about myself? Was I afraid they'd judge me? Pity me? Try to give me advice?

I took another bite of the delicious salad and reminded myself of the ways these women already had opened up and accepted my family and me. Why wouldn't I want to be honest and open with them?

"Let's be our own small group," Jennalyn said with a finality in her voice. "I can still host other gatherings with lots of women. But let's be our own little hive. My home is always available as our haven."

"I like that idea," Sierra said. "Does everyone else?"

I nodded, and so did Christy.

"We should come up with a name for ourselves, if we're going to keep gathering regularly," Tess said.

"*If* we're going to keep gathering?" Jennalyn repeated.

"Okay. Since," Tess stated firmly. "Since we're officially a group, what should we call ourselves?"

Chapter 15

*T*he suggestions for a name for our group were all over the place. We couldn't say we were a book club because, as we had proved tonight, those dots hadn't connected for any of us. Sierra tossed out "The Hive," based on Jennalyn's comment about being our own hive. That prompted a bunch of silly and cute bee-themed names.

But, as Jennalyn said, none of those names "stung" us just right.

"We should figure out what we are to each other." Christy had kept silent during the "bee" buzzing ideas but now spoke with confidence. "We are women who are figuring out how to be what each other needs. We're becoming the sister we don't have or the mother we lost or the friend we want to be."

"That's it," Sierra agreed. "That was beautifully said."

"I love that," Jennalyn chimed in. "It's true. We're sort of nurturing each other."

"That's what I felt the first time I came," Sierra said. "Usually it's hard to break in when a few women are already friends, you know? That certainly was true the whole time I was in Brazil. I mean, I had some friends, but I always was trying to break in to established circles. And the language was a problem for me."

"How long were you in Brazil?" I asked.

"Almost five years. That's a long time to be trying to give and serve and follow God's leading and not feel connected to any other women at the heart level." She brushed a runaway blond, curly tendril off her forehead. "At the very end of my time there, I did connect with a Brazilian friend, Marianna. But right after that, I moved back to the States and had to start all over again."

"I'm glad you called me as soon as you knew Jordan and you were moving to Irvine," Christy said.

"I'm glad Jennalyn and you invited me to your fun little watermelon fest the first week I was here. Most women who are already in sync with each other would say, 'Sorry, no room at the inn. We're good.' But from the moment I walked in, I felt welcomed. I think both of you have the gift of hospitality."

"I felt that way too," I said bravely. "I was so nervous about coming the first time and—"

Before I could make a further confession, everyone started talking at once, pointing out what a loss that would have been if I hadn't come that first time. They continued saying kind things about me and how they couldn't imagine the group without me.

For a woman whose heart feels permanently starved for affirmation, their words went deep.

"I don't want to even try to imagine what would have happened if you hadn't come that night and then showed up at just the right time to pick up your cookie plate!" Jennalyn said.

"I feel like we're doing life together," Tess said. "Real life. With all the good things and unpleasant things that come at us. It's not fluffy life."

"What is fluffy life?" Sierra asked with a laugh. "Do you mean like what some of my friends post on social media? Because I never have had, nor do I think I ever will have, a fluffy life."

Christy grinned. "Do you mean the posts of infinity swimming pools and palm trees? Those kinds of social media posts?"

"Exactly. Fluffy life," Tess said. "I have a friend from my modeling days who loves to post pictures like that. She travels all over the world and has an entire album of all the exotic spas she has visited."

"You were a model?" I asked.

Tess nodded. "I'll have to tell you about it sometime. I only did it for five years."

"What do you do now?" I realized I was getting us off track, but I wanted to know.

"I'm a personal stylist."

"What is that, exactly?"

"I help women to develop their wardrobes and—"

"She's being humble." Jennalyn interrupted Tess and positioned Alex over her shoulder to burp him. "Tess has a very successful business working with a short list of high-end clients. Is that what you call them?"

"High profile," Tess said.

"As in, movie stars and other performers." Jennalyn cradled Alex back in her arms. "But don't ask her about her clients because she won't tell."

"They value their privacy," Tess said. "And I value keeping their business."

I looked at Tess's flawless skin and blue eyes and took note that she did seem to always wear nice-looking outfits with just the right amount of jewelry. I thought she was classy when I first saw her, but now I viewed her as classy and elegant. I was curious how she and Jennalyn first met, but that bit of information would have to wait. The others had returned to the topic of a good name for our group.

"Does the Non-Fluffies work as a name for us?" Sierra grinned. "Or maybe the Just Us Group."

"We're like Eve," Christy said.

"Like Eve?" Jennalyn echoed. "What do you mean? Like, we all mess up?"

"Yes," Christy agreed slowly. "We are very much human. But it's more than that. I was thinking of how in the Chronicles of Narnia Aslan calls the children Sons of Adam and Daughters of Eve because they're human. Not fluffy." Christy leaned in, warming to the thought. "They struggle to trust and not be afraid and figure things out along the way."

"I like that." Tess sat back and took in Christy's comment.

"Daughters of Eve." Jennalyn's expression lit up. "That's what we are. All of us can relate to Eve in different ways."

Jennalyn looked at me and smiled. "Eve didn't have a mother to be there when she gave birth or help her to know how to raise her children."

"Eve and her husband had to figure out how to start over," Sierra said.

"That's a good point," Christy said.

I drew in a deep breath. "Eve knew what it was like to have everything and then lose it."

"It sounds like all of us qualify as Daughters of Eve." Jennalyn thought a moment and added, "We can call ourselves the DOEs. Get it? Daughters of Eve?"

Sierra burst into song. *"Doe, a deer, a female deer."* Her singing, followed by our laughter, caused Ella Mae to stir. Sierra rested her arm on the carrier and rocked it back and forth.

Jennalyn looked at me, smiling and lifting Alex. "Would you like to hold him?"

"That's a question you never need to ask twice." I went over to Jennalyn, taking her little love along with his blanket. I changed chairs, this time sitting at the other end of the table in a chair that had arms and a cushioned seat.

Alex cuddled up, wrapped in his soft blanket, gazing at my smiling face and looking beyond, at the hanging candles.

The moment was dripping with sweetness. I loved being with these women. I loved the way I felt around them.

"I have something I want to say." Christy sat up a little straighter. "You know how I always ask God for a word for the year? Well, I wanted to share that my word for this year is *listen*."

"What a great word," Sierra said.

"I know. It kept coming back to me," Christy explained. "I know I'm usually private about how a theme for each year is just between the Lord and me. This year, I felt like I needed to tell you guys because I want you to help me to be a better listener."

"Goals," Tess said as decisively as if it were a word with a hashtag in front of it.

"We were just saying that we are each other's sisters, mothers, and friends. So I want to ask you sisters that if you see me interrupting or not paying attention, take me aside and tell me. All you have to say is, 'Christy, what was your word again this year?'"

"Are you sure that was supposed to be your word?" Sierra asked.

"Yes, no doubt about it."

"Because I think that should be my word for the year." Sierra added, "I'm the one who runs ahead in conversations and misses the important parts. Are you sure God didn't give you that word so that you would give it to me?"

We chuckled. Sierra was fun to watch. She reminded me of a fairy princess out on a holiday among the common folks.

"I'm happy to share my word with you," Christy said. "There's no reason we can't have the same word for the year."

"See what I mean?" Sierra looked at the rest of us. "Why would God give you the word *listen*? You're the kindest, most intentional one in the group. I don't think you need to listen more."

"Yes, I do," Christy said resolutely. "As soon as that word surfaced in my thoughts, I knew that was it. I haven't been very intentional about listening to the Holy Spirit when He's nudging me to do something or say something. Things in my life always go so much better when I listen to Him."

"I know what you mean," Jennalyn said.

"The other way that word hit me was with my family. I definitely need to listen to my children more. I tune them out way too much." Christy lowered her eyes. "And it's been a long time since I've stopped everything and sat and listened to Todd the way I used to."

The circle of women grew quiet. I imagined all the Daughters of Eve were evaluating their own listening habits. I knew I had room to improve when it came to listening to God and to my husband and daughter.

"I'm glad you told us, Christy," Jennalyn said. "I can't say that I've sensed God giving me a word. The last two months, the only word that keeps recurring in my head is *sleep!*"

As the others laughed at Jennalyn's comment, I felt an unexpected rustling in my spirit. It was the return of the familiar, pulsating thought that had come to me in December when the word *release* seemed to rest on me. I hadn't thought about it for weeks. But right then, sitting in Jennalyn's backyard, as I held baby Alex and felt the warmth of his little body bundled up in my arms, I knew that was my word for the year.

Release.

What happened next was unplanned. I didn't think of it as something I would do, nor was it something I had longed to do.

I didn't tell the Daughters of Eve my word for the year. Instead, I told them my story.

What tumbled out like a waterfall was the whole, unfiltered version of how Trevor and I had been told that we fell into the category of "secondary infertility." We had optimistically followed all the well-meaning advice that led us down a trail of hope. I told them about all the money we had spent on the infertility treatments. All the shots Trevor had to give me. All the doctors, tests, charts, and procedures.

I cried as I told them how interwoven Trevor's family had been in the journey over the years, how high their expectations were, and how painfully difficult it was for me to accept the final defeat over a year ago. And how we were officially bankrupt.

Then, because I had gone that far, I told them about the worst day.

"We were living at my in-laws' because, as I said, we had to sell our house." I handed Alex over to Jennalyn because he was fussing. I was grateful because I was beginning to feel uncomfortable holding him while divulging the details about our non-baby status.

"Go on," Sierra said. "What happened?"

"I was talking to Audra in her room about something unrelated. I know now that for months—years, actually—I had pushed everything down instead of processing it in the moment. All that compression hadn't diminished any of my emotions. It just made them compacted."

"Like a spring ready to pop," Sierra added.

I nodded. "Like a spring. I didn't realize how tight it was. Then, on that ordinary afternoon, Audra and I were talking, and I realized I didn't have any feeling in two of my fingers. Then my arm went numb. I felt a sharp pain in my neck, and I thought I was having a heart attack."

"How terrifying," Tess murmured.

"We were the only ones home, so Audra had to dial 911. She thought I was dying. I wish I had never put my daughter through that traumatic experience." I felt my throat tightening.

It seemed the others were all practicing Christy's word, *listen*. They waited for me to finish saying all that I wanted and needed to express.

"It wasn't a heart attack. I had a panic attack. I was holding my breath and not realizing it. My hands and arms tightened and curled in. I couldn't feel my legs. My whole body silently was screaming and going into a slow paralysis. I couldn't stop the process.

"That's when Trevor started talking about making a big change and moving to California. The doctor had referred me to a counselor, and she thought it would help if Trevor and I could distance ourselves a little from his family because that's where so much of the pressure was coming from, at least for me. In my mind, I felt trapped."

I caught my breath. "Trevor didn't see it that way at first, but the counselor explained to him how enmeshed we were with his family. We were living in their house, Trevor worked for his dad, and we ate our meals with them and sat together in a long row at church every Sunday."

"I understand," Sierra said sympathetically. "It's hard to figure out how to be your own family when you're part of your husband's bigger family."

I nodded. "The situation wasn't bad. They're wonderful people. We just needed space." I explained about Trevor's uncle giving us the used-car business for a dollar and how difficult it had been. Then I told them how Trevor's parents were in the process of buying a house for us back in North Carolina and that his dad was holding a job open for Trevor.

"We're still trying to figure out what we should do."

A solemn quiet settled around the table. I laughed the sort of nervous cough-chortle that comes after you've squeezed every last drop out of your heart and then stop long enough to see the big mess you just made.

Sierra asked about my job and whether I had considered finding a different one to make more money so we could stay.

Jennalyn and Tess chimed in that they wanted us to stay too.

Christy stopped them from going on. "I want to say something." Her expression made it clear that she wasn't interested in being part of an intervention team, ready to solve my problems.

"I think as Daughters of Eve, this is a moment when we all should listen and not try to offer advice. It sounds like Emily was given more than enough advice from sisters over the years."

I felt a calm covering me like a blanket as Christy spoke.

Jennalyn agreed. "Speaking as a woman who knows what it's like to have a paramedic wheel her out the front door, I agree that silence can be the better part of healing."

Tess nodded and offered me a compassionate look. Not an "oh, bless your heart" look but one that seemed to say, "I'm here for you. That's all. Just know that I'm here."

"What would you think," Christy said slowly, "if we all prayed? Not aloud. What if each of us bowed and silently talked to Jesus about everything Emily just shared with us?"

The answer to Christy's suggestion came in the form of nods around the table. As the two infants slept quietly and the Daughters of Eve all bowed our heads, I could hear deep breaths being drawn in and released slowly around the circle.

Never in my life had I felt more supported or more understood.

That was what I had needed, long needed. Silent companionship and unmoving support. The space around us seemed to echo back the calming words I had spoken to Jennalyn in her most vulnerable moment.

Just breathe.

I'm here for you.

You can do this.

I leaned my head back and looked up through the protective tree branches, up into the vast cosmos above us. The inaudible prayers bolstered me, and I realized these women were laboring with me. They were with me as I was being delivered from the pain of my deep soul wound.

It's going to be okay. Breathe.

Release.

Chapter 16

The time I spent with the Daughters of Eve that night changed me. Trevor noticed it right away. Audra said I was a happier mom. I slept better, and I did more around the house and for my family because I felt strong. I didn't feel locked up or tongue-tied. My spirit felt lighter. I knew I had been released somehow. I had been delivered from the pain that I had carried way beyond its due date.

I no longer worried whether this apartment was going to be our permanent dwelling or whether we would be breaking our lease early and moving out when school ended. The freedom I felt after that beautiful night with the Daughters of Eve prompted me to nest. I wanted to feel like we were "home" in our apartment regardless of how long we stayed there.

Trevor had a good week at the car lot. When I told him what I wanted to do, he told me that we had a little extra cash that month, and I should feel free to spend it on "whatever makes your heart happy."

Several times after work I stopped at the local vintage thrift shop Sierra had told me about. On half-off Friday, I found a huge outdoor rug that fit beautifully under the patio table and covered up the uneven cracks in the concrete. The colors in the rug were lapis blue, light brown, and emerald green with some touches of sunny yellow. I kept a photo of the rug on my phone and was elated when it took me only three visits to other secondhand shops before I found nice cushions for the chairs that coordinated with the rug.

Audra persuaded Trevor to string the Christmas tree lights back and forth across the patio covering. I brought home a big bucket from work that Mr. Sanchez was going to throw out because it was cracked on the bottom and the handle was missing. Audra painted the bucket. Mr. Miller provided us with some potting soil.

At my request, he also supplied me with nicely rooted cuttings from the beloved night-blooming jasmine, which I planted in our recycled bucket planter.

I hoped that if I could keep up with the fast-growing bush, I could train it to climb around the patio post and grow along the line of the covering so that, as Audra described it, we would have our own enchanted garden.

Our small backyard was far from looking like an enchanted anything. But it looked cheerful and much more inviting than it had.

Trevor and I were seated on the nice cushions on the chairs one evening during the last week of February, and I was commending him on the great job he had done stringing up the twinkle lights. Audra was in bed already. The night was ours.

"Emily?"

"Yes."

"I have to tell you something."

"Okay." I braced myself. All the nesting might have been an exercise in futility. A chasing-after-the-wind sort of activity. Based on my husband's expression, this was serious.

"I talked to my uncle." Trevor gave me a side glance. "He told me that if I sold the car lot, he would split the profit with me fifty-fifty."

I was stunned. This possible solution to our financial dilemma had seemed obvious to me months ago, but Trevor, who had a difficult time admitting defeat to anything, hadn't been open to the possibility.

"Are you going to sell then?"

"I'm thinking about it. What do you think?"

"Well . . . yes! That means we would stay, right?"

"Possibly."

My mind was racing. "What are you thinking?"

"I'm thinking we should figure out how we can live in California. Selling the lot is the first step."

I wanted to jump up, wrap my arms around his neck, and kiss him good. He was still so serious, though. He needed to say more, so I held back and listened. I wanted him to feel like I understood how difficult this conclusion had been for him. It seemed he was viewing this route as a failure in the same deeply painful way I had viewed my inability to produce more children.

Remembering the word that Christy, and possibly Sierra, had taken on for the year, I leaned back to listen.

Trevor talked for some time without stopping. He had thought through everything. How he would conduct the sale, what would happen to Carlos, what the estimated profit would be, and what we should do with our half. He had even thought of a special way to thank his uncle, who now lived in Montana.

"He asked if I still had the old green Cadillac on the lot because he wanted me to hold it for him. I don't know where I would park it long term until he could fly down to pick it up. So I told him I would ship it to him. It's pretty expensive, but he appreciated my offer. I think it's the least I can do for him."

Trevor hadn't yet reached the next part of the topic, as in what would he do for a job after he sold the lot. I spoke up and said I thought he should look for a sales position at one of the luxury dealerships in Newport Beach, since he had experience with those types of cars. And I knew he could make good money if he had enough clients.

He had other ideas. "Todd said a few positions might open up at the school where he teaches. I could use some of the money and go back to college to earn a teaching credential."

I blinked. I had never heard my husband say he wanted to be a teacher. "What would you want to teach?"

"I'm not sure yet." Trevor still looked serious. He didn't look enlivened at the idea of teaching the way he used to look when he came home after a good day of selling cars. He didn't seem as happy about going back to school. He had the same expression that had shadowed his forehead for weeks, as he was trying hard to figure out what to do.

Once I realized that he was thinking aloud, I relaxed and listened without trying to give input or become the beacon of reality he seemed to need. Trevor had always been a dreamer. I knew that. I'm sure Audra got her wish mind-set from him.

The difference between Audra's wishes and Trevor's dreams was that Audra's wishes were precise. I think she inherited the sense of orderliness from my side of the family. Trevor's dreams were all over the place, like a puppy let loose to run around the yard. His eagerness, optimism, and hard work had convinced me of his dream to make a life in California as the owner of a used-car lot.

I ached as I watched the dream dying in him.

We sat together quietly, both letting the magnitude of his unexpected declaration sink in. I could hear the distant hum of the steady traffic several blocks away on Newport Boulevard. A few houses down, a dog barked. I felt safe. Covered. Our patio cloister wasn't the same as Jennalyn's lush backyard, but this was becoming a haven for us.

Under the twinkle lights, with our coffee mugs resting on the blue woven place mats that I had brought home that day, I didn't feel anxious about what Trevor's next step would be. We were making something new together. Not a baby, as had been our goal for more than half a decade. We were making the next version of our married lives and possibly the next version of ourselves.

Trevor kept thinking aloud, and I kept listening. He came up with four other career opportunities he had been considering.

"These are just options," he said. "They're possibilities. That's all."

"I understand." Any of them would suit him and his outgoing, tireless personality. The challenge was figuring out how long the finances would hold until he managed to make a living at one of the endeavors.

"I love hearing you dream," I told him that night when we finally went to bed.

"I love watching you dream aloud," he countered.

"How do I dream aloud?"

"You make things." He ran his thick hand over the curve of my hip. "You're turning this place into a home for us with the cushions, pictures, and stuff. I liked seeing how happy you were today about the place mats."

"It's been a long time since I've had a chance to decorate."

"I know."

I scooted closer. "I actually have had more fun shopping in the second-hand stores than I think I ever had shopping for furniture online."

"That's because you always had my mom or my sisters telling you which company they bought their furniture from and giving all their suggestions."

"I needed their suggestions."

Trevor pulled back and looked me in the eye. "I didn't see it before."

"See what?"

"The things the counselor was saying when I went with you on that last appointment."

"What did she say?"

"She talked about how influenced you were by all the women in my family. That you needed space to let your own personality develop before going back to spending every day with the clan."

"I miss your clan," I said. "You know that, don't you?"

Trevor hesitated. "I miss them too. But since we moved here, you've started doing things differently. I like it."

"What have I done differently?"

"You cook differently. It's getting better."

I grinned. "Glad to hear that."

"You have been dressing differently, and I like the way your hair looks. You're different with Audra too. It's like you're able to focus on being her mom more because we're not so caught up in trying to make our tribe increase, as my dad used to say."

"Audra is getting to be so fun. Today, when I picked her up from school, she chattered nonstop as usual. Then she paused and said, 'You and I never used to talk this much, did we, Mom?'"

"That's because she was always with her cousins after school."

"I think she could use more time with her friends from school." I ran my fingers through Trevor's hair. "But for now, I don't mind being the one she chatters with."

"We should tell her we've decided to stay," Trevor said.

"She doesn't know we were waffling on what to do, does she?"

Trevor gave me an "oh, come on" look. "She picks up on everything. If nothing else, I would guess she has some idea that things have been tense for us. I think we should find a good time to talk with her and let her ask questions. She'll feel more secure."

"Okay. I'll come up with something special for us to do with her. A picnic, maybe. Or a walk down Balboa Pier."

Leaning closer, I kissed Trevor lightly. In a whisper I asked about that one part of all this that he hadn't talked about yet. "What about telling your parents?"

The corner of Trevor's eye fluttered, as if he had a nervous tick. "I was thinking about that."

"And?"

"I need to do it. I'll call my dad tomorrow."

"What do you think you'll say?"

"I don't know. Any ideas?"

We kept talking about how he could phrase the announcement, trying to imagine what his parents would say. Both of us agreed that Trevor would need to make the announcement airtight this time. We didn't want his parents to think we were putting our return move on hold again.

Instead of our closeness as we talked leading to an amorous night, we ended up praying together and fell asleep in each other's arms, emotionally spent.

The next afternoon, when Audra and I returned home, we saw Trevor's car in the apartment parking lot.

"Why is Dad home?"

"I'm not sure. Let's go find out."

I opened the front door and saw Trevor out on the back patio, pacing and with his phone in his hand. I knew then that he had decided to come home to have the important conversation with his dad.

Noticing the rent check on the kitchen counter, I quickly handed it to Audra and asked her to take it down to Mr. and Mrs. Miller's. Shooing her out the door, I knew Audra was likely to find something to chat with them about, and that would give Trevor a bit more time.

His head was down as he paced. I waited in the kitchen, and since the sliding door was open, I could overhear him say, "Yes, Dad. We both prayed about this."

Based on Trevor's tone, the conversation didn't sound like it was going well.

"No," Trevor continued. "The decision was mutual. Emily and I are a team, just like you and Mom."

I felt a familiar sinking feeling. A memory came to mind of a conversation I had with Trevor's mother early in our marriage. My timid personality had prompted me to turn down a chance to attend a pottery-painting class with all the Winslow women. The next day, when my mother-in-law found out I hadn't declined because I was ill, she told me I needed to be more of a team player. I wasn't sure at the time what she meant by that. But I tried.

As Trevor assured his father that this was a permanent decision, I realized that if I had to come up with a motto to define our first decade of marriage, it would be "I tried." Ever since we had moved to California, I felt as if I didn't have to try so hard at everything. I could simply be Trevor's wife, Audra's mom, and now, a friend to the other women in Daughters of Eve. I felt released from a tangle of expectations and disappointments. Now it was Trevor's turn; he needed to feel released as well.

It didn't look as if his parents were going to let him go with grace and their blessing.

Audra came in at close to the same time that Trevor finished his call. I knew that she could hear the last few lines as clearly as I could.

"Okay, Dad. Thanks. I appreciate that. Tell Mom we love her. Love you too."

I could tell by Trevor's expression when he put down the phone on the patio table that he was hurting.

"Hi, Dad!" Audra waved.

He put on a half grin for her and came inside. Leaning down to look her in the eye, he asked, "How about if we do something special tonight?"

"Like what?"

Trevor looked over at me. "Like whatever clever, fun plan your mom comes up with. It will be a surprise."

Audra glanced at me skeptically. "Are you willing to take suggestions?"

"Always."

Audra's suggestion included ice cream. Trevor and I exchanged glances. "All your best ideas tend to include ice cream," he said.

"That's why they're my best ideas!"

We grabbed our sweaters and took Trevor's car down to Balboa Peninsula. The weather had been gorgeous all day. It was four o'clock on the first day of March, but to me it felt like a perfect summer day. We walked to the end of Balboa Pier, stopping half a dozen times to gaze down at the ocean and to watch the scattering of fishermen who had their long poles in the water.

Squawking seagulls circled above us, keeping a close eye on the fishermen and monitoring their progress.

I had slipped my hand into Trevor's at the start of our walk. He gave it a long squeeze, which I took to mean that he was okay.

"Should we?" Trevor asked when we hit the end of the pier.

"Should we what?" I asked.

Audra knew the answer. "Should we go inside this restaurant and see if they have ice cream!"

I looked up at the sign over the old-fashioned diner. "Ruby's," I repeated as if it were supposed to mean something. "Sure, let's go inside."

It felt odd for me to enter another diner since I was so familiar with Peggy's Pies and the layout of their tables. I almost felt like a spy.

"This is the first time we've gone out to dinner since we moved here," Audra said excitedly.

I was certain she was wrong. Trevor and I studied each other's faces for a moment, both of us trying to name a restaurant we had eaten at in the last seven months. Neither of us came up with an answer.

"Then I'd say it's about time." Trevor held up three fingers to the hostess who was heading our way with some menus. She led us to a booth in a prime location by the window where we could watch the surfers in their wet suits, catching the late afternoon waves.

"I love this place!" Audra was beaming.

"Why didn't we come here before?" Trevor asked me.

I didn't remind him of our solemn agreement to be ultrafrugal—our near vow of poverty if compared to the standard Southern California cost of living. With a big grin and a happy heart, I said, "This can be our new place to come."

He winked at me.

I always loved it when Trevor winked at me. It meant he saw me. He knew what I was thinking, and best of all, he was thinking the same thing.

"Look at all the kinds of shakes they have!" Audra had disappeared behind her opened menu and was reading off the yummy-sounding milkshakes. "And then, look. It says you can create your own flavor." She peered at us from around the side of the menu. "May I? I always wanted to create my own milkshake. It's my . . ." She seemed to try to come up with the right event excuse to tag what would inevitably be one of her famous wishes.

"How about spring?" Trevor suggested. "It's time for us to celebrate new beginnings."

She nodded eagerly. "It's my spring wish."

"So what is your special spring wish flavor going to be?" I asked.

Our little artist reviewed all the standard flavors again as well as the combinations listed on the deluxe shake menu. When our waitress arrived, Audra was ready. Her concoction sounded like a sugar overload to me. She wanted strawberries, bananas, crushed cookies, and caramel drizzled on top of the whipped cream.

The end result looked decadent, and she was elated. Trevor and I stuck with water and ordered two hamburgers to split between the three of us. We also asked for "frings," listed on the menu as a french fry and onion ring combination. Trevor requested that the waitress bring the frings first as an appetizer.

"It's a spring fring!" he said when the combo basket arrived.

Audra and I groaned at his joke.

"Speaking of spring and fresh starts and—" Trevor chomped into one of the onion rings and immediately fanned his open mouth.

"Hot?" I asked in the way that only a wife knows how to ask such an obvious question.

He nodded and then tilted his head as if handing over to me the baton so I could finish this race to tell Audra that we'd decided to stay in California. I gave him a glinty-eyed side look and took the baton anyway.

"Your dad and I have been trying to figure out what's best for our family and . . ." I handed the announcement back over to Trevor.

He swallowed and said, "We've prayed about it a lot, honey. We think we should stay here. So I'm going to sell the car lot and find another job that hopefully provides us with more money."

Audra wasn't surprised, of course. She said she was glad we were staying, and she hoped that meant we would be happier.

"I know people aren't happy all the time," she said. "But I like it when you're both happy at the same time. Like now."

Trevor leaned over and kissed the side of my cheek. "You know that you have the best mom in the world, don't you?"

Audra nodded. Her eyes were opened wide, and her lips were pursed around the straw that she held daintily between her thumb and forefinger.

"Do you have any questions for us?" I asked.

She nodded again and held up her first finger on her other hand, indicating that she wanted to finish her slurp through the straw.

I glanced at Trevor, feeling good about how all this was going. We could relax a little and work together to build our future while enjoying these sweet moments with our little girl.

Audra swallowed and cleared her throat. "I have one question."

"Okay, what's your question?"

"Where do babies go?"

re you asking where do babies go when they leave their mother?"
Trevor lowered his voice and leaned in so that the people around
us would be less likely to hear our conversation.

"No, when they die," Audra said. "Do they go right to heaven?"

Trevor nodded. "Yes. Remember the story in the Bible about David
and Goliath?"

Audra took a slurp of her shake and nodded. I thought she might have
rolled her eyes a bit because the answer was so obvious. I was startled at the
gesture, which seemed to announce we were entering the preteen phase.

"When David grew up, he had a baby that died. In the Bible it says that
David knew he could one day go be with his baby in heaven."

"So when I go to heaven, I'll get to meet my seven brothers and
sisters?"

Trevor and I shot side glances at each other.

"Your brothers and sisters?" Trevor asked.

Audra pushed the shake away and took on one of her grown-up expressions. "From the seven viable embryos."

"How did you know there were seven?" he asked.

"Aunt Sally told me."

I glanced at Trevor. He and I had tried to talk openly with her while we were going through the in vitro process. She knew a lot more than I ever wanted her to know, but we had purposefully left out specifics that we felt weren't important for her to be aware of.

She repeated her question. "Will I get to meet all of them in heaven?"

I swallowed and turned to Trevor. He dipped his chin and looked at Audra with the warmest, kindest fatherly expression. His eyes were clear when he told her, "Yes, you will. I believe you will."

Audra began to cry. "I wish they had all lived here first." Her voice was soft and low.

I dabbed my tears, and Trevor handed Audra a napkin.

"So do we," Trevor said.

Audra didn't look up.

Trevor smiled at me, as if trying to infuse me with the courage I needed in that moment. Audra wiped her eyes and blew her nose, loudly. Folding the napkin, she placed it in her lap instead of on the table, ever the little lady she had been taught to be.

"I don't think I can eat anything more," she said.

"Why don't we take this home?" Trevor lifted his arm to motion for the waitress. As he lowered his hand, I saw him wipe away a tear.

The three of us walked down the pier back to our car without talking. The sky had turned a baby-soft shade of spun sugar, and the clouds in front of us looked like enormous puffs of cotton candy. As the sun was setting behind us, the light tinged the tops of the clouds with a golden lining. A promise of heaven.

The beauty that covered us and hemmed us in was heartbreaking. The sky was so filled with glory that instead of getting into our car, the three of us stood there close together. Trevor put his arms around both of us. We gazed up at the magnificent clouds and then looked behind us at the pier and the big, orange sun ball as it melted into the ocean.

"I hope we can go back to that restaurant again," Audra said once we were buckled up and on our way home. "I liked it a lot."

I was glad she said something more typical of the way she usually started one of her chatty sessions. I couldn't help thinking, though, that Ruby's would always be associated with a distinctly somber memory for all of us.

When we arrived home, we noticed an envelope wedged in the side of the screen door. My name was written on it, and the handwriting was distinctly Jennalyn's. I didn't feel any twinges of embarrassment that she had seen where I lived. That's how I would have felt several months ago. Now all I felt was a wave of regret that I wasn't home when she came by.

"What is it, Mom?"

"An invitation. From Jennalyn. Do you want to see it?" I handed the card to Audra. A twist of long branches with tiny green buds ran up the side of the paper. Safely nestled at the top was a nest with two blue eggs. The invitation read,

Daughters of Eve

Let's welcome spring

Bring a

Zing Thing

(no humans)

March 10, 7:00 p.m.

Jennalyn's Nest

"What is a zing thing?" Audra asked.

I smiled at Jennalyn's cleverness. I also marveled at how she had time to create such detailed and adorable invitations when she had a newborn and a toddler. I was reminded that we always found time to do the things we love. Jennalyn clearly loved to create note cards.

"A zing thing is something that makes your heart go zing," I said.

"I've never heard of that."

"Our group made it up." I placed the invitation on the refrigerator and used a magnet shaped like a starfish to keep it in place. Over the last few days, the DOEs had run a string of text messages. Tess had reported that she'd gone on a coffee date with a guy named Joe. Sierra, always ready to dive to the core of the matter, asked Tess if Joe made her heart go zing.

Tess's response was a question mark. The rest of us chimed in with our thoughts on how one should gauge the level of zing-ness and exactly how much zing-ness one should feel before accepting another date.

Christy had commented on how she had found a new herbal tea that was making her mouth go zing and asked if that factored into the discussion in any way.

Jennalyn pounced on the concept and announced that she was going to host a Zing Thing party, and we would all be required to bring our favorite thing that made our heart go zing. And no, none of us could bring someone we loved. Hence, the added "no humans" line on the invitation.

"I wish I could go." Audra gave an exaggerated pout. "I already know what my zing thing would be."

"What?" I asked.

"I would take you and Dad because you're my best zings. But, if I couldn't take you because you two are humans, then I would take my milkshake creation."

I didn't comment.

Trevor already had put the shake in the fridge. He had pulled out a plate and warmed up the rest of his burger and some of the onion rings. He was seated on the sofa with the remote in his hand.

"Come here, Buttercup." He patted the couch next to him, and Audra joined him, saying she was still too full to eat anything else that night.

I wasn't hungry either. I decided to take a bath and use the rest of the bath salts I had been given for Christmas. The steaming water felt good, as I stretched out and let the fragrant salts minister to my body.

Closing my eyes, I thought about our conversation at Ruby's Diner and Audra's question about where those seven viable embryos were now. My focus during all the procedures had revolved around tests and injections, temperatures and charts, baselines and doctor's appointments. I felt like a walking human laboratory more than I ever felt like a cocreator with Trevor of tiny sparks of life that carried our DNA.

Trevor believed those seven souls were in heaven. We were going to meet them one day.

The concept messed with my mind.

Feeling the effects of the hot water, as well as the thoughts that were searing my heart, I sat up in the tub and rested my arms on the sides. For such a long time, I thought I was grieving the vacancy in our family that would have been filled by the second child we longed for. Tonight, perhaps for the first time, I felt a maternal need to grieve the loss of those seven little possibilities.

I needed to talk to someone about this. This was heavy.

My bath left the scent of lavender and vanilla on my skin when I crawled into bed next to Trevor. He was sitting up, his back against the wall, literally, because we didn't have a headboard. He looked deep in thought. I hoped we could process all the thoughts that had circled me in the tub.

"I don't think my dad took the news very well," Trevor said. "I know it's the right thing for us. We made the right decision. I'm not changing my mind."

He seemed to be coaching himself more than starting a conversation with me. If he was processing this tangled-in-the-net conversation with his dad, I didn't think he would be ready to talk about the issues swirling around my head and my heart.

In a way, I felt relieved. I wanted to rest, deeply rest.

"They're good parents," he said. "They just want what's best for us. I get that. That's what I want for Audra. But I think they need to let us go. They need to see us as a couple. A family."

I rested my head on his shoulder. "I agree. We're in a different stage of life now."

"That's right. We're adults."

"They need to release you."

"That's the word I was trying to think of. Yes. They need to release me." He was picking up steam. "We're no longer the twenty-something newly-weds who didn't know how to apply for a credit card. You know what my dad said about our decision to stay here? He and my mom thought that this was my wild-hare dream—coming to California. He said it reminded them of when my brother took off to backpack around Europe for the summer. Dillon got the wanderlust out of his system, and then he came home and buckled down. He was ready to run the dealership they put him in when he was twenty-one."

"The difference between your brother and you is that this isn't just a wanderlust break, and you're not going back to run the dealership they want to put you in."

"Exactly. My parents didn't expect that." Trevor moved his arm so that he could wrap it around my shoulder and draw me closer. "It's still the right thing."

"Yes, it is."

"We should be joyful and confident. Isn't that what your verse says?"

I pulled back and looked at him, confused. "My verse?"

"The framed verse by the sink. You would think we both would have it memorized by now after reading it so many times. We'd looking forward to becoming all that God had in mind for us all along. Something like that."

I let the thought settle on me. "You're right. We are becoming more of a family. It's a different version of us, but we're still us."

"I think we're more us than we've ever been."

I patted his broad chest. "By the way, you did a great job with Audra at dinner. I did not see those questions coming."

Trevor chuckled, causing his chest to rumble. I sat up and smiled at him. "If the school Todd teaches at needs a sex ed teacher, I'd write you a recommendation."

Trevor took my comment in a different direction. It's funny how we'd been married for so long yet I still said things that to me didn't have a deeper, more amorous meaning, but he heard an invitation every time.

The interaction between us that followed left no place for me to talk about how I felt when Audra asked if her seven siblings were in heaven. That conversation would have to wait for another time. I was fine with letting it rest.

The weather remained beautiful through the next week. We were busy at Peggy's Pies and everyone, including Mr. Sanchez, seemed to be in a good mood.

Mr. and Mrs. Thompson said they might take me up on the invitation to come to my apartment for lunch one day. I had told them how I was fixing up the patio and had planted some jasmine.

"We'll wait until summer," Mrs. Thompson told me on Friday morning that week. "That will give your jasmine a chance to grow, and we can sit outside when the weather is nice."

"Okay, I'm going to hold you to that, Mrs. Thompson. We'll get a date on the calendar."

Right before I left on Friday afternoon, I told Mr. Sanchez that I had some ideas about how he might make some changes at the diner. Our dinner at Ruby's had inspired me to say something about the idiosyncrasies at Peggy's Pies that had bugged me since my first workday.

"If you ever wanted to move the bench in the waiting area over to the other side, up against the window," I suggested, "it would help a lot with the traffic flow. The way it is now, whenever anyone opens the door, they walk right in and bump the legs of the people waiting on the bench. If someone comes in with a walker or wheelchair, it's even more crowded."

"Humph." He looked at the bench and the two possible places for it going back and forth, then back and forth again. "What else?"

"I wonder if you could have the toasters cleaned out at least every day. Maybe even a couple of times during the morning shift. It always smells like burned toast when you walk in. Probably bread crumbs have fallen through to the bottom of the toaster's tray and burned there."

"Is that all?"

I decided to go ahead and toss out my last idea.

"Have you considered making and selling little pies? You know"—I made the shape of a small circle with my hands—"the size of a tart."

"Why?"

"Because customers look in the case at the pies, and they say they couldn't eat a whole pie. Then they walk away, even though they really wanted one."

"Never done it that way."

"I know. But if you had pies that would feed two people, I think you would have steady sales from the Ivy Glen folks. I could ask some of them if they would buy a little pie to take with them, if we offered that size."

"No." Mr. Sanchez shook his head. "Don't ask them."

"Okay."

"Is that all?"

"Yes." I offered him a smile. "For now."

"Get outa here." He was presenting himself as his joking, grumpy persona. The older clientele loved it when he told them to get out. I had a theory that some of them enjoyed being around someone who was grumpier than they were.

I told Trevor about my suggestions on Saturday morning when he was getting ready to go to the car lot. His uncle's green Cadillac had shipped out the day before, and he had two dealers coming that afternoon to cherry-pick the lot before he started negotiations with an interested buyer. It felt like a good day for fresh starts and spring cleaning.

"How did Mr. Sanchez take your ideas?"

"For him, pretty well, I think."

"They're good ideas. It'll be interesting to see what he does."

"Mom?" Audra came out of the bathroom dressed as if she were going to school. "Can I go to work with Dad this morning?"

"May I," I corrected her.

"May I go to work with Daddy, and then you come pick me up at lunchtime?"

I looked at Trevor. He shrugged, indicating it was fine with him.

"Sure. Any particular reason?"

Audra looked at Trevor as if she wasn't sure if she could tell the reason. Then she seemed to throw caution to the wind. "I wanted to go to the car lot because Carlos always brings in churros on Saturday mornings."

"Oh?"

"They're like doughnuts."

"I know what churros are."

"They're so good. Do you want me to bring one home for you?"

"No, that's okay." I kissed the top of her head, thanked her for thinking of me, and sent her out the door with Trevor.

It felt strange to have the morning to myself since this was a rare Saturday when I wasn't scheduled to work all day. My first instinct was to open the windows and start cleaning. I began with the kitchen counter and moved on to wipe off the windowsill. When I picked up the round glass dish I had placed in the window a few weeks ago, I looked at the contents and tried to decide what to do.

In the dish were the roses Trevor had given me for Valentine's Day. The seven rosebuds hadn't opened. I had done everything I thought I should do by cutting the stems' ends at an angle, dissolving an aspirin in the water, and putting them where they would get light.

They never bloomed.

I had plucked the rosebuds and placed them in the dish on the windowsill so I could still enjoy them. They had dried up now, still in their original rosebud shape. I was about to toss them in the trash when I felt a warmth pressing against my chest.

Seven.

They never bloomed.

I can't throw them away and just forget about the love that gifted them to me.

I knew what I needed to do. With the gentle pressure still resting on my heart, I took perhaps the bravest step I had ever taken during the entire process of our secondary infertility.

I went outside to our slowly-becoming-beautiful patio, and I said goodbye to the seven little possibilities. The souls that Trevor believed were waiting for us in heaven.

I released them.

My ceremony was simple. I stood beside the potted jasmine plant and thought about Mrs. Miller's admonition to "plant the sweet things" from my past into my new life. I plucked a petal from each of the buds and tucked them into my apron's pocket. Then, digging my fingers into the warm earth, I placed the rosebuds in the soil and said goodbye to what might have been but never was.

In that spontaneous, holy moment, I felt they released me. I hadn't failed. I had tried. That was enough. I was enough. Our little family of three was enough.

Chapter 18

The evening of the Daughters of Eve zing thing party, I took a small ring box out of my top dresser drawer. That jeweler's box had made my heart go zing the day Trevor pulled it from his pocket, went down on one knee, and looked up at me as if I were the only woman he would ever love for all his days.

Carefully opening the lid, I looked at the seven dried rose petals. I had tucked them in the box on Saturday, one from each of the buds I had pressed into the soil at the base of the jasmine plant. The sight of them brought a sense of melancholy. I didn't feel fresh pain but rather a soft touch of nostalgia.

I closed the ring box, put it in my purse, and pulled a sweater from the dresser drawer in case Jennalyn had set up our place of gathering in the backyard. Slipping into the bathroom, I checked my hair in the mirror one more time and added another layer of gloss to my lips.

"I'm going now."

Trevor and Audra were watching a movie, and both called out "Have fun" without looking up.

"I will. Love you both."

I was at the door when Trevor hopped up from the couch. "Why don't you take the Mercedes?" He fished the keys out of the bowl on the counter. "It's a nice night to put the top down."

"Are you sure?" I knew Trevor had added me to the insurance for this particular car because he thought it would be fun for me to have one last chance to enjoy a "fancy" car before all the sales for the lot had gone through.

He placed the keys in my hand. "Sure. Why not?"

"Okay." I kissed him and gladly took the keys to the silver Mercedes convertible. Smiling as I strolled to the parking area, I noticed that a sprinkling of tiny white flowers had begun to bud on the jasmine bush.

I paused long enough to draw in a deep breath. My nostrils caught only a wisp of their fragrance. I knew the heady scent would soon fill the air every time we came or went from this place that had become a haven for us.

After settling into the driver's seat, I adjusted the mirrors and the steering wheel. The engine started with a purr. I pushed the button and watched the top go down. I couldn't stop smiling. I had forgotten how much I loved the feeling that came with driving a classy car.

My senses were on high alert as I drove to Jennalyn's. I kept checking to make sure the car behind me wasn't too close. I parked in her driveway and twice pressed the remote on the car alarm after double-checking that the top was up all the way and the windows were secure. Funny how I rarely worried about those details in my little white sedan.

The other Daughters of Eve were already there when I went inside. We exchanged hugs and smiles, and I felt happy. Calm and happy. These were my women. We had a lot of catching up to do since our last gathering under the protective trees in Jennalyn's backyard.

I joined the others on the sofas and added my dish of chocolate-covered macadamia nuts to the treats on the coffee table. A client at Trevor's work had given him a big bag, so I had filled a bowl and brought them with me.

"Are those what I think they are?" Christy reached for one of the dark chocolate balls and popped it in her mouth. "These are so good. They are the only nuts I like."

"You probably would like other nuts if they were covered in dark chocolate like that," Jennalyn said.

Christy shook her head and reached for a second one. "Nope. Only macadamia nuts. I think it's because they remind me of my honeymoon."

Listening to the background music that floated around us, I turned to Jennalyn. "I feel like I'm in a forest."

"Do you like it?" She grinned. "I put on the chirping birds and babbling brook mood music because I decided I wanted to stay inside tonight. I thought the woodland music would give us a bit of the enchanting springtime feeling we had in the backyard. What do you think?"

"I feel like I'm back at the spa where I used to work," Christy said. "The speakers in here are amazing. The birds sound like they're all around us."

"It's the perfect zing-thing music," Sierra said. "Although the sound of the running water is doing a Jedi mind trick on me. I'll be right back." Sierra made a hasty dash to the powder room. She called over her shoulder, "Tess, don't divulge any details until I come back."

"Okay," Tess responded. "I'll save all the juicy details."

Christy looked intrigued. "Now you have my attention."

Tess kept a straight face and plunged a round cucumber slice into the yogurt and fresh dill dip Jennalyn had made with herbs from her backyard garden.

"This is so good!" Tess dabbed the corner of her mouth with one of the bright floral napkins that added to the springy floral theme of the get-together.

"Anyone else want iced tea?" Jennalyn reached for the pitcher in the center of the coffee table. "This one is new. It's peach flavored."

"That sounds good," Christy said.

I nodded when Jennalyn looked at me and then helped myself to one of the pastel-colored macarons lined up like a row of springtime tulips on the tiered serving tray. "These macarons are so good."

"I bought them at a bakery," Christy said. "It's a place my aunt really likes. The pale yellow ones are my favorite."

"Favorite what?" Sierra asked, returning to the group.

"Macarons. I was saying that I like the yellow ones."

"I had a pink one," Sierra said. "It was strawberry, I think. Or maybe it was raspberry."

"You better have another one so you can figure it out." Jennalyn slid the dainty tiered tray across the coffee table so it would be closer to Sierra.

Christy turned to me. "By the way, before I forget, Emily, do you think you could give me a ride back to my parents' place? Todd dropped me off here, but my mom borrowed my car today, so I need to pick it up."

"Sure." I wanted to say something on the bragging side like, "Only if you don't mind riding in a convertible." But no sassy words came out. They would have been imitation sassy words because it's a little silly to brag about a borrowed car, and a used one at that.

"Okay, Tess," Sierra said. "Tell all. How did your date go? Where did he take you?"

"We just went for coffee." Tess leaned back, her tall glass of peach tea in her hand, her long, thin legs crossed. She was wearing a floral, blousy top and skinny jeans. Her long hair was twisted up on top of her head in a feathery bun. She looked like she was striking a pose for a clothing magazine.

"Well?" Sierra asked.

"I had a jasmine green tea, iced. He had a hazelnut latte. He paid for his; I paid for mine." Tess's expression didn't reveal how she felt about any of the details as she continued the report. "We sat outside by a noisy street. He kept his sunglasses on. His phone buzzed nonstop. He asked me to excuse him as he sent at least three text messages."

"This isn't sounding very promising," Sierra said.

"After fifteen minutes of awkwardness, he said he had to return a call to his agent and walked away. I sat there for another ten minutes, watching him on his phone call in the parking lot. Then he got in his nice car and drove off."

"No!" Jennalyn spouted.

"Yes."

"That's terrible!" Sierra said.

"What did you do?" Christy asked.

"I finished my iced tea and went home." Tess uncrossed her legs and kicked off her shoes, using her toes to release the straps from across her ankles. "Worst date ever. Although I'm not sure I can even call it a date. His mom wanted us to meet. She's one of my clients. We met. End of story."

"I can't believe how rude he was." Sierra followed Tess's example and slipped her feet out of her shoes. "Are you going to tell us who he was? If he was calling his agent, he must have been an actor, right?"

"I'll never tell." Tess's expression made it clear that she wasn't kidding. She kept her client list top secret and apparently maintained the same privacy policy for her clients' sons. Even if they deserved to be called out for their behavior.

"How do you feel about it now?" Christy asked.

"Fine."

"Really?" Jennalyn asked.

"Yes, really. I'm not interested in being involved with anyone right now. Especially someone like him. I kept my promise to his mom. I'm glad I did that."

We all sipped our peach tea silently. I tried to imagine what I would have done in a similar situation. Not that anything like that had happened to me or would happen to me.

Tess reached for one of the yellow macarons. "The thing is . . ."

Our attention was fixed on her, waiting. She hadn't shared a lot in our past gatherings. I wondered if this might be a spilling-of-her-heart moment like I had experienced when I shared my story.

"It's just that . . ." Tess put the uneaten macaron on the flowery napkin resting on the arm of her chair.

"That what?" Jennalyn asked.

"Did any of you ever feel like the possibility of being pursued was more enjoyable than the possibility of being caught?"

"Yes." Sierra looked around to see if the rest of us were going to chime in. When we all kept our thoughts to ourselves, she dove in and told us about a guy named Paul. She had met him at the airport in London, and she was hopelessly caught up in the dream of what might happen between them.

Tess leaned forward, listening.

"He always gave me just enough hope to think something might be growing between us. I thought of him all the time. I was so sure he would wake up one day and realize what a wonderful person I was and decide he couldn't live without me."

"What happened?" Tess asked.

"Nothing." Sierra gave Tess an "if you can believe that" look. "Except I introduced his brother to my sister, and now they're married and have two kids."

"You're kidding!" Tess laughed, and the tense sympathy we had felt over her bummer of a date lifted from the room.

Sierra popped one of the strawberries in her mouth. "Yup. So we're quasi-related now, and here's the fun part. I ended up going to Paul's wedding because of my sister, and that's how I met my husband. Jordan was the wedding photographer."

"That's crazy." Tess reached for the abandoned macaron and pointed at Christy. "You have a pretty romantic love story too. The way Todd and you met on the beach when you were only fourteen, and you ended up together. It's a classic."

"We had our ups and downs," Christy quickly added. "I mean, it wasn't all carnations and kisses."

"But it was real, and it's lasted. That's what I admire." Tess took a nibble of the macaron. "I've seen way too many shallow relationships and ugly marriages. To be honest, I'm so content right now with how things are going in my life, I don't want to change a thing."

I followed Tess's lead and took another macaron. I wondered how old Tess was and was especially curious how she had connected with this group. It was good having her in the circle.

"Emily, how did you meet your husband?" Sierra asked.

"Trevor and I met at a summer camp."

"And?" Sierra prodded. "Did you notice each other right away? Did he pursue you?"

"Trevor is a lot more outgoing than I am. All the girls at camp were flirting with him. I was so shy. He told me later that he liked the challenge of trying to get my attention." I smiled at the memories. "By the end of the week, he had my full attention. So, yes, I guess you could say he pursued me."

I decided to add the part of our story that always raised eyebrows. "We were married ten months later."

"Ten months! Were you still in high school?" Sierra looked at the others.

"No, I worked at the camp. I wasn't going to the camp. I had worked there for two years. It was in North Carolina, which was far enough away from where I grew up in New Mexico for me to feel like I was really seeing the world. Trevor was a counselor. We were young, but we weren't high schoolers."

"Summer romances," Christy said with a subtle grin. "They really are the best, aren't they?"

"You know," I said as I reached into my purse, "I should probably share my zing thing since it goes with my story."

"Yes," Jennalyn said. "Perfect."

I held out the ring box in the palm of my hand. "My engagement ring came in this box." I couldn't help but smile. "I didn't expect Trevor to propose when he did. The moment I saw him pull out this box, it was like my whole future opened in front of me. I didn't care where we lived or what we did as long as we could always be together. I had it bad for him. Most days, I still do."

Jennalyn reached for my left hand and took a good look at my simple yellow-gold engagement ring. The small center diamond was flanked by four diamond chips on both sides. "It's so sweet and feminine."

"I love it." I thought about the times Trevor said he wanted to upgrade the diamond or replace my ring with something more showy like his sisters' engagement rings. I didn't tell the others about that or the way I always refused. My ring represented who we were when we got engaged, and I wanted to remember us in that beginning season.

"Are you saying that Trevor picked out your ring and surprised you?" Christy asked.

I nodded.

"You didn't have any say in what you wanted?" Tess asked.

"No. He saw it and liked it and decided to use all his savings to buy it." I glanced down at my ring. "It's what I would have picked. When I saw the ring, I felt as if he knew me. He knew what I liked."

"That's so sweet," Jennalyn said.

"I'll go next with my zing thing." Tess stood up and slipped her hand into the back pocket of her jeans. She pulled out a piece of paper, unfolded it, and held it out for us to see. "This is the thing that made my heart go zing a few months ago. I kept it, and to be honest, I still feel giddy when I read it."

"What is it?" Sierra asked.

"It's a handwritten prescription from the counselor I went to for many years. It says . . ." Tess turned it so she could read the exact words. " 'Take care and take chances, and call me whenever you need me.' "

I looked at the others, who seemed to understand why those words made Tess so joyous.

"It feels like a diploma," she said. "When I see it, I feel as though my counselor cleared me to move ahead after I had been stuck in all the twisted places in my life for so long."

It surprised me that Tess was talking openly about going to a counselor. When I went to the counselor, the topic was hush-hush, and I only went a few times. Tess seemed to have dug in and done a lot of hard work.

I wondered what would have happened if I would have relaxed and gone to more sessions with the counselor. If I hadn't felt the urgency to prove that I was okay and nobody needed to worry about me, would I have handled the disappointment better?

In the same way that Tess felt she had received a diploma for graduating from her counseling sessions, I felt as if time had led me to the point that the seven rosebuds I had pressed into the earth represented my release.

Sliding the ring box back into my purse, I decided it was enough for me to know that the rose petals were inside. When I decided to bring the box, I wasn't sure how I felt about opening it to these women and sharing the contents. At our last gathering all the focus had been on me. My hurt. My journey. It seemed better to privately savor the settledness my heart felt at this moment and let Tess be the one to receive the concentrated attention of the kind-hearted women in the group.

Sierra asked Tess a question about what it was like to meet weekly with the counselor, and that led us down a trail that Tess seemed grateful to talk about.

"My mom never married. She has always been with a guy, though. The list of her live-in boyfriends is long. From watching her life, I avoided having a serious relationship with any guy for a long time. It messed me up. More than I realized."

As I listened to Tess talk about her disconnected relationship with her mother, I saw similarities with my relationship with my mother. I understood when Tess said she discovered early on that the best thing she could do as a child was to learn how to become invisible.

"One of the breakthrough sessions I had was the day my counselor helped me to see that I never was nor would I ever be invisible to God." Tess looked at Christy as if that was the face in this room that gave her the most courage to share openly. "She showed me in the Bible where it says that my heavenly Father knows what I'm thinking and what I'm feeling. He knows what I'm going to say before I even say it."

Christy nodded. "Psalm 139. It's one of my favorite chapters in the Bible. God knows everything about us, and we can never hide from Him."

"I love how it says God saw me when I was in my mother's womb, and He knew all my days before there was even one of them," Tess added.

I pulled out my phone and made a note to read Psalm 139. I didn't know how I hadn't heard of that chapter before. Maybe I had, but it didn't mean anything at the time. Tonight it felt like an echo of comfort resting on me when Tess said that God sees us in our mother's womb.

God sees. He knows.

"I'll tell you what really helped me," Tess said. "When the counselor told me that God knows the number of hairs on my head, I broke. I mean, I lost it right there in her office. I never had anyone pay attention to me like that. I mean, down to the number of hairs on my head. It was a breakthrough moment because I realized that if God loved me that much and was that intimately in tune with all the details of my life, I could trust Him. I mean, truly trust Him."

Tess took a deep breath. She looked around the circle.

"So that's what makes my heart go zing," she said.

Chapter 19

*R*eady?" I clicked my seat belt in place.

Christy watched from the passenger's seat as the convertible's top automatically slid back. "What a fun car!"

I put the car in reverse and backed out of Jennalyn's driveway with extra caution, even though it was almost eleven and it appeared everyone in her neighborhood had gone to bed.

"How's the selling of the car lot going?" Christy asked. "That was such a great text update that you sent to the group last week. I thought we might end up talking about it tonight."

"Tonight was Tess's night," I said.

"Yes, it was."

I checked for cars twice in both directions before making a left turn on Orange Street. "Trevor is still in the process."

"Did he tell his parents yet?"

"Yes."

"How did that go?"

"Not very well. But we both know it's what's right for us. Staying here, I mean."

"I'm so glad." Christy pulled her shirt closer to her neck and clutched her hair in a ponytail as the cool night air picked up around us.

"Here." I turned on the heater to warm our feet and turned the dial up to four on my seat. "The seats are heated. If you want, you can press the button right there."

"This is nice." Christy leaned back.

"It is fun, isn't it? Southern California is made for a car like this. Or maybe I should say a car like this is made for Southern California." I rolled up the side windows, and that helped to keep the chilly night air from feeling like it was going right through us. I realized then that my exuberance over giving Christy a ride in a convertible hadn't been thought through. The night air was too cold for us to drive with the top down. Even with the heated seats and heater on our feet, we both were shivering when we arrived at the apartment parking lot.

I pressed the button and the roof returned over our heads. With the windows up and the seats still warm and our toes fairly toasty, it felt like we were in a cozy cocoon. I looked at Christy in the glow of the security lights that lit up the parking lot. She looked back.

Both of us started laughing. It felt so natural and spontaneous.

"I don't know what I was thinking," I said. "That was the coldest I've been since we moved here."

"I didn't want to say anything because it was so fun." She laughed again. "I felt like we were a couple of runaway moms out on the town past our curfew."

"We'll have to try this another time when the sun is out and it's at least seventy-five degrees." I confessed that I had checked the temperature on the panel display when we were turning down the street that led to the apartments. It was fifty-two degrees. If I had checked before we left Jennalyn's, I never would have subjected Christy to the arctic-blast drive.

We laughed again, and Christy said, "I think we don't get out enough."

"That's for sure."

Christy leaned against the headrest. Instead of getting out of the car, now that we were snug and warm, Christy asked, "What does Trevor want to do?"

"He has a few ideas. One of them is teaching where Todd teaches."

Christy looked as surprised as I had felt when Trevor told me. "Does he like teaching?"

"He says he wouldn't mind, but he hasn't looked into how much schooling he would need to qualify, and he doesn't even know if a position would be open. I think Todd must have made it sound appealing."

"That's probably because he likes what he does so much." Christy shook her head. "I never would have guessed he would end up being a teacher."

"So you're saying there's a possibility Trevor will like teaching too?"

"I don't know. What is Trevor good at?"

"Sales. He's a fantastic salesman. I thought he should apply to some of the luxury car dealerships in this area."

"That sounds like a good idea. What did he think?"

"I have discovered with Trevor that it works best to toss out my ideas casually and then hold back and let him figure things out. If I'm too enthusiastic, he pulls back." I shook my head. "I don't understand because, in the end, my suggestion is what ends up being the way to go, and he's completely on board, as if it were his idea to start with."

Christy nodded her agreement. "We've gone through a lot of decision-making that was like that. I think it's a guy thing. Todd needs to process ideas down to the last detail. He's always been that way. You would think I would be used to it by now."

Christy paused. I thought she might reach for the handle and get out. Instead, she said, "I love that you shared your engagement ring box tonight."

"I thought what you shared about your ID bracelet that Todd gave you was really touching."

Christy held up her arm and gave her wrist a shimmy so that the gold bracelet caught the light. "'Forever,'" she said. "That's what he had engraved on it, and as each year goes by, it seems to take on a deeper meaning."

I smiled. "It was fun hearing everyone's love story tonight. That was pretty spontaneous."

"Everyone but Jennalyn's," Christy mentioned. "Next time we'll have to ask her to tell us."

"You don't know how she and Joel ended up together?" I asked.

"No. I've only heard little bits here and there. When Jennalyn and I met, she and Joel had been married for a while. Eden was just a baby."

"Her zing thing was so touching." I placed my hand on my heart and thought I might get teary again. We all had when Jennalyn showed us the handwritten recipe for peanut butter cookies.

"I know," Christy agreed. "That was so, so sweet when she said it was one of the few things she has in her mom's handwriting. And all the little hearts and Xs and Os at the end . . ." Christy couldn't finish.

I thought Jennalyn was immensely brave to share the recipe card and then tell us it made her heart go zing because she knew her mom was thinking of her with a wellspring of love when she wrote out the recipe and mailed it to her. Neither of them knew that she would be gone within a month.

"I can't imagine what it would be like navigating this season of life without my mom," Christy said. "I always regret that I didn't appreciate her more when I was a teenager."

"Your mom is a lovely woman," I agreed. "She's so patient and kind."

"I know. She's always been that way. I have a lot to learn from her." Christy turned to face me. "You know what's interesting to me, though?"

I turned toward her.

"I feel like I've been waiting a long time for a group like ours," Christy said. "It's a rare thing for me to be comfortable sharing openly with a group of women. I've always been sort of a one-close-friend person. And I have to say, I've been blessed with some very precious women in my life. My mom is one of them. And so is Jennalyn. My other two closest friends moved away."

"Where did they move to?"

"One is in Oregon. The other is in Kenya."

"Africa? Wow, that is a long way away."

Christy's expression took on a sensitive, sad look. "I know. We try to keep in touch at least every month, but it's getting more difficult. She has three little boys. They are all only about a year and a half apart, and they are adorable. We went through so much together in high school and college. I've been sad for a long time that she and I can't do life together during this season."

I couldn't relate to having a close friend for so many years. Clearly Christy was the sort of loyal friend who would stay connected no matter what. I admired that quality.

"I was telling Todd before I came tonight that this group is more important to me than I ever guessed it would be," Christy said. "I didn't know how much I needed a circle of friends. It's like we were saying when we came up with the name for us: we are becoming the sisters, mothers, and friends that some of us never had."

"It's true."

Christy's voice took on a fuller, more rounded tone of heartfelt confidentiality. "I've been wanting to tell you that I deeply appreciated what you shared with us last time about your secondary infertility. I wanted to call you the next day and see if you were doing okay, because I know that sometimes when I open up that much in a new situation, I end up having a vulnerability hangover."

I let her term sink in. "That's a good way of saying it."

"Did you feel that way after you shared?" Christy looked concerned.

"I did and I didn't, if that makes sense. It felt cathartic, and I felt safe with our group. That probably sounds crazy since it's not like we've been friends for years and years. Maybe it helped that I felt like Jennalyn and I got so close so fast."

"Delivering another woman's baby will do that." Christy grinned.

"I didn't really deliver him."

"You know what I mean. You were there for her when it mattered," Christy said.

"And I felt like all of you were there for me when I needed to tell my story. It was an important step for me. You were there when I needed your support."

"I know I'm not the only one who felt honored that you shared your story with us."

"Thanks, Christy. Thanks for saying that. And thanks for asking if I had a vulnerability hangover. I didn't feel that way, though. I thought about it, but it didn't settle in on me that way. Trevor calls it 'buyer's remorse'— when people drive off the lot with their shiny new car and then the next morning wake up and worry about how they're going to make payments. I didn't feel that way."

"Good. I'm glad you felt safe and that you didn't have regrets the next day."

Our hushed conversation in the car reminded me of one of the few sleepovers I had gone to in junior high. I had only listened that night, as the other girls whispered their secrets around the circle, revealing which boy they liked with lots of giggles and flashlights turning off and on so that the lights darted around the room. That night I didn't have anything to contribute.

Tonight, with Christy, I felt as if I had things to share that were personal and yet not embarrassing.

"You know when Sierra showed us her zing thing?" I asked.

Christy nodded. "I wondered if that was difficult for you."

"No. I thought it was so sweet the way she had framed her first sonogram image of Ella Mae. I loved that she shared it with us and told all the details about the way Jordan was so mesmerized by the image."

"It must be the photographer in him," Christy said. "Like Sierra said, he was always trying to use his camera lens to capture natural beauty around him, and the sonogram had captured the deep natural beauty that was hidden inside Sierra. It was so poetic the way she said it."

"I think that's one of the things I like about being invited into this group," I said. "Everyone in the Daughters of Eve is open about what really matters in life. The deeper things. We don't sit around and talk about hair, diets, and cars."

"Well, I hate to disappoint you, but I'm definitely going to talk about this car the next time we get together," Christy teased. "I think I'll suggest a field trip. We need to all jump in your car and go cruising down to Laguna Beach." She looked into the back seat. "How many can we fit in here?"

"Legally?" I asked.

"That's probably the responsible way to go."

"I think we could get all five of us in." I squinted to see if there were enough seat belts. "The skinniest ones would need to squeeze into the back."

"And we would need to come with our hair pulled back."

"We could wear scarves," I suggested playfully. "Like the women in those vintage movies used to wear along with the big sunglasses when they drove the winding roads of Monte Carlo."

Christy laughed and pretended to toss the tail of a chiffon scarf around her neck. "Like an Audrey Hepburn movie."

"I'm picturing a different actress. What was her name? She had white-blond hair. I saw something about how she married a prince."

"I know who you mean," Christy said. "What was her name?"

We both reached for our phones and entered into a friendly race to see who could come up with the actress's name first.

"Grace Kelly?" Christy asked.

"Yes, that's the one. Grace Kelly."

"We'll call it our Grace Kelly Day." Christy continued to warm up to the idea. "Scarves and sunglasses required."

With a cute expression that looked like she was about to tease me, she added, "Guess what? We just talked about cars, skinny girls, and hair after all."

I grinned and decided not to make a comparison between the fun conversation Christy and I had just had and the kinds of conversations I used to have with my sisters-in-law. Ever since we moved, I had found my-self doing far too much comparing. I needed to let the different seasons of my life stand on their own. The first decade of our marriage had been wonderful in so many ways. Trevor's family had welcomed me in, even though I was so different from all of them, and they had included me in their lives.

The same was true now of the Daughters of Eve. I was included. Life was very different in California, but that didn't mean everything from the last ten years had been difficult and oppressive and now I was free. Who I was and who I was becoming were both important.

Christy and I had slid easily into a lull in our midnight car chat. The night chill had snuck in since I hadn't turned the motor back on, and I was feeling cold again.

"I really should get going." Christy reached for her purse and leaned over to give me a hug. "Thanks for the ride, and thank you for being my friend."

"Thank you for being my friend."

I felt so happy as we got out, and I locked the car.

"See you soon." Christy waved, and I waited in the parking lot until she drove away.

Trevor was already in bed when I tiptoed into our little nest. He must have been sleeping lightly because he rolled over when I slipped into bed and rested his arm across my midriff.

"Have a good time?" he murmured.

"Yes," I whispered. "It was really good. I love you."

"I love . . ." He drifted off, and I remained still, feeling the weight of his protective arm across me. Wisps of the multilayered conversations of the evening seemed to float in a circle above the bed.

I was glad I hadn't opened the ring box or shared about my cathartic experience in saying goodbye with the symbolic rosebuds. I was glad that everyone else had shared in meaningful ways, with most of the focus on Tess. I was especially glad that Christy and I had a chance to extend our conversation. The idea of a Grace Kelly Day was a good one. I started to think about how that might happen.

As my body relaxed and the circling wisps of conversations evaporated, I thought about how much had happened in my heart and mind over the past year.

Now all that needed to happen was for Trevor to finish the sale of the business and get established in a new job, and for us to have a steady income. We needed enough income to feel at peace about our decision to live here. That's all.

My thoughts had turned into a prayer. I felt like I wasn't asking God for too much. Just direction for Trevor at this crossroads. I silently thanked

God for the gift of my new friends, for how well Audra was doing, and for the ways He had led us here.

I didn't pray for a baby, the way I had for so many years. My spirit felt resolved.

Everything is settled in me, God, isn't it? I can be at peace and . . .

Something didn't feel right. It was as if I wanted a big bow to tie up the box of all my emotional experiences from the past few months. Then I could hand it over to God, making a gift to Him of all the emotional shards that had cut my soul for years and left scars. It would be a fine and noble thing to do . . .

Why do I not feel settled? What is still unresolved in me?

I was too tired for a soul-searching inventory. All I knew was that I was feeling what had become a familiar nudge.

Release.

I opened my eyes wide in the dark bedroom and scanned the ceiling above me as if I could read the answer to the "release" message written in invisible ink.

Release what? What am I missing? Do You want more of me, Lord?

Trevor shifted his position, removing his arm and rolling over onto his back. I turned on my side and let the easy pace of his breathing become the metronome that lulled me to sleep.

The next morning we were in our usual early morning scramble when my cell phone buzzed. I saw on the screen that the call was from my mother. I hesitated before answering. My stomach had tightened when I saw her name. I felt a clench of fear, as if I had done something wrong and was going to hear about it now.

I cleared my throat and answered, "Hello?"

"I hope I didn't call too early. I wanted to catch you before Audra went to school."

"This is fine. How are you? Is everything okay?"

"Yes, everything is fine. I'm calling to let you know that I would like to come see you."

I paused.

Trevor walked into the kitchen, buttoning up the front of his shirt. He was heading for the coffee maker, which had just finished Trevor's daily brew with a spurt and puff. He gave me a questioning look when he saw that I was on the phone and mouthed the word, "Who?"

"That would be great, Mom," I answered loudly enough for Trevor to pick up on why I was standing in the middle of the kitchen with a deer-in-the-headlights look.

Trevor stopped to watch me closely.

I can't say exactly how I knew, but in my knotted gut I realized that, somehow, this call was connected to the word *release* that had returned to my thoughts so many times.

"When are you planning to come?" I asked.

"Two weeks from yesterday."

"Okay, great."

"Sundays are good for you, aren't they? You said at one point that Trevor doesn't work on Sundays."

"That's right. He'll be home." Trevor and I had locked eyes. I hoped I sounded upbeat.

"We will only stay for lunch, so I hope we won't be a bother."

"No, that's fine. It's not a bother at all." It struck me that my mother had just said "we" so I asked, "Did you say 'we'?"

"Yes. It will be Karl and me."

"Karl?"

"Yes. Karl. It's time for you to meet him."

Chapter 20

Once again my mother was implementing her superpower of with-holding. She withheld the identity of Karl and hung up before indicating why the time for me to meet him was now.

All day my thoughts spun through every possibility. As soon as Audra was in bed that night and Trevor and I had a chance to retreat to the patio, I plugged in the overhead twinkle lights in the hopes that they would bring some cheer.

"Who do you think he is?" Trevor asked.

"I don't know. Do you think I might have a brother I never knew about?"

"Could he be your dad?" Trevor seemed to have been spinning the options as much as I had. "Maybe he didn't pass away when you were little."

The thought disturbed me more than I wanted to admit. "That would be terrible."

"You hear stories about things like that happening. The dad goes off to prison or abandons his family, and years later he returns to make amends."

"Do you really think my mother would have lied and said he was dead if he wasn't?"

Trevor put up his hands in defense to the tone of my voice. "Hey, I'm just trying to make sense of her game. I think it's terrible she is doing this to you. She's controlling all the pieces and keeping you guessing. Why?"

I didn't want to say what I was thinking about how manipulative my mother could be. I agreed with Trevor. Calling up and announcing that she was coming with some man in two weeks was cruel.

"What if your mother is in a relationship?" Trevor ventured. "What if he's her boyfriend, and she wants you to meet him?"

"My mother doesn't have boyfriends."

"The more I think about it, the angrier I am with your mom."

"We can't go down that trail. You and I will be a mess by the time she arrives."

"I think we're both already a mess thinking about it." Trevor pushed back from the table and crossed his arms. "What if we told her she couldn't come?"

"I already told her we would be home. I said she could come."

"What if we have other plans?"

"I'm not going to lie, Trevor."

"I'm not asking you to lie. Todd has been saying that we should go over and hang out with them sometime. What if we make plans to go to Todd and Christy's that Sunday and tell your mom we won't be able to have lunch with her and her mystery man."

"Then we'll never know who he is."

Trevor shrugged and stuck out his lower lip. "I can live with that."

I sipped the hot tea I had brought out with me to the table and stared at the potted jasmine plant. It had made a conservative but steady effort to wind up the post at the corner of the patio. Mrs. Miller's words from months ago came to me.

I shook my head. "No. I only want to plant sweet things. She might be happy playing some sort of game with us, but I don't want to play games back."

I thought about Jennalyn and how her mom had passed away unexpectedly. I told Trevor, and he asked, "What happened?"

"I don't know. Jennalyn didn't say how her mom died."

"Is that why you want to be nice to your mother? Because you at least have a mom, but Jennalyn doesn't?"

"That could be part of it. I don't know."

"You can be the gracious one. I'm just mad at her."

Trevor stayed mad for the next week and a half. It wasn't only my mom and her "antics," as he was calling them. Trevor also was mad about how things were going at work. He thought the deal he had negotiated was a sure thing and that everything was in place with his uncle.

But, like most business arrangements with the men in the Winslow clan, it was tangled. Trevor had meetings with attorneys and some long calls with his uncle. Every night he brought home thick folders of paperwork and stayed up late. He evaluated each car that remained in inventory and adjusted the price so it would hopefully sell quickly but still leave him a profit.

"How much is the Mercedes listed for?" I asked late one night when he was working on his iPad.

Trevor was standing at the kitchen counter as he worked because standing helped him to stay awake. He tapped on the screen and turned it so I could see a picture of the car and its slashed price.

"Any interest in it yet?" I asked.

"No. Why? Are you hoping we can keep it?"

"No. I know you need to sell it. I just wondered if I could drive it one more time."

The tense expression on Trevor's face seemed to melt when he heard my request. I think it was in his blood to be pleased whenever anyone showed interest in a car, especially a luxury car.

"I'll bring it home tomorrow," he said. "The insurance runs until the end of April. We should take Audra out for a drive in it. Maybe we can put down the top and drive up the coast."

I wasn't sure when a leisurely drive like that might happen for Trevor because he was giving every waking hour to finalizing the sale. He seemed to have simultaneously come to the same conclusion. I watched the corners of his mouth turn down.

"Why don't you drive it for about another week and a half."

"Thanks."

Trevor came closer and wrapped his arms around me. "I wish I could give it to you. I really do."

"I know. But I don't need a fancy car." I circled my arms around his middle and rested my head on his chest. "I have a fancy husband and a daughter who thinks she's very fancy." I smiled. "I'm content."

"I'm not." He kissed the top of my head and pulled away. "At least not yet. I hope I will be content, though, once I make it through all this."

"Let me know if I can do anything to help."

"There's one thing you can do." Trevor had returned to his stack of files on the counter.

"Sure. What?"

With a half grin he said, "Stop trying to distract me." He raised an eyebrow and then gave me a wink.

I read his message and adored him for making me feel desirable even in my late-night, ready-for-bed, disheveled state. "Okay, I'll leave you alone."

Heading for bed, I called over my shoulder, "At least for now."

"To be continued," he echoed.

As promised, Trevor brought the Mercedes home, and I took advantage of driving Audra to school by putting the top down. I enjoyed exiting the grocery store and remembering what car I was looking for. I especially loved slipping into the convertible when work ended and feeling the flow of air around me with the sun shining on the top of my head.

After driving the car for two days, I referred to her as BB, which stood for "Borrowed Bliss." I added to the luxurious experience by using the last of my Christmas gift certificate money to buy a pair of stylish sunglasses. I loved driving around, looking like I was living the California dream.

Christy texted me the afternoon that I had bought the sunglasses and said she saw me when I was heading down the street to our apartment. I waved, but you must not have seen me. Either that or you're too cool now in your fancy car to wave back.

I assured her that I hadn't seen her.

That's a relief.

She added a smiley face and then texted, Have you given any more thought to doing something with the DOEs? With you driving, of course.

I replied that we needed to plan something soon because I only had BB for another week.

Christy wasted no time starting a conversation with a group text. The others didn't know what she was talking about when she said we needed to plan a Grace Kelly Day. Christy was the only one who knew about BB, and apparently Tess had never heard of Grace Kelly. Christy explained everything, and I followed her long text with the reality notice that the only day I could do it would be this Saturday.

Within minutes, our outing was all arranged. None of us could manage to spend an entire day away from our real lives. We had no problem, though, juggling all our schedules, ending up with plans for a drive down the coast to Laguna Beach. We would spend a leisurely morning drinking coffee and munching on pastries at a place Sierra wanted us to try.

On Friday I asked Audra to help me to wash the car after school. Mr. Miller agreed to let me pull BB into a restricted space so we could use his garden hose. He ended up pitching in and helping us dry BB with old beach towels he provided.

Mr. Miller didn't say much while Audra chattered and the three of us worked together. When we were finished and BB was sparkling, he stood back and said, "It's nice the way you girls take care of each other."

"That's what moms do," Audra spouted off.

"I meant the group Christy is in. The Eve Girls, or whatever you call yourselves." As he rolled up the garden hose, I had an idea.

"Mr. Miller, would you and Mrs. Miller like to go for a spin in BB?"

He looked surprised that I suggested it.

"One of you will have to sit in the back seat with Audra, and it can get a little breezy."

"I'll ask Margaret."

I returned BB to her regular parking spot, and Audra climbed into the back seat, ready to go.

"You know who else you should take for a ride?" Audra said. "Mr. and Mrs. Thompson from the restaurant. You keep asking them to come over for dinner, and they keep saying not now. Maybe they would want to go for a ride."

"That's a good idea. I'll ask them."

"You should also ask Carlos and his family if they want to borrow the car for a day before Dad sells it."

"Why Carlos?"

"Mom, don't you remember? Today is his last day. He probably is really sad. Maybe if he could use the car, it would be like a going-away gift for him."

I had forgotten about Carlos leaving that day. When Trevor let him know he was selling the car lot, Carlos found another job right away, and I know that was a relief for Trevor. Audra had spent so much time at the car lot she had picked up on all the details, as usual.

"I'll ask Dad," I told her. "I like the way you think about other people, Audra."

"That's what you do. Didn't you hear Mr. Miller? All of us Eve Girls have to look out for each other."

Mr. Miller came striding through the parking lot. I couldn't tell by his expression what he was going to say.

"Margaret said to tell you she appreciated the offer but she has dinner on the stove."

"Oh, okay," I said. "Maybe another time. Although I won't have the car much longer."

"Well, I would like to go," he said.

"Now?"

"Isn't that what you were offering?"

"Yes," I said quickly. "Hop in. Where should we go?"

Mr. Miller adjusted the passenger's seat to better suit him and ran his big hand across the dashboard, as if we had missed a spot when we were cleaning the car. "It's your choice," he said. "If you end up going by the hardware store, I need to pick up a nozzle for the hose. You probably noticed how much it was leaking."

I hadn't noticed, but I was happy to drive Mr. Miller to the hardware store. I asked Audra to take my phone and look up the nearest big-box home improvement store. Mr. Miller stopped me and said he preferred the small, haphazardly stocked local hardware store on Tustin Avenue, which was only two miles away.

My favorite part of the short outing was watching the slow smile that lifted his weathered face. He rested his arm on the rolled-down window and kept looking up at the overhanging traffic lights and the tall eucalyptus trees that lined Ocean Parkway.

"I don't want to compare him to a dog," I told Trevor that night when I gave him the full report of our outing. "But he did remind me of a faithful Labrador sticking his head out a truck's window."

I kept my voice low as I told Trevor because we were out on the patio, and I didn't know if any of the neighbors had their windows open and could hear what I was saying about our apartment manager. I thought Trevor would at least grin at my update. It had been a happy afternoon for Audra and me, as well as for Mr. Miller. Trevor's thoughts seemed to be fixated on the car lot.

"I should tell you that I added a bonus to Carlos's final check when he left today," he said.

"That was nice of you." I was proud of my generous husband and praised him some more.

Then he told me the amount of the bonus, and I felt the earlier happiness go poof.

"I thought that was the amount you budgeted for us. To make sure we had enough to cover expenses through the summer."

Trevor already had told me that he was going to have a lot less profit after the sale than he had first predicted. He originally planned to have enough to cover living expenses for four months. Now it sounded like we would only have enough for a month or two. That is, if everything sold off the lot.

"I thought it was the right thing to do," Trevor said.

"But Carlos already has a new job. You don't."

"I know." His jaw tightened.

"Then why didn't you think about us first in all this? It's great that you're concerned about Carlos and his family, but what about you and your family? Aren't you supposed to take care of us? Why aren't you protecting us?"

What followed was the worst argument we had had in a long time. We kept our voices low, but that only added to our words' intensity. They came out with a gravel sound, and we used our facial expressions to emphasize what might possibly be lost in the growling whispers.

"You're one to talk about protecting our family!" Trevor's eyes narrowed. "You were the one who unilaterally agreed to let your mother come for lunch with a stranger."

"What was I supposed to do?" I could feel my face burning.

"You could have said you needed to check with your husband, look at the calendar, and then call her back."

I had no reply. I knew he was right. I let my mother hijack me.

We stopped talking. Full stop, as if we had slammed on the brakes at a stop sign. We sat in silence, taking time to calm down.

It struck me that we had managed to come to the conclusion to stay in California after months of stressful conversations and wavering indecision. Through all those discussions, we had remained fairly polite and considerate of what the other person was thinking and feeling.

All those previous courtesies were missing tonight. They seemed to have no place in the way we were treating each other now. To have come through all those months and now be in such a place of terrible disconnect with Trevor was sickening. It made me mad.

"I'm late." Trevor pushed back his chair and picked up the dinner dishes that still remained in front of us.

"For what?"

"Friday night. The Gathering. I told Todd I would be there."

Something wicked in me wanted to throw out a cruel comment about how I hoped the Bible study would do him some good. I kept my lips closed.

Trevor lingered a moment before opening the sliding door.

"Hey, I apologize," he said.

"So do I," I mumbled. I think both of us knew it wasn't the sort of apology that solved anything. It was more like each of us was saying the other person should be understanding and excuse the flare-up. We each had our reasons. We each had strong feelings.

He left, and I sat alone on the patio, feeling the slow burn of my anger without doing anything to snuff it out. Neither of us had said, "I'm sorry." We only said we "apologized." In our marriage, we understood those two terms as different entities.

Audra came out on the patio a few minutes later with tears in her eyes.

"What's wrong?"

"My stomach hurts."

I went inside with her and asked all the usual questions a mom employs to evaluate such a complaint. My stomach was unsettled as well. I thought it was from the tense conversation, but now I wondered if the spaghetti sauce had been too acidic. A child's antacid followed by a bubble bath and my hand on her head for Audra's nightly blessing seemed to be all she needed.

"You're a good mom," Audra said as I closed her bedroom door. "I love you."

"I love you too. Sweet dreams."

If she had heard any of our argument after dinner, she didn't let on or ask about it. She had been in her bedroom watching a show on Trevor's iPad, so I doubted she could hear us since the sliding door was closed.

I thought about the plans I had with the DOEs in the morning and wished I could move it to the following Saturday. My mother and Karl would be in our home on Sunday, and I needed to shop for food and do some serious cleaning.

Plunging my hands under the running water in the kitchen sink, I planned our Sunday lunch menu. Thoughts of Trevor's extravagant gift to Carlos kept overriding my menu thoughts. I remembered what it was like to be recipients of Mrs. Thompson's extravagant Christmas gift. It had been a godsend for us. Maybe Carlos needed the money more than we did. Maybe Trevor knew that.

Ignoring all my flittering thoughts, I loaded the dishwasher, turned on the TV, and wrote out a grocery list. About half an hour later, I thought about what I had said to Trevor in my anger. How he was supposed to be the one to take care of us and protect us. I remembered how Audra had said that I was a good mom after I did what I could to make her stomachache go away.

That's when I knew where all the anger came from.

I'm angry at my mother!

I had brushed off Trevor's frustration with her, but he was right. She had pulled us all off balance with her announcement that she was coming with a mystery guest. The more I thought about it, I could see how deep the roots of my anger went. They ran all the way back to when I was the child with the stomachache, longing to feel her cool palm on my forehead.

I was angry at my mother. Angry at her about many things. I had been for a long time.

The door opened, and Trevor came in. I turned off the TV. He looked at me on the couch and came closer before saying, "Hi."

My sincere apology tumbled out before he even sat down. "Trevor, I'm sorry. I was taking out my frustration on you earlier, and I shouldn't have. Please forgive me."

He sat beside me and reached for my hand. "I forgive you. Will you forgive me?"

"Yes, of course."

"You were right," he said. "I haven't done a good job of caring for you and Audra and protecting you both the way I want to. And on top of that, I was mad at your mother."

In a small voice I said, "I'm mad at my mother too."

"I know. You have reason to be mad at her. I have reason to be mad at her. But our anger at her has only messed with *us*. She probably doesn't even know we're angry. I don't want to mess with us. I'm sorry."

"So am I." My hand felt so warm and sheltered under his.

"I want you to know that I'll protect you on Sunday," he said. "You don't have to worry about my saying anything out of line to your mom. I'll show her the respect I should give her as my mother-in-law. But listen, if she comes in our home and starts doin' anything that I think is harmful to you or Audra, I'm just gonna ask her to leave." Trevor reached over and touched the back of his thick fingers to my cheek.

I hadn't realized that I had started to cry.

"What do ya think? Is that a good plan for us?" Trevor's drawl had kicked in, so I knew he was hoping I would agree to whatever he was trying to sell me.

I nodded.

He leaned back. "I have a lead on a job. Todd gave it to me tonight."

My lips parted, but as often happened, nothing came out. I never had been able to switch gears quickly the way Trevor could. I knew that Trevor had given up on the idea of teaching at Todd's school when he found out how many classes he would need to take before he could teach in California.

"The job is for a guy Todd knows. He's looking for an experienced luxury car salesman. I'm gonna call him tomorrow. I don't know what kind of dealership it is, but I'm hopin' it's either Lexus or BMW since that's where I have the most experience."

"Trevor, that's great."

"Yeah, it is. Makes me feel like God is going to take care of us."

We sat calmly, side by side. Trevor stroked my hair and twisted his finger around one of the relaxed curls. I felt like we were two weary warriors who had fought hard but now had surrendered to each other, fully aware that we needed to join forces for the battle looming before us Sunday.

Chapter 21

When the alarm went off at seven the next morning, I groaned. Then I remembered it was Saturday. Coffee. Eight a.m. Sunglasses. Scarf. Grace Kelly Day.

Why did I agree to this? Do I even own a scarf?

Trevor was as worn out as I was. We both had expended a lot of emotional energy during our fight the night before. He got up when I did, though, put on some music, and made oatmeal, which is one of the three things he excelled at making. His version of oatmeal included whatever tasty additions he could find in the cupboard. This time his hunt-and-gather expedition resulted in the addition of raisins, maple syrup, a handful of dried cherries, and his usual dollop of peanut butter on top.

I left him to his masterful creation and took a shower. Audra knocked on the bathroom door and called out, "Do you want me to find a scarf for you? I heard you telling Miss Christy that everyone was supposed to wear a scarf."

"Yes!" I called back. I had no idea what she would find.

Audra turned out to be the second family member that morning who had creative success on her hunt-and-gather mission. She found a pale pink chiffon scarf I didn't even know I owned. When I finished my shower, I found the scarf smoothed out full length on top of our bedspread. Next to it was an old top that had always been a little tight under the arms. The top was a combination of all of Audra's favorite colors so I could see why she had selected it to go with the scarf.

"Audra, where did you find this scarf?"

"It was in one of the purses you only use for fancy dinners."

I walked into the kitchen in my robe, amazed that she knew where my two clutch purses were located.

"If you want to use a fancy purse today, I put them back on the left side of your bottom dresser drawer."

"You are a wonder, daughter of mine." I returned to the bedroom and heard Audra ask Trevor if being a "wonder" was a good thing.

"Yes," he assured her. "It's a very good thing. Are you finished eating?"

"I can't eat it all, Dad. I mean, it was good. Well, except for the raisins. I don't think I like raisins anymore. Besides, I need to save room for a churro."

I stopped dressing and listened to Trevor's answer.

"You know that Carlos doesn't work with me anymore. He won't be there this morning so there won't be any churros."

"I know. But that doesn't mean we can't still have churros on Saturdays, does it? Mr. Carlos used to say that he paid me in churros whenever I helped on Saturdays. So if you aren't going to pay me in churros, what are you going to pay me with?"

Trevor's laugh sounded good floating through the paper-thin walls. It had been a while since I had heard his happy laugh. My husband's chipper attitude and Audra's contentment were like gifts to me that morning. I left the house aware that I had their blessing to go have fun and laugh with my friends.

Audra's fashionable choice for me made me feel young, tightness under the armpits and all. I climbed into the Mercedes, lowered the top, slipped on my sunglasses, and looked up at the clear blue sky the way Mr. Miller had taken in the view. This was the perfect morning to go freewheeling with the Daughters of Eve!

The others were already at Jennalyn's when I arrived. I pulled into the driveway and smiled at all of them lined up wearing sunglasses and scarves around their necks. Jennalyn had added a fabulous big floppy hat, and Sierra was wearing a beautiful, long, flowing, gauzy dress that was embroidered across the bodice and had wonderful, big bell sleeves.

"And here I thought I was early!" I exclaimed.

"You are," Jennalyn said. "I think we must have needed this because all of us were ready ahead of time."

"I don't know about you guys, but I always feel like I'm on borrowed time," Sierra said. "I have four hours, and then Ella Mae is going to need me to be home. How about everyone else?"

Jennalyn agreed as she slid into the back seat and Tess followed, taking the skinny spot in the middle. "Four hours exactly," Jennalyn said. "How fast can you drive, Emily?"

"Not so fast that I get a speeding ticket."

"You don't have to drive fast." Christy settled into the remaining spot in the back and insisted that Sierra take the front. "This isn't the Monte Carlo Speedster Race Day. This is our elegant and sophisticated Grace Kelly Day. Decorum, ladies. Chins up."

Sierra cracked up, as she buckled her seat belt, and I playfully revved the engine. "Christy, you do realize, don't you, that you just sounded like your aunt Marti the way you said that?"

"Good. Because that was what I was going for."

"It reminds me of when Marti took us to Switzerland, and she was mortified the whole time with my manners," Sierra added.

"Christy's aunt took the two of you to Switzerland?" Tess asked. "I've always wanted to go there. Do you think Marti would want to make a repeat trip? Because I would be her travel partner in a minute."

"I would too," Jennalyn said.

Sierra turned around and must have exchanged a humorous expression with Christy that I missed. The two of them burst into laughter, making it seem that traveling the world with Christy's wealthy aunt wasn't exactly the dream-come-true adventure the rest of us thought it might be.

I slowly backed the car out of the driveway, a maneuver that was more difficult with three heads and a hat blocking my view. Fortunately no cars were coming in either direction, so we had the street to ourselves as I put the car in drive and headed for the Pacific Coast Highway.

"Scarves, ladies!" Sierra sat up straight and did her best to imitate a woman of high society by giving her ivory scarf an exuberant toss around her neck. The excessive fringe on the tail of her scarf brushed the side of my face.

In the rearview mirror I saw the others imitating her posh gesture. Jennalyn had her hand on top of her floppy hat as we rolled up to the first stoplight. An older woman in the car next to us studied us curiously.

"Hello, dahling!" Sierra called out, waving as if she were in a royal procession. "Beautiful morning, isn't it?"

The DOEs in the back seat laughed and joined the waving.

"We must look like a bunch of overage sorority sisters carrying out an initiation event for Tess, since she's the one sitting in the middle of the back seat." Jennalyn laughed in a way I never had heard her laugh. It sounded like pure joy, holding out all the high notes until they squeezed crystallized happy tears from all of us. I had heard Jennalyn wail, cry, growl, and chuckle. But this full-throttle laughter was absolutely the best sound ever.

I kept my eyes on the road and told myself to be extra careful. The merriment continued with rounds of silliness as I cruised down the Pacific Coast Highway, heading to Laguna Beach. We rolled past all the cute shops in Corona Del Mar and a darling restaurant on the right side of the road called the Five Crowns. It looked like an old English pub and had a red phone booth out front.

Everyone was chatting at once, like birds on a wire. I would have preferred being a passenger because I missed most of the conversations as I focused on the road and the cars on either side of me.

I did hear Sierra say that we should change the name to a Grace Kelly Morning because we weren't spending the whole day together roaring up and down the coast like women of leisure.

Christy had shouted back, "Let's just pretend we are."

"Agreed," Jennalyn added. "Think of this as our four-hour movie, and we get to be the stars."

Once we drove past Pelican Point Drive, the road opened up, and we had clear views of the pristine, springtime blue of the Pacific Ocean on our right.

"I haven't been down this way in so long," Christy called out over the breeze that had picked up now that we were going a little faster. "It's so beautiful!"

"I'm glad we did this," Tess shouted. "Who came up with the idea? It's genius!"

Christy reached between the seats and patted my shoulder as if giving me full credit for the playdate idea, as Jennalyn had called it in one of her texts. I pointed back at Christy, making sure all the accolades didn't fall on me. "Group effort," I shouted.

The scarf around my neck felt like it was dancing as it fluttered in the wind. I felt so happy. So full of life. What brought me the most joy was realizing I had done something that brought elation to my sweet friends.

"Todd used to surf down there," Christy called out.

The sign said Crystal Cove State Park. I wanted to remember it so that maybe Trevor and I could take Audra there sometime. We could bring a picnic. The area where we lived was congested, and the houses were close together; I had no idea that not far down the highway, miles of undeveloped coastline with a state park existed.

As soon as the sale of the car lot was finalized, we'd have to come here. We wouldn't have BB anymore, but it would still be fun.

We rolled on down the highway into a densely developed area. "This is Laguna Beach," Sierra told me. She had her phone out and was checking directions for the café she had selected for us. "Turn left at the next light. The café is going to be about a half mile up the street on the right, I think." She turned her phone. "Maybe it's on the left."

"So it's not by the beach?" Tess asked. "I thought you wanted to walk on the beach."

"I thought we could do that afterward." Sierra turned to the women in the back seat. "This place has fair-trade coffee and features work from local artists. It sounded interesting. I called and reserved the alcove for us, but if you guys want to go someplace else, that's fine with me."

"No," came the reply in unison.

"It sounds enchanting," Jennalyn said. "I love little hideaway places."

"Me too," Sierra agreed.

I put on my blinker and turned left at the light. "So is it on the right or left from here? What did you finally decide?"

"It's down there." Sierra pointed for me to turn onto a narrow, one-way street that angled off in a Y from the main street, which explained why the map was confusing.

"Look, there's even a parking place out front," Sierra said. "Perfect!"

I stopped and sized up the parking space, making sure there weren't any red curbs or signs indicating that I shouldn't park there.

"What if everybody gets out now?" I suggested. I wasn't the best parallel parker on the planet. I figured they could go on to the café, and I could complete what was bound to be an embarrassing and time-consuming maneuver.

Everyone disembarked. But instead of going inside, they seemed to think I had requested they provide 360-degree parking assistance. Since the top was down, each of them could give directions in whatever manner suited her personality.

"Isn't this one of those cars that parks itself?" Sierra asked.

"I don't think so." If it was, I hadn't figured out where that secret button was, and I wasn't going to attempt it now.

Tess was standing tall in her stylish summer pants and off-the-shoulder top. She positioned herself behind the car, using both hands like a traffic controller inching an enormous jet into an airport gate with two glowing batons.

Christy stayed right beside me, walking slowly with the car the way a circus trainer keeps close but not too close to the dancing bear. Her voice was soft and too encouraging to be of any specific guidance. "You're doing great, Emily. You have plenty of room. Don't be nervous."

Jennalyn stood in front of my car issuing precise commands and using her hands as if I couldn't hear her and she needed to pantomime each move with exaggeration. "You have two feet at the front. A foot and a half now. One foot. Okay, stop. You'll need to go that way and then come this way and back in at more of an angle. Crank the wheel. You have this much space."

Sierra was no help at all. She stood in the middle of the street on her phone, occasionally looking up and nodding or shaking her head without any indication of what the shakes and nods meant.

BB had one helpful feature that contributed to the comical effort. Her backup sensor beeped louder and louder the closer I got to the car behind me. Every time it beeped, Sierra looked around as if the alarm was going off on someone else's car.

"Do you guys hear that?" she asked.

"It's the car," I called out.

"Which car?"

"This car."

"Your car?"

"Yes, my car." I put my foot on the brake and sat there. BB was angled like a jackknife. I was getting nowhere in spite of the crazy choreography and slapstick routine going on all around me. I mean, if anyone had been filming us during the last four minutes, we would have had viral video footage for sure.

"I'm going to find a different parking spot," I announced. "You guys go on in. I'll find you."

None of them protested the decision, and none of them seemed to think our antics were as funny as I thought. Maybe because they didn't have the center-ring view that I did.

I maneuvered BB out of the alleyway and drove until I came out at a main road. To my relief, a public parking area appeared half a block away and had nice wide spaces. I pulled into one with no problem. I was happy to pay whatever rate they charged for the luxury of pulling into the space nose first.

I trotted back to the café, past lots of interesting boutiques and art shops. The DOEs stood at the café's front counter, waiting for their beverages and pastries.

I had a hard time deciding what to order. It had been a long time since I had been in a coffee shop. The menu was handwritten on a large chalkboard, and each of the coffees and teas was given a whimsical name like "Midsummer Night's Dream." The drink was described as chamomile tea with a "puck" of orange rind and a lavender-laced sugar cube.

The others had gone to the alcove, which was outside, behind the building. I knew it would take me twenty minutes to read the entire storybook menu. All the pastries looked delectable.

"And for you?" the barista asked.

"I would like whatever you have that's closest to a chai latte," I said. "And one of those."

"An apricot oat bar," she said, reaching into the case with the tongs. "And a Spice and Nice with Cream."

I'm still not sure why I went for the chai latte, but I was glad I did. I took a sip before carrying it to the alcove since the ceramic cup was filled to the brim with foam, and I was afraid I might spill it on someone in the tight quarters. The drink was unlike any chai latte I had ever had. Much smoother and with lots of cinnamon, which I love.

Christy pulled out a chair for me as I approached. The five of us just fit with our feet tucked under the rustic, round wooden table. We had the alcove to ourselves, thanks to Sierra's foresight in reserving it for us.

The walls were made of adobe and gave the cool little courtyard the feel of a secret hideaway in the middle of a Spanish hacienda. Bright springtime perennials spilled over the sides of the large clay pots that were clustered like old women gossiping in the corners. The air carried a fine scent of freshly ground coffee beans mixed with the earthy aroma that came from potting soil and deep purple petunias in full bloom.

"Don't you love this?" Christy said in a hushed voice. "We were all just telling Sierra that she picked a winner."

Sierra leaned in with a forkful of gooey cinnamon roll. "This is incredible, you guys. I mean, I know my cinnamon rolls, and this one is off the charts."

"Better than the cinnamon rolls you had at your wedding instead of wedding cake?" Christy asked.

"You remembered." Sierra stuffed the whole bite in her mouth and nodded, making a yum expression. She swallowed. "Almost as good as Mama
Bear's."

For the rest of us, she explained, "I worked at a bakery when I was in
high school. Mama Bear's. Their specialty was cinnamon rolls. That's why
we had their cinnamon rolls at our wedding."

"We had carrot cake," Jennalyn said with a reminiscent look. "Joel loves
carrot cake."

"By any chance did Joel make your wedding cake?" Christy asked.

"No, a friend of his made it for us. It was her wedding gift to us."

"Was it scrumptious?" Sierra asked.

"Joel said it was. I don't remember eating more than the little bite we fed
each other for the picture." Jennalyn looked at my apricot oat bar. "How is
that? I almost ordered it."

"It's amazing. Do you want to try it?"

I held out my plate, and soon we had a throng of forks circulating around
the table as we lifted our plates and all took nibbles of everyone else's pastry.
Christy's cherry tart was nice, but I was glad I had selected the apricot bar.

I leaned back, sipping my chai latte and enjoying the conversation and
spurts of laughter. I loved our little haven. I loved the way we all looked a
little silly with our scarves still draped around our necks.

Most of all I loved being able to simply be myself with these women.

Chapter 22

J contentedly listened to the hum and pitch of the conversation, feeling like a sailor who learns the sounds of his ship once he has been at sea long enough. This was not my maiden voyage any longer. I was on board with these women and felt that wherever we were going, we would sail there together.

Jennalyn made a comment that drew me out of my thoughts and prompted me to ask her to repeat what she had said.

"I said that I think we're all twelve-year-old girls at heart."

"I've thought that before too," I said. "It's like something in us gets stuck at that stage of life."

"Why did you say a twelve-year-old?" Sierra asked.

"Because I think that's the age when we realize we want to be included and accepted," Jennalyn explained. "We hope we're special and exceptional in some way. Yet by the time we're twelve, we have a pretty good sense of how others see us, so we start to believe the messages, spoken and unspoken. We form our sense of identity, and usually we're pretty critical of ourselves."

"That's definitely the age when I started to feel the most insecure," Tess said. "All the hormones that kicked in didn't help."

Sierra took the coming-of-age topic by the horns and provided us with a little too much information regarding one of her most embarrassing moments.

"TMI!" Jennalyn put up her hand to stop Sierra from saying anything more.

"You're right. Too much information," Sierra said, "Sorry about that. This is why I need all of you to keep me in line. I think I lost a few of my cultural filters during the time I spent in Brazil. The point I was trying to make was that I'm glad I had a mom who was very patient with me at that age and explained everything that was happening to my body in clear detail."

"I think we all needed patience when we were twelve," Christy said.

"I agree." Tess licked the back of her fork, enjoying the very last crumbs of her chocolate éclair.

"Now that I have a daughter," Sierra said, "I've already thought about how I want to do whatever I can to make her transition during that time in life less traumatic and more natural."

"I've thought about that with Hana too," Christy said. "She is growing up so fast. I want to help her to understand what's happening when her body changes, but not too soon. I want her to stay young and naive as long as possible."

"I feel that way with Audra," I said. "She knows enough, I think. I hope. I don't know. Trevor is really good with explaining things to her. But I want to make it easier for her too, like you said."

"You seem like such a nurturing mom with Audra," Sierra said. "Was your mother that way with you?"

I paused, thinking about what I wanted to say. I hadn't talked much about my mom to the DOEs, and I didn't want to bring her into the center of the conversation. I had a feeling it would be too easy once I got started on my mom to spill my guts about our complicated relationship and that she was coming tomorrow. I didn't want her to be the focus of today.

"My mom was reserved." I left my comment at that. My response to the question was honest and respectful, but it didn't dip into too many details.

Jennalyn asked, "Reserved in what way?"

"I'll put it this way: I was sheltered as a child, and when I matured, I had no idea what was happening to my body."

"Oh." Jennalyn looked sad for me. "That must have been frightening."

"It was."

I didn't want to get the TMI signal from Jennalyn the way Sierra had, so I didn't tell them that I had feared I had cancer because that was all my innocent imagination could come up with.

"I agree with Sierra and Christy," I said. "I don't want Audra to ever feel the kind of shame and fear that I felt."

Jennalyn had pressed her hand to her heart. "My mom was wonderful about it all. She took me to lunch and told me I was pretty and sweet and that my body was developing just the way it should. She made me feel very feminine."

"That's how a young girl should feel," Tess agreed.

Jennalyn smiled at the memory. "After lunch we went for a walk in a beautiful rose garden. When she was certain no one else could hear us, we sat on a bench, and she talked to me as if she was passing on the ancient secret of womanhood. She told me that when my body changed, it would be a blessing because it meant that one day I would be able to have babies. She said that having me was one of the biggest blessings of her life."

"That's so sweet," Sierra said.

Christy agreed. "I love that your mother found a way to turn everything into a celebration."

"She did. That's where I get it from. She loved to host a party."

"Your mom and my mom sound like opposites," Tess said. "My mom just went to parties."

Tess wrapped both hands around the curves of the rounded mug as if savoring the last touch of warmth that it offered. "Emily, I have a feeling you and I have a lot in common with our mothers."

"Except for the parties. My mom didn't go to parties," I said.

"She probably didn't bring all kinds of men home either."

I shook my head. "Like I said, my mom was reserved."

"How is your relationship with your mom now, Tess?" Christy asked. "You were saying earlier how much the counseling had helped you to view your relationship with her differently."

"The counselor told me I had magical thinking with my mom," Tess said. "I kept expecting her to change. I thought one day I would wake up and suddenly she would start being a real mom to me. The kind of mom I wanted her to be."

I glanced at the others to see if any of them could understand what Tess was saying. I certainly understood.

Trevor would probably say I still have magical thinking about my mom.

Tess was looking at me as she continued. "The counselor helped me see that my mother might never change."

She paused. "But I could change. And I did."

"How?" I asked.

"I had to step back and develop a realistic view of my mother. When I did that, I realized that whatever it was that had fractured inside her long ago had never healed properly. Or maybe it healed in a way that had left her crippled emotionally."

"That's an intense concept," Sierra said.

"It is. I started to think of it this way: If my mom had somehow damaged her spine and was confined to a wheelchair, I wouldn't keep saying to her, 'Get up. Give me a hug.' I would recognize that something was broken in her, yet I was asking her to do something she couldn't."

Tess leaned in. "My counselor helped me to see that I had a choice. If I wanted to, I could be the one to give her a hug without expecting her to get up and come to me."

We all seemed to be nodding, slowly taking in the concept.

"That's powerful," Sierra said.

"It's your superpower," I murmured.

"What did you say?" Tess asked.

I paused, letting my thought form completely. "By being the one who was making the choice in the relationship, you got your strength back. Your ability to choose became your superpower."

"Exactly! I like that." Tess grinned and struck a cute pose. "Look out, world. It's Wonder Tess and her superpower!"

Her cuteness lightened the moment. I smiled, wondering if she had any idea how adorable she was.

"It's really all about choosing to love, isn't it?" Jennalyn said. "I mean, we all have that power, don't we?"

"I think the power is in the choice," Christy added. "Like Emily just said."

"Right, because if you're a victim, you don't have a choice," Sierra said. "But if you take back your ability to choose how you're going to position yourself in a relationship, you aren't at the other person's mercy anymore. It is a superpower, Emily. I like that. I'm going to remember that."

Tess's complexion picked up a warm glow from the filtered light entering the alcove. "Where were all of you when I was working through this a few years ago? I would have graduated a lot sooner from my therapy sessions if I had friends I could talk to like this."

Jennalyn reached over and placed her hand on Tess's arm. "Didn't I tell you? The real reason I gathered everyone is because I needed group therapy. You all have been part of my self-prescribed intervention group."

We laughed but then agreed that we all felt that same way.

Sierra pulled out her phone, checking the time or perhaps checking for any SOS messages from home. I remembered that both she and Jennalyn had said when we left that they were on the clock when it came to returning home to their little ones.

"So," Sierra said brightly, "not that I wouldn't love spending all morning sitting here psychoanalyzing each other, because I do love our group therapy sessions very much, but does anyone else feel the need to get a little vitamin s-e-a before we head home?"

"I get it," Jennalyn said. "Vitamin sea. That's clever."

"Haven't you heard that before?" Sierra asked.

"No, but now I want to do some fun lettering with it and put it on a card or sign." Jennalyn had pulled out her phone and was tapping herself a note. She looked up with a wide-eyed expression.

"I didn't tell you guys!"

"Tell us what?"

"I got a big order from one of the shops on Balboa Island that sells Christy's aprons and pillows."

"Did she finally call you back?" Christy asked.

"Yes. And she wanted to see some of my other work. Particularly the lettering I do on reclaimed wood. She said she has a market for small pieces like that."

"Yay!" Christy said. "I've been wondering why she never got back to you. Your work is so much better than a lot of what she carries. That's great news, Jennalyn."

"It probably won't be as lucrative as my watercoloring class was," Jennalyn said. "But it means I can do my side hustle from home. That's what I was hoping for."

We started to discuss work, careers, and the pressure we all felt to bring in more income. To my surprise, Tess talked about the second business she had along with being a personal stylist. She sold oils like the Slippers roll-on fragrance she had given us at the Favorite Things party.

The others all knew about her oil business. I was grateful that it wasn't something Tess had tried to pitch and sell to me at our first gathering. It assured me that Tess saw me as a friend and not a potential customer.

She and Sierra talked about lavender oil, and that made me want to become a customer and buy some. Not that we had extra money for anything. But Sierra's enthusiasm over how much the lavender had helped Ella Mae to fall asleep caused me to want the lavender fragrance to lull me to sleep every night.

"I really should sign up with you," Sierra said. "I could sell oils like crazy. Adding to the income would be a boost for us right now."

"Let's get together next week," Tess said. "I'll give you all the information, and you can see if that's something you would like to do."

Sierra turned to me. "Emily, you should sign up too. We could both have home side businesses."

I put up my hand before the discussion could go any further. "Trevor is the salesman in our family. Not me. I wish I was a work-from-home kind of woman, but I'm not."

Jennalyn checked her phone. "Not to change the subject, but does anyone else want to do a little browsing in the shops here?"

"I do," Tess said. "I need some inspiration for one of my clients. She's a bit . . ." Tess glanced at Christy.

"Yes," Christy agreed. "She is."

They exchanged a grin. I had a feeling that even though Tess made it a practice not to reveal the identity of her high-end clients, Christy obviously knew about this particular one. That meant it probably was Christy's aunt Marti. I wondered if Marti had been the connection between Tess and this group.

"Let's go!" Sierra popped up from the table. "We can save the vitamin sea beach walk for another Grace Kelly Morning. This meals-on-wheels mama has only two hours before it's letdown time."

"TMI," Tess said with a laugh.

The next two hours were a lark. We took a fabulous, carefree jaunt through as many of the specialty shops as we could find in that part of Laguna Beach.

Jennalyn discovered an inexpensive oil painting the size of a cell phone and bought it without hesitation. Christy took photos of various fabrics and designs in one of the home interior shops. Sierra had a sparkling comment about everything. I realized, as we were on our merry trek through the shops, that Sierra must have been a lot like Audra when she was growing up. She was highly attuned to everything around her and had no trouble catching every side conversation.

Tess was the most fun to watch.

"She should have her own reality show," Jennalyn whispered to me when she caught me standing near the curtained dressing room in a boutique. The others were holding up tops and examining the necklaces hanging from a custom-made display in the shape of a cat. I was watching Tess rather than shopping.

Tess held up a flowing, flowery kimono. "What do you think?" she asked Christy.

"Doesn't she already have one like that?"

"The other one is teal. I like the rose tones in this one. She can only wear certain shades of pink, and this one works well on her." Tess checked the tag. "It's labeled 'dusty rose.' Perfect."

Christy burst out laughing. We all looked at her, trying to figure out what was so funny.

"Dusty rose," Christy said. "I painted a bookshelf years ago with a paint called dusty rose. I can't believe the name is back in style."

Tess had moved on to the rack where the individual silk tops were lined up by color. In a wink she had pulled the right matching shell and was holding the shell and kimono up to the long line of pants that came in a variety of lengths and colors. "These," she said, pulling out a flowing pair of dark gray pants.

I would never have given the gray pants a second look. When Tess held them up to the tops, it all worked together beautifully.

"Impressive," I whispered to Jennalyn.

"See what I mean? I'm telling you, she has a gift. I wish I could pick out paint colors the first time the way she does. I usually have to see the combination of colors next to one another on paper before I'm happy with the watercolors for a design that I like enough to want to duplicate it."

Tess bought the outfit and asked the shop attendant to hold it for her, saying she would pick it up within the hour. Her method worked nicely. When we were finished shopping, I went for the car while she and the others returned to the various shops to gather Tess's bounty. We met at the street where I had turned for the café, and all the garment bags and shopping bags were stuffed into the empty trunk.

Jennalyn slipped into the back again and slid behind my seat. This time Sierra insisted on taking the middle seat, saying Tess should have the front.

"And if it wouldn't be a problem," Sierra said, "do you mind going back through the canyon and dropping me off in Irvine? I came with Tess, but if you guys are okay with going back through Laguna Canyon, it's a straight shot to my place."

Reaching for her phone, Tess said, "I've got it." She pulled up directions from where we were to Sierra's address, and the voice that had been leading me all over Southern California ever since I arrived started telling me how to get to Sierra's in-laws' home.

Tess turned on the radio as I was coming to a stop. The car faced the ocean, and the quintessential beauty of Southern California spread out before us. We gazed at the sand volleyball courts filled with tanned, athletic enthusiasts; long stretches of golden sand; the deep blue Pacific shimmering in the morning sunlight. If I weren't driving, I would have taken a picture.

"I love that song!" Jennalyn spoke up from the back seat. "Leave it there, Tess."

Tess upped the volume as the light turned green, and I made a left onto Pacific Coast Highway. The three back-seat DOEs sang along at the top of their voices. In between the laughter and the mismatched lyrics, the five of us seemed to have invented our own version of Carpool Karaoke.

The smile on my face kept getting bigger as the hits just kept on coming from the back seat. Tess was playing the role of disc jockey, changing the station if there was the slightest protest over one of the songs. I joined in singing along on one of the tunes but didn't even try to match the volume of their voices.

As we cruised through Laguna Canyon, I noticed that the rains from earlier in the year had been a blessing to this area. The two-lane road was flanked on either side by hills covered in shrubs and pale green tufts that grow in arid regions. It didn't appear lush by any means, but the hillsides didn't look parched. Just dry. Every curve in the road revealed something new in the foliage as well as in the sparse buildings. As the back-seat singers kept their groove going, we wound our way past old stores that sold livery goods, as well as gated driveways that no doubt led to some hideaway homesteads.

As we emerged into the familiar world of freeways and intersections, I stopped at a red light at Lake Forest Drive. The singspiration had come to a natural slowdown. Tess turned the radio off and twisted around to offer her appreciation and playful applause to our choir girls.

"I wish I had recorded that," Tess said.

"We're glad you didn't." Sierra had nearly lost her scarf in all the fluttering about as we were twisting and turning through the canyon. In the rearview mirror I could see her wrapping it around her neck with an extra loop, the fringe adding to the tangle.

The car next to us had its windows down, and the infant in the back seat suddenly let out a cry, followed by a convincing wail. With the top down on our car, and after the rush in our ears of the wind and loud music for so many miles, the baby's cry seemed especially loud.

"Oh, oh," Sierra cried. "No, no, no! Don't cry. Don't cry. Roll up the windows! Quick! Roll up the windows!"

"Why?" Tess asked. "What good would it do? The top's down."

I glanced again at Sierra in the rearview mirror. She had crossed her arms and was pressing against her chest. Memories I had long forgotten came back to me of how I had soaked more than one T-shirt during my stint as a nursing mother when another baby's cries had done what they were doing to Sierra right now.

The light changed, and I pressed on the gas pedal, getting a dash of a start. I didn't realize how much power this car had.

"Undo the tie," Sierra squealed. "Christy, undo the tie on the back of my dress. This is new. It's my favorite. Dry clean only. There. Help me pull it down."

I glanced in the mirror long enough to see Jennalyn and Christy pulling on the top half of Sierra's embroidered dress. Sierra was untangling her scarf, and the fringe hit Christy in the face the way it had grazed me when Sierra had been in the front seat on our outbound journey.

"Hurry!" Sierra shouted.

I didn't know if she was talking to me or to Christy and Jennalyn. I was aware that the people in the car next to us were watching the flurry of activity in the back seat. I tried to go a little faster so that my car wasn't neck and neck with theirs.

The stoplight in front of us turned red. I didn't dare sneak through. Jennalyn took off her floppy hat and held it in front of Sierra as if that would draw less attention to the three of them in the back seat of the open convertible.

Tess pulled off her scarf and offered it to Sierra. "What just happened? Are you okay?"

"Hashtag, nursing mother issues," Sierra shouted.

Christy took off her scarf and offered it to Sierra as well. Just before the light turned green, I pulled off my chiffon scarf and handed it to Tess to pass to the back.

"It's working!" Sierra hollered. "Drive like the wind, Emily. Don't get a ticket, but get me to the church on time, sister!"

I asked Tess to turn up the volume on her phone and followed the directions through the residential neighborhood to Sierra's in-laws'. In less than five minutes, I pulled up in front of a nicely kept single-story home.

Tess hopped out and pulled back the seat to speed Sierra's exit. Christy tumbled out, followed by Sierra. That's when we all got a full view of the flustered new mom as she hurried toward the front door.

Sierra had used the donated scarves to stuff her bra and fend off the leakage. The top of her dress remained untied and was hanging down from her waist. To cover her top, she had managed to wrap her scarf around her bodice in a very fashion-forward manner so that the fringe dangled in a gathered knot under her bustline.

The only problem with the clever wrap was that it was so tight across her overly scarf-stuffed bra that the extra padding made her look like a lumpy cartoon character. From the back, she resembled a walking pinwheel, with the tails from all our scarves flapping in all directions in the breeze.

"Only you, Sierra," Christy called out, wiping the laughter tears from her eyes. "Only you."

Sierra turned and blew us a kiss, and we all broke into wild belly laughs as we took in her voluptuous bust and fluttering tails.

Christy scrambled into the back seat. Tess returned to the front seat. She leaned her head back and said, "Best. Day. Ever!"

We broke into another round of laughter. It was the sort of laughter that rolls over a group of friends who know they will have excellent teasing material for years to come.

s wonderfully relaxing and restorative as our Grace Kelly Morning had been, I had a hard time sleeping Saturday night. I kept thinking about my mom's impending visit, just as I had ever since her phone call. The steamed-up train of thoughts was on a different track now, though. What Tess had said about not expecting her mother to get out of a wheelchair to come hug her rolled through my mind again and again.

I knew so little about my mom's childhood or about her marriage to my dad. I had to wonder if something in her became damaged emotionally—to the point she simply couldn't be the one to get up and come to me.

She is coming to you. Remember? She's the one who initiated this visit.

A midnight game of mental volleyball began. I didn't start with the question about who Karl was or why she was bringing him. This time I asked myself why I hadn't come right out and asked my mom, *Who is he? Why do you want me to meet him? Why now?*

Jennalyn's comment about how we're all twelve years old at heart seemed to fit the way I had handled our phone call. I reverted from an adult to a child and told myself to make sure I didn't do anything wrong.

*What if I decide to act like an adult around my mom when she comes?
I don't cower around other women her age, like Mrs. Miller or any of the
customers at the diner. I'll always be my mother's daughter, but why can't I
be her adult daughter?*

The concept was basic: She's an adult. I'm an adult. Why couldn't we
start a new era in our relationship?

I didn't have anything to feel ashamed of or anything to apologize
about. I could be the one to extend to her the kindness and affection I always
had longed for her to give me.

Opening my eyes, I rolled on my side and squinted at the dim light
coming from the bathroom nightlight. Even with our bedroom door closed,
the light found a way to sneak in and make the way clear. The image
matched my thoughts.

*Light finds a way to slip into the darkness. Love can find a way too. I
can give my mother love tomorrow instead of becoming painfully timid and
waiting for her to initiate the conversation.*

As with all endeavors of the human heart that are decided in the dead
of night and then sound foolish by morning light, my inspiration to be the
one to shower my mom with love seemed like a bad idea the next morning.
Most days it took everything I had to remain intentional about showing lots
of love and kindness to Trevor and Audra.

And I really liked them.

"Why don't you stay home from church," Trevor suggested after I had
changed for the third time. He and Audra were ready to go, and Trevor had
agreed to help Todd at a table in the courtyard. All they were doing was
passing out information about a fund-raiser for a mission trip to Kenya that
Todd was taking students on that summer. But Trevor took his commit-
ments seriously, and he had promised Todd he would be there.

"Fine." I pulled the shirt over my head and rejected it as a wardrobe option by tossing it in the laundry basket. I thought I had washed it, but it didn't smell fresh. I definitely needed to at least start out this day smelling fresh.

"Emily." Trevor placed his hand on my shoulder. "It's going to be okay. You stay here, relax, and get lunch ready. Audra and I will be home in plenty of time to help with whatever other details you need."

"Okay." I hung my head.

"Hey, no shame here," he said. "It's going to be fine."

As soon as they were out the door, I went into a busy-bee frenzy, cleaning the house even though I had done the heavy cleaning yesterday afternoon. I ran a load of laundry, swept off the patio again, and made sure the towels on the rack in the bathroom were folded in thirds and not just folded in half. Then I took everything out of the refrigerator, wiped off the shelves and put everything back. I turned each item just right so the labels faced forward.

Oh dear.

I looked at my reflection in the shiny clean door of the microwave.

I have become my mother.

Retreating to the bedroom, I sat on the edge of the bed and felt as if the room were swaying.

Breathe. Deep, slow, calming breaths.

My heart gave a flutter as my lips moved in whispers. I prayed that God's Spirit would draw me close and fill me with peace and clarity. I asked for love and grace. I closed my eyes and could almost feel a distinct calm cover me like a shawl.

Release.

I opened my eyes, and the world around me seemed to have righted itself. The fear was gone. My thoughts lined up like a row of daffodils in springtime. It was one of those sweet and rare times when God's Spirit actually felt present in the space around me as well as the space within me. His light was slipping through.

Forgive.

The thought was so precise, I felt as if I could taste it the way a pinch of baking soda smarts on the tip of the tongue and then almost immediately soothes the canker sore it was applied to.

Releasing my mother from all her shortcomings, forgiving her for not being who I thought she should be, extending grace to her from out of the abundance that had been poured all over me—this was what was being asked of me. I knew in my heart that's what I needed to be healed.

Releasing her meant I was choosing, from my heart, to forgive.

Forgiving my mom meant I was willing to release my list of hurts.

A slow trail of tears coursed down my face, as if they had escaped from a crack in a deep cistern where my insecurities were hidden. I knew they would be the last of the tears I had kept stored in my little-girl heart. It was time to release. To forgive. To engage my superpower and choose love.

The single word *yes* rumbled up from my heart and burst out in a prayer. "Yes, Lord, I release her. Heal me. Heal her. Heal us."

The tears stopped. I drew in a long, deep breath and sat in the stillness, inwardly quieted and at the same time curious. *What just happened? What's going to happen next?*

I walked into the kitchen with a lightness in my step. I put on the apron Christy had made and turned on some music, the way Trevor had started doing in the mornings.

Humming along, I went to work arranging the place mats, silverware, and napkins at five places around the patio table. I checked the time and calmly put the last of the chopped cucumbers and tomatoes into the big salad. I lined up the salad dressing options on the counter and put out a bowl of spicy pulled chicken. The cornbread was ready to be warmed up. A fleet of ice cubes floated in the pitcher of mint iced tea.

I felt like I was becoming me. The grown-up version of me, entertaining in my home and no longer afraid that my feelings would be hurt by anything my mother could say or do. I was ready to serve up a big slice of love, no matter what happened.

Those courageous thoughts prevailed when Trevor and Audra came home. They were still surrounding me and fortifying me when the doorbell rang. Audra hopped up and accompanied me. With a smile on my face, I pushed open the screen door and invited my mother and a tall, slender man with gray hair and oval-shaped glasses to come into my little haven.

Then I guess I was feeling so strong I did what I'd do for other guests whom I loved but had rarely done with my mother. I looped my arms around her and hugged her.

She kept rigid and was surprised by my outburst of expression. Her short blond hair looked good. She looked good. She had on a bubble-gum-pink jean jacket over a crisp white collared blouse. I couldn't remember ever seeing my mother wear pink. Certainly not Barbie Dream House pink.

"Hi, Grandmother." Audra came out from her halfway hidden position behind me and followed my lead. She hugged my mom hesitantly and looked up at the serious-looking man beside my mother.

"Emily, may I introduce Dr. Karl Roycelle." She turned her open hand first to me, Audra, and then to Trevor who had joined us in the crowded entry space next to the closet that hid the washer and dryer. Her gesture was formal. His expression was not.

"Dr. Roycelle." Trevor politely extended his hand and offered his usual extroverted, friendly greeting. "Good to meet you! Come on in."

"He's a dentist," my mother said as if the doctor part needed to be explained. Then she added, "My dentist."

Audra shot me a side glance as if to say, *Why in the world is Grandmother bringing her dentist to visit us?* I had the same thought, as I studied Dr. Roycelle's profile while he stepped past me and followed Trevor out to the patio. He was composed, comfortably engaged in the moment, and giving off the vibe that this was exactly where he wanted to be.

That's when I knew.

He loved my mother.

I don't know how I knew, nor could I explain it later when I was recounting the moment of silent revelation to Trevor. All I knew was that this tall man, with his hands behind his back and a pleasant expression across his closed lips, had found something irresistible about the no-nonsense woman who had given me birth. And he was going to follow her wherever she wanted to go for the rest of their lives.

It was a marvel to me.

The pitcher of iced tea and my best glasses were waiting for us on the patio. Trevor poured and casually asked all the usual questions with ease. Did they have any trouble finding our place? Was the traffic bad? Wasn't the weather nice? During the catches and pauses between their answers and Trevor's next question, we all took sips of tea. The ice cubes made the faint sounds of a fairy's wind chime.

Audra seemed to have warmed up to our company and asked, "Grandmother, would you like to see my room?"

"Not now."

The reply was curt, and Audra's expression showed her surprise.

My mom looked up at Karl, and I knew she was about to make her announcement. With a quick clearing of her throat, my mother turned and let her gaze rest on me with an uneasiness I'd rarely seen. Her tone was as direct as she had been with Audra, and her words were delivered with conviction.

"Karl and I are married."

It was as if she had expected shock and silence to follow her declaration, so she stopped to clear her throat again.

My response was immediate, and I think the enthusiasm surprised her. "Congratulations! I'm so happy for you. For both of you."

"Thank you, Emily," Karl said with a polite nod of his head. "We are quite happy as well."

Trevor regained his composure and started a round of hugs for both of them, along with a convincing handshake with Karl. "Congratulations!" Audra followed Trevor's hugs, and I brought up the rear.

"We met several years ago," my mother said quickly, as if she needed to explain herself. "As I said, he was my dentist. We found we had quite a lot in common and decided to get married."

"When did you get married?" Audra asked. "I wish I could have gone to your wedding."

Karl gave Audra the sort of smile I imagined he used with all his young patients. "It was a civil ceremony before a justice of the peace at the county courthouse. Not the sort of elaborate wedding ceremony you might be thinking of."

"Oh." Audra looked at my mom. "Because if you wanted, I could have been your flower girl."

"You would have made a lovely flower girl." The affirming reply came from Karl, not from my mother. She seemed to be fixed on me, still surprised at the way I had received her news.

"Did your brother tell you?" she asked me. "I specifically requested that he not say anything."

"No, he didn't tell me."

I still felt calm and very much like I had activated my new superpower. Instead of being stuck at twelve, letting my sense of hurt and disappointment rule my emotions, I felt like I had grown up. This was the way I chose to respond to her announcement, and it felt good.

"Why don't we go inside and dish up?" I suggested. "I thought we could bring our food out here to eat, if that suits everyone."

"Sounds good," Trevor said. I loved that he was always my cheerleader. He seemed to be keeping a wary eye on me, though, as if my cool, calm confidence were an act and not reflective of what was really going on inside me.

After our simple lunch, we lingered at the table for another hour and a half. Both Trevor and Audra seemed eager to ply Karl with questions about himself. He answered as if he had nothing to hide and was grateful to have found such an ideal life partner at this stage of his life. They had moved into my mother's place for the time being but had purchased a lot in a newer part of Albuquerque and were working together with a contractor to build what sounded like the nicest place my mother had ever lived in.

"Maybe we can come visit you," Audra said. "Do you think your new house will be finished by Christmas?"

"No." My mother shook her head. "They are already behind. We'll be glad if they finish by next year at this time."

"Then maybe we can come for Easter next year," Audra said optimistically. "How long does it take to drive there?"

None of us seemed to be able to agree on an answer for Audra. Karl and my mom had flown into Long Beach that morning and rented a car. They said they planned to drive down the coast to a condo they had rented in a coastal town I wasn't familiar with. My mom kept referring to the week ahead as their "vacation," as if "honeymoon" would have been too sophisticated for Audra.

When they were ready to leave, my mother seemed to still be examining me. She helped me clear the plates as Trevor went with Audra, who wanted to show her bedroom to Karl.

"Are you sure your brother didn't say something?"

"No, he didn't. I just somehow knew when you arrived. Karl seems . . ." I was going to say he seemed to be in love with her or that he seemed happy to be with her. This wasn't a girlfriend I was talking to, though. The words that came out were, "He seems like a good man."

"Oh, he is." Her expression was that of a woman ready to defend her man against any unjust accusations.

"I'm happy for you, Mom." We were standing side by side in my tight kitchen and had placed the dishes in the sink. She was looking at the items lined up on the windowsill, and I noticed that I was a little taller than my mother. It wasn't that I'd grown since my teen years. Maybe I was simply standing up straight. I felt as if I had met her eye to eye, adult to adult. It felt different.

I quickly discovered that whenever one part of an ecosystem changes, it affects another part. If a relationship that had always been a teeter-totter, with one person up and the other down, was now a wobbly balance with both participants creating a straight line, one of them would resort to her previous position.

"Trevor made it sound as if you plan to stay in California," my mother said. "Even though he doesn't have a job."

The teeter-totter tipped, and I felt a flash of a twelve-year-old insecurity but recovered quickly. "He's meeting with a dealership owner this week. I don't know if you heard him explain about the interview during lunch."

"I heard him. After he explained what happened with his uncle's car business, I expected him to say that you'll move back east to be with Trevor's family again."

"No. Like I said, he has an interview coming up with a dealership here. If that doesn't work out, he'll look for something else. He'll find something. I'm sure of it."

"I don't know how you can be so optimistic in this economy." My mother looked hard at me, the way she used to when she was giving me important instructions. "If things don't work out here, I imagine you'll want to move to Albuquerque."

"Probably not. We want to figure out how we can make it on our own. But thank you for the offer."

She looked surprised. "I wasn't offering for you to move in with us in our new house."

"Oh." I scrambled to clear the air. "I should have said thanks for the suggestion."

"But you said offer."

"I did."

"Just so there's no misunderstanding about our new house being your backup plan if things don't work out for you here."

"Mom." I reached over and touched her shoulder in an effort to calm her. She froze. "Mom, don't worry. That's not what I was thinking. Trevor and I are committed to finding a way to make it work for us in California. God has taken good care of us. I believe He will continue to take good care of us."

"The problem is that the two of you married too young." She made her statement with finality, as if it were her last comment for the day.

"We were young," I agreed. I still didn't feel ruffled. Why did she seem to need to be combative? I wasn't asking to live with her. I wasn't asking anything of her. And I certainly didn't regret the past. "Trevor and I have never regretted marrying when we did."

My mom shifted her position to make it clear that she wanted me to remove my hand, which I did. "I have never understood you," she said.

I didn't know what to say. The statement was true. And I had never understood her. Although I would never say that aloud.

The more rational, newly sprouted adult version of me asked a question that I knew could have disastrous results. I planted my feet on the rug in front of the kitchen sink and asked it anyway. "Mom, what is it about me that seems to aggravate you so much?"

Her eyes narrowed. I knew she was going to let me have it. This was it. I asked for the truth, and after all these years, I was going to get it.

Chapter 24

"What did your mother say?" Christy's head was turned toward me as we walked on the beachfront sidewalk two days after my mom and Karl had come to visit.

Christy had suggested we get some fresh air since the weather had been so nice. I had picked up Audra from school, and she was elated to find that Christy wanted her to "babysit" Hana for half an hour while Christy pushed Cole in the stroller and we talked.

I was grateful to have the chance to process the conversation with my mother after a very busy day at Peggy's Pies. "My mother said she never understood my choices. She said that I had a chance to work my way through school and have a career, but instead I chose to get married when I was too young. She said I could have made something of myself the way my brother had." I adjusted my sunglasses and glanced at the long stretch of unspoiled sand at Newport Beach dotted with lifeguard stations.

"My mother repeated twice that I had far more chances than she ever had, and yet I didn't take advantage of any of them. I didn't have to tie myself to a man or burden myself with a child the way she had. She made it sound as if my birth, followed by my brother's birth fourteen months later, was the reason she has never had the life she wanted to live."

"Oh, Emily, I'm so sorry she said all that to you."

"I know that life was hard for her. When my dad died, she was overwhelmed, and she had to go on food stamps." The knot that had been in my stomach for the last two days cinched tighter. "She asked me if we're on food stamps yet."

"Why would she ask that?"

"Because Trevor told her he's selling the car lot. She is convinced that Trevor is going to fail at finding a job. And since we made it clear that we're not moving back to North Carolina, she made it clear that we would not be welcomed to live with them just because she and Karl are building a four-thousand-square-foot home."

"Four thousand square feet. That's quite a new house."

"Audra asked her if we could visit them, and my mother made it sound like that was the last thing she ever wanted." The thought brought tears to the corner of my eyes.

"I thought I was doing so well," I said. "I felt strong when she was there. I went to her, you know. The way Tess had explained about her mother. I reached out and hugged her and congratulated her. I was kind to her."

"You activated your superpower," Christy said with tenderness in her voice. "You showed her love."

"I did. And it was so freeing."

We walked another dozen steps before I said, "So why did she have to be cool and dismissive of Audra? I don't get it. If she wants to be mean to me, I can handle it. I'm used to it. But why does she have to be like that with her only granddaughter?"

I thought of the hurt look on Audra's face when my mom and Karl left on Sunday. I told Christy how Karl had politely told Audra it was a pleasure to meet her. Then Audra tried to give my mom a hug, but she just stood there.

"It hurts," I said. "It hurts me, but it hurts Audra even more when my mother withholds like that."

Christy stopped walking and put the brake on the stroller. With misty eyes, she threw both her arms around me and gave me a hug. It was the kindest, most supportive expression of understanding I think I've ever received. I didn't care that I had started crying into her hair or that my shoulders were shaking. Christy let me hold on to her until I was ready to let go.

I fished for a tissue in the pocket of my jeans and tried to sop up the mess I had made of my face.

Her calm demeanor as she stood beside me, waiting for whatever I needed next, prompted me to say the thing that perplexed me the most. "You know, I thought I was strong enough to take whatever my mom said. I invited her to say it. That's because I felt strong. I felt like God had done some really deep and essential healing in me right before she came. I thought I had successfully released all my twelve-year-old little girl fears."

I caught my breath.

"I don't know why I let her words get to me right at the end. I haven't been able to shake the thought that she could be right. Trevor and I could be headed for failure."

"No. Emily, don't do that. Release that thought right now," Christy said. "Don't hold on to that. It's a lie. You don't know what's going to happen. God has done some amazing things for you guys already. He will make your path straight. I know He will."

I nodded slowly, feeling the truth of Christy's words fall on me like raindrops. Those last few minutes of my mother's visit were when the teeter-totter of adult to adult shifted. I emotionally reverted to a child again and let myself stay suspended there for two days.

Drawing in a deep breath, I thought of all the truth Christy had just spoken. As I exhaled, I forgave. I released once again.

"Okay?" Christy asked.

I nodded. We started walking again. Cole looked like a little cherub sitting in the stroller and proudly holding his sippy cup. He waved at a woman who passed us with her fluffy little dog on a leash.

"Doggie!" Cole exclaimed.

"That was a cute doggie," Christy repeated to him.

"I really thought I was past all this," I sputtered.

"Don't start beating yourself up," Christy said. "Forgiveness and freedom is a process. I'm sure you know that."

"I'm learning."

"Todd says that forgiveness is like taking a shower. You feel all fresh and friendly right at first and want to go out and take on the world. Then a few days later, you realize you have to get cleaned up all over again, as if nothing was accomplished earlier."

"That's what it feels like with my mom. With other people it seems like I pray about it, and it's resolved. I move on."

"One and done," Christy said with a grin.

"Exactly. With my mom, it seems like it's an ongoing process for the life of the relationship."

"That's how I feel about my relationship with my aunt," Christy said. "I haven't told you much about Aunt Marti, but for years she had the ability to say things that leveled me. Things about how I looked or what I chose to do. When I was younger, I especially felt inferior, like I was always doing something wrong. I tried hard to conform to her ways."

"You just described my childhood. I never would have guessed you had that struggle with your aunt. How did you get past it?"

Christy glanced at me. "This is going to sound really bad, but my aunt became a Christian. I mean a fully surrendered, transformed, in-love-with-Jesus, brand-new Christian."

"Why is that a bad thing?"

"Because when she did that, things between us got worse."

"Worse? How?"

"I thought she would be different. I mean, she was different. She is different. But she's still herself, if you know what I mean. She still has the same ideas and ways of doing things and the same personality. I realized I was still in the habit of keeping a secret list of all the things I did that irritated her and all the things she did that irritated me. Todd helped me to see that I had to tear up the list. That's what he had to do with his mom. That's where he came up with his analogy of the shower. With some people, we just have to choose to release them and forgive them seventy times seven, as Todd says. If they're not going to change, then we have the choice. Like Tess said. We can change."

I kept in step with Christy. "What's your relationship like with your aunt now?"

"It's good for the most part. But then, I usually only do things with her in a group. She's great in a group."

"That's how she seemed at Christmas and at Jennalyn's shower. The blessing and reading Marti did for Jennalyn was beautiful."

"I agree. There are lots of amazing things about my aunt. She's very generous, and she loves a good party." Christy was the one drawing in a deep breath now. "But if she were to invite me to go shopping, just the two of us, to buy clothes for me, I would say no. It's those one-on-one times when I feel like she still sees me as a fourteen-year-old girl from Wisconsin who needs a makeover."

Christy continued, "There are some things I know I will end up being ferocious about when it comes to protecting Hana as she gets older. But I think it's easier to make good decisions about what's best for our children and for me if I'm not doing it out of hurt or anger."

"Once again, release," I said. "That has definitely become my word for this year."

"It's a good word. You're doing well, Emily. You really are. This is all big girl stuff, isn't it?"

I chuckled. "Yes, it is."

We walked past three more beachfront houses before I said, "I'm so glad I could talk with you like this. Thanks for suggesting the walk."

"Todd told me he had talked to Trevor earlier today, and Trevor said you were still in a funk after your mom's visit. I thought a walk would do both of us some good. My mom has this little saying about planting the sweet things."

"I've heard her say that," I said. "She told me about the jasmine plant that your dad transplanted from your old house."

Christy paused and bent over because Cole had dropped his sippy cup. He had taken to waving both hands at everyone we passed and lost interest in the cup.

"What I was going to say," she continued, "is that I've been trying to do that with Aunt Marti. Plant sweet things, I mean. Like that verse in Philippians about whatever things are good and lovely and true, those are the things we should think about."

"Daddy! Daddy!" Cole struggled to exit the stroller, turning as far as he could to watch the guy that had just gone past us on a beach cruiser bike. The surfer had blond hair and was managing to balance an orange surfboard under one arm as he pedaled toward the pier.

"That's not Daddy, Cole. He looks like Daddy, but Daddy is at work."

Cole started crying. It was a fake wail, but sweetly sad nonetheless.

Confiding in me, Christy said, "Todd has been so busy with all the plans for the mission trip to Kenya, I think it's taking a toll on the kids. Plus, I don't know what it is with Hana and Cole, but they moved out of this cute, snuggly phase as siblings and now are competitive over toys, food, and everything they can think of. I feel like a referee. I need a whistle."

Cole had stopped crying and was waving to two girls who were passing us on in-line skates. "Hi! Hi!"

One of the girls turned and waved back with a big grin.

Christy said, "I think separating the two of them for a while in this phase is what I need to do."

"I'll go for a walk anytime you want," I said. "And you know that Audra loves coming over and entertaining your littles."

Christy checked her phone. We had left my phone with Audra and gave clear instructions that she should call immediately if she needed us for any reason. Audra hadn't called. Christy seemed to be checking, though.

"You have a darling little girl," Christy said.

"So do you."

"I'm glad they enjoy each other so much."

We had turned around and were heading back to Christy and Todd's beach cottage for the final loop of our walk. We had kept ourselves within a six-block distance, even though the walkway stretched out much farther in both directions. We wanted to be close enough to sprint back to our girls if necessary.

Christy and Todd's home was only a few short blocks from the sand. It wasn't nearly on the level of her aunt and uncle's luxurious and spacious beach house. The way Christy had decorated it with a coastal shabby chic design made it feel like the sort of place where you were at home the minute you stepped inside.

"You know," Christy said, "when we had coffee last Saturday at our secret clubhouse—"

"Our secret clubhouse," I repeated with a grin. "I like that. Sierra did a good job of finding that hideaway for us."

"She did. And she provided the best entertainment I've seen in a long time with her memorable exit!"

We both laughed at the memory.

"Do you think we'll ever get our scarves back?" I asked.

Christy laughed. "Do you really want yours back?"

"Ah, no. I guess I don't." I remembered that I had interrupted Christy and asked her what she was going to say about our coffee time.

"I was thinking about how you told us that your journey into womanhood was frightening and how Jennalyn said her mom had turned the important conversation into a celebration. So what if . . ." Christy seemed to still be collecting her thoughts. "What if we had a Welcome to Womanhood party for Audra?"

"Okay." My reply wasn't exactly an agreement as much as a consideration of her suggestion. The truth was, I didn't know what a celebration like that would look like. Christy had some ideas, though. They were good ones.

By the time we arrived at her front door, we had a plan in place. Audra's party would be the Daughters of Eve's chance to make this passage into womanhood a smooth transition for her. Christy stated that Hana, Eden, and Ella Mae wouldn't be far behind. I told Christy I liked the idea a lot but wanted to wait until I was sure the timing was right for Audra.

"Then let's talk about it the next time the Daughters of Eve get together," Christy suggested. "There's no rush. I was remembering the way Audra ate up every moment at Jennalyn's shower. If we could do a party like that and bless her and welcome her into womanhood, she would be . . ."

"Over the moon," I said, finishing Christy's thought for her.

"That's what I was thinking."

Christy unlocked her front door, and we found the girls contentedly sitting on the rug under the living room coffee table, stringing necklaces made of large beads. Hana couldn't wait to show her mommy the colorful loop around her neck. She leaned into the stroller and spoke to her brother sweetly, showing him her work of art. As Christy said, the separation had put the happiness back into the two siblings.

"Let me know how it goes," Christy said about twenty minutes later when Audra and I were about to leave. "I know this interview Trevor has with the car dealer this week is a big deal."

"Thanks."

Audra and I headed back to our apartment. She chattered all the way, telling me about her idea for an art project she wanted to do with Hana next time and how we needed to buy more glue sticks and pink tissue paper.

I nodded, only half listening because my thoughts were darting in a dozen different directions. I couldn't remember if we had enough leftovers at home for dinner. I didn't want to stop at the grocery store.

Taking a chance, I went directly to the apartment since Trevor would probably be home soon and I liked the routine of having dinner ready every night.

A praiseworthy memory washed over me.

And the way my mom always had dinner for us at exactly six o'clock every night. And the way she always had meals planned so that even on her limited income, we had nutritious food three times a day.

A wobbly smile came to my lips. It was a smile of understanding. My mother had done some things well. Her nurturing wasn't with words of praise or affectionate hugs. She showed my brother and me that she cared about us by making sure we were well fed and had clean clothes, and that we learned the value of always doing our chores and finishing our homework. She kept the house meticulously tidy and changed the sheets on our beds every Saturday morning. She worked long hours at a variety of low-paying jobs and was good at making sure we stayed in bed when we were sick. Her expressions of motherly love were hidden in her acts of goodness toward us.

I got it.

I understood. These thoughts were what was true and honorable and lovely about my childhood and my mother. Those were the things I would choose to think about.

I realized I hadn't seen those qualities of hers as strengths in the past. Many of them had transferred to me. I felt happy when I had dinner on the table at six or when the sheets were tumbling in the dryer before noon on a Saturday.

It had taken an uncluttered heart that had released the long, ongoing list of grievances to see the good that had been there all along.

My attitude was the best it had been in a long time when Audra and I bounded into our apartment. Trevor was already home. He was in the kitchen, unloading the dishwasher. Not something he normally did.

I took one look at him and knew that something was wrong.

He waited until Audra had given him a hug and a full report on her day before he met my concerned gaze. Audra trotted off to her bedroom, and I waited.

Leaning against the counter, Trevor said in a low voice, "The BMW dealer canceled the interview."

"Why?" I felt my heart racing.

"He said they thought one of their guys was leaving, but he changed his mind, and they don't have any openings."

I stretched out my arms, inviting Trevor to find solace in my embrace. Stroking the side of his hair and kissing his neck, I whispered all the things I knew he needed to hear. "It'll be okay. You'll see. Something else will work out."

I let him linger in my hug the way Christy had let me linger in hers.

With all my heart, I hoped the words I had just spoken in Trevor's ear were true. God would take care of us. We were at His mercy.

We are excellent candidates for a miracle, Father God. Lead us. Please. Show us what You want for us. We are Your children. You take good care of Your children. I know You do.

Chapter 25

*J*n the days that followed, I watched my husband tough it out. That's the only way I can explain what he had to do. He worked hard to complete the final steps for the car lot's sale. He made trips to the bank, signed papers, and checked that the green Cadillac had arrived at his uncle's in Montana. He even sold BB to a woman who insisted that her Chihuahua cosign the papers after putting his paw on an ink pad. I was sad to see BB go. I hoped the lady and her comfort pup enjoyed it as much as I had.

The final day, when Trevor drove away from the lot, Audra and I accompanied him. We stopped on the way home for ice cream cones, not as a celebration but as more of a consolation.

I had made soup the day before and planned to have leftovers for dinner. By the time we got home, Trevor said he wasn't hungry. I teased him about spoiling his appetite with the ice cream.

Audra jumped into the conversation with what seemed like sympathy pains. "My stomach kind of hurts too. It's been sore all day."

I took her complaint to be one of the many she had come up with lately. She had been moody and cranky for several days. I had a feeling she was picking up her daddy's vibe of discontent and was finding her own way to process the stress we were all feeling.

I served the soup anyway, and we ate together on the patio. Our meal-time was so depressing that I asked Audra to clear the dishes as soon as she and Trevor pushed away from their half-eaten bowls of tomato soup. She complied with a scowl and left Trevor and me alone, as if she knew this was going to be one of those nights when he and I would sit outside and talk under the twinkle lights.

We sat, but we didn't talk. Everything that could be said had been discussed in full over the past few weeks.

"I heard from Todd today," Trevor said. "He asked if I had given any more thought to the idea of becoming a teacher."

"What did you tell him?" I asked the question cautiously.

"I haven't thought about it anymore. I don't think I would be a good teacher."

"You're an excellent salesman," I said. "You'll find a new job where you can use those skills. Even though the opportunity with the BMW dealer fell apart, it seems to me plenty of other car dealerships around here would be grateful to have someone with your experience and abilities."

Trevor sighed. "Thanks, Em."

I knew he knew that I was his biggest cheerleader. I always had been and always would be.

"It's a little more complicated than that," he said slowly, as if he were carefully choosing his words. "I've learned a lot during the process of selling the car lot. I didn't tell you some stuff because you didn't need to know."

"Like what?"

"I discovered that the dealerships, at least the luxury dealerships, are pretty much a closed circle."

I knew what he meant. People at our church in North Carolina had tried to obtain jobs in one of Trevor's dad's dealerships, but when they hadn't been able to squeeze into one of the rare openings, they accused my father-in-law of nepotism. In some ways, they were right. The business was family-run and had been for more than fifty years, starting with Trevor's grandfather. I attended a women's event at church once and heard someone call my father-in-law the "godfather" of all the local car lots. Unless you married into the family, you couldn't work at any of the Winslow dealerships.

Thinking about that uncomfortable moment reminded me why I had withdrawn from doing things with other women during that season of life. I found it less stressful to do everything with the women I was related to.

"It sounds like things here are similar to how they were in North Carolina," I said.

Trevor nodded. "I didn't see it when I was in the middle of it, but I understand how it works now. It's going to be difficult for me to find a way into the system." He paused and turned to me with a positive look. "But I can do it. God will open a door somehow."

"I believe that," I said. "We just don't know how yet."

Trevor looked down at his hands and rubbed them together. I knew he wasn't telling me something else.

"What is it?" I asked.

"My dad called today," Trevor said finally.

I braced myself.

He nodded. "He's been checking in on me. I appreciate it. He's a great dad."

"Yes, he is."

Trevor rubbed the back of his neck. "He said something interesting today, though. Something I took to heart."

I expected Trevor to finish his thought by saying that his dad had presented him with another job offer and maybe we should consider it.

Instead, Trevor said his dad told him he was proud of the way Trevor had handled the sale and settled the deal so generously with his uncle.

"My dad said that he and my mom are starting to understand why we made the decisions we did. He said they want us to know that they support us."

I waited for the "but" to come.

"He said something I had never heard from him before. He said that ultimately I have to answer to God for how I lead my family. I don't have to answer to him. Just to God."

I let the words sink in. "He's releasing you."

"Is that what you hear in that statement?"

"Yes. I don't think that's a guilt-trip statement. Your dad is all about integrity and shooting straight. I think he's saying that he's releasing you."

Trevor nodded slowly. "It did feel different. It was like he was talking to me the way I've heard him talk to my brothers. Do you think he's viewing me as an adult now? And not the baby of the family anymore?"

"It sounds like it."

Trevor let that thought sink in. I thought about how I, too, was figuring out how to enter into a new, even teeter-totter balance with my mother. Karl's influence over her seemed to be having an effect, rounding off some of her sharp edges. She had mailed me a thank-you note for the lunch, and Karl had added a PS in a wide-lettered scrawl, saying that he hoped he would see us soon.

Trevor and I talked about how strange and yet freeing it felt to finally be in a place where both of us were being viewed by our parents as adults.

"Now all I need is a job." Trevor stated the obvious with a half grin and a huff of a laugh, as if he were asking for the impossible.

"I'm praying," I said.

"So am I." Trevor looked over my shoulder, into the house. He motioned, and I guessed that Audra had appeared and wanted to come outside to join us.

She opened the sliding door and stepped out on the patio. Instead of sitting down, she stood between us with an expression of subtle wonder mixed with the terror of the unknown.

"What's wrong?" I asked.

"I started," she announced in a quavering voice.

"Started what? Your homework?" Trevor asked. "Do you need help?"

The motherly, womanly, sisterly instinct in me woke up. I reached for Audra's hand. I knew what she meant.

"Sweetheart." I stood and gave her a big hug. A squeeze of her hand wasn't enough for a moment like this. I couldn't believe she was so comfortable making the announcement in front of both of us. I wanted this to be a positive, affirming moment for her and not carry any of the feelings of shame or fear that I had felt when my body began doing what it was created to do.

Glancing at my still-confused husband, I said, "Our little girl is becoming a woman."

Trevor caught on and reached for Audra, hugging her and giving her a big kiss on the forehead. He clearly seemed to be at a loss as to what to say. He fumbled to come up with something and finally said, "You know you'll still always be my little girl, though, don't you?"

Audra gave him an "oh, Dad" look and then turned to me with tears glistening in her eyes. The newness of what was happening to her body seemed to have set in, and she looked as if she was asking for me to do something.

"Why don't we go to your room," I suggested. I knew she had everything practical that she needed, but I wanted her to feel the freedom to keep processing, girl to girl, woman to woman.

What followed was a very special bonding time while my talkative daughter recounted her moment of discovery. Then she let loose with a wave of emotions mixed with questions including, "Does this mean I can start wearing makeup?"

"No." I grinned at her cute face and added, "Nice try."

She snuggled herself into bed half an hour later than usual that night. Trevor and I both blessed her. We prayed with her and kissed her. Closing the door behind us, Trevor and I stepped into the living room and turned to look at each other with thin-lipped smiles.

"Well done," Trevor whispered to me.

"Well done, you," I whispered back.

We held each other for a while, swaying as if we heard the same music. Trevor kissed the side of my head and murmured, "You make me want to lead our family with excellence. You are such a great wife and mother. I love you."

"I love you too."

We kissed. Simple and sweet, like a couple about to cut the cake at their thirtieth wedding anniversary party. We were established. We were us.

Trevor had done the dishes while I was having girl time with Audra. When we pulled apart, I thought he would sit in his usual corner on the couch and see if we had anything interesting recorded on TV. Instead, he pulled out his phone. "I'm going to check a few job sites."

I decided to take a leisurely bath. While the hot water filled the tub, I sent out a group text to the Daughters of Eve. **SOS! Christy had a great idea about having a Welcome to Womanhood party for Audra. We need to do it pronto!**

Tess was the first to reply: **What are you talking about? I'm lost.**

I tapped back a more detailed explanation, and the comments streamed in for the next twenty minutes. By the time I slipped into bed, we had the whole event planned. I told Trevor the party for Audra was going to be a week from Saturday, my one Saturday off that I had each month. I also told him that I wanted to have it at our house.

"And I'm going to try to keep it a surprise," I said.

"Good luck with that. Have you met our daughter? She doesn't miss a thing. She's probably listening in on us right now."

We both stopped moving and listened, as if we expected to hear her answer us from her bedroom.

"I just remembered something." I tossed back the covers and slipped out of bed.

"What did you forget?" Trevor was propped up on his elbow. He was badly in need of a haircut. The tousled look made him appear young again, like the wild, tanned, summer camp counselor he had been when I first met him.

With what I hoped he would recognize as the beguiling grin of the wife of his youth, I whispered what had become our secret code in this apartment. "I need to put some towels in the washer."

Trevor grinned. "Then you'd better turn that dial to the longest cycle, darlin'."

I was glad to see that he hadn't slipped into a depression, which was the direction he seemed to be heading at dinnertime. We were good together, Trevor and me. He had spent many years bolstering me up when I was worn down in spirit and body. Now my turn had come to love my husband well.

As the days flowed into a full week and then edged into the second week of Trevor job hunting, I noticed how patient he was with Audra and how much he was helping out at home. He helped Mr. Miller plant a row of Italian cypress bushes along the side of our small backyard, giving the patio even more privacy and the feeling of an enclosed garden. The jasmine in the repurposed container had begun to climb up the post, and the honeysuckle

Mr. Miller had planted several months earlier along the back fence were aggressively stretching out and taking over, which had been the intent.

I was glad I had decided to have Audra's Welcome to Womanhood party at our place. It was truly becoming a haven, and I wasn't ashamed of where we lived. I loved that we had a chance to make such a sweet memory here.

Jennalyn created beautiful invitations and mailed one to Audra. It arrived several days before the party, but I didn't give it to Audra until breakfast on the day of the party. When she saw her name on the envelope and knew by the handwriting and the watercolor flowers in the lower left-hand corner that the invitation was from Jennalyn, she was ecstatic and started crying.

She had done a lot of that lately. Crying, laughing at odd moments, and stomping around the apartment. We even had one night with a slammed door. Trevor came down hard on her and that, of course, produced more tears. Audra's tears over the invitation were happy tears. Especially when she saw that the party was for her. And it was to be held that afternoon at two.

As Trevor had predicted, she wanted to know everything, which is why she didn't receive the invitation until a few hours before the big event. Audra gave one of her nearly extinct little girl twirls as she asked all her questions. Who was coming? What were we eating? Were we going to play games? What should she wear?

The sweetest question of all was when she asked if I had invited Mrs. Miller and Miss Marti because she had decided that they were her adopted grandmothers. Or, as she called them, her "fairy grandmothers."

The answers to almost all of Audra's questions were yes. Christy's mom and aunt had both been invited. Jennalyn was bringing my favorite baby boy, and Sierra probably was bringing little Ella Mae. The answers continued to be yes, as she asked whether we were having fancy treats like pink macarons and whether she could wear the dressy outfit I had bought her for Easter.

With a mix of a regal, chin-up posture and a nibbling of her lower lip in eager anticipation, Audra took off for the shower.

Trevor grinned at me. "This is going to be a day she'll always remember."

"I hope so."

He glanced at the clock on the microwave. "I have to go. See you back here after your tea party." He called his goodbye to Audra through the closed bathroom door, and she called back a cheery goodbye.

I noted a bounce returning to Trevor's outlook and to his step. The last few weeks had been rough. Yesterday Christy's uncle Bob had called and asked if Trevor could meet with him at his real estate office on Saturday to talk about some part-time work he thought Trevor might be interested in. Trevor told me that whatever work Bob had in mind, he planned to take it.

I had a few qualms about mixing work with friends after all the years of mixing work with family. But I decided to wait and see what Trevor had to say after meeting with Bob.

My focus easily turned back to setting up everything on the patio. The table was pushed to the side next to the potted jasmine. I had covered the round table with an ivory brocade tablecloth Trevor's mother had given me the first Christmas we were married. It hung to the floor and gave the space an elegant feel even without any of the food items adorning it yet. The chairs formed a large oval around the rug. Mr. Miller had brought over four folding chairs with padded seats.

Trevor had helped me to pull the corner armchair from Audra's room and place it in the most prominent location. A mini-throne for our honored guest.

All we needed now were the decorations and the flowers that Jennalyn insisted on being in charge of. She promised to come over early and transform my patio into a bower for my little princess.

It was 12:45. All I could do now was wait.

Chapter 26

*T*rue to her word, Jennalyn arrived just before one o'clock with baby Alex in a sling and pulling a toy wagon stacked with bins of party-prep goodies. I reached for Alex and balanced his chubbiness on my hip as Audra begged us to let her help.

"You're the guest of honor," Jennalyn said. "Don't you want to wait in your room, come out, and be surprised?"

"No. I would like to help. I want to learn. You are my favorite artist, Miss Jennalyn. I want to learn how you make things look beautiful the way you do."

Jennalyn glanced at me. I gave a nod, and my creative daughter was in heaven as she strung garlands, arranged tiered tea trays with bite-sized brownies and cookies, and added her own touch of throw pillows from her bed as backrests on the folding chairs Mr. Miller had brought over.

Jennalyn pointed to one of the small cookies on the top of the tea tray. "Try one."

Both Audra and I popped the single-bite cookies into our mouths. I let mine melt on my tongue. "Mmm. Peanut butter. But it's so moist. I love it."

"It's my mom's recipe." Jennalyn's face turned rosy. "It's the first time I've made them."

I knew what that meant. Those cookies were a sweet reminder of her mom. They would play a special role in our celebration today and would probably become a staple at many celebrations to come.

"I love that a little bit of your mom is here today," I said.

"Me too. She would have liked that."

"This party was basically inspired by her, you know."

Jennalyn smiled. "She would have liked that too."

The Daughters of Eve arrived at my front door at two o'clock, sounding like a fluttering flock of happy birds. Audra eagerly asked if she could greet the guests, so I stayed on the patio, contentedly rocking Alex who had fallen asleep in my arms. My heart was happy on so many levels.

The serving table soon was laden with all sorts of scrumptious treats. I asked Christy to pop my bruschetta bites into the oven long enough for the cheese on top to melt. Audra floated among the women, pulling out all the southern charms she had learned in her childhood. She graciously thanked each of them for coming to the party.

Christy's mom and aunt arrived together just as Christy was adding the plate of bruschetta to the already abundant spread on the table. Marti was carrying two medium-sized pastel boxes. The first box contained a treasure trove of pink, yellow, and pale green macarons. Jennalyn went to work, arranging them on the serving table so that they looked like a scattering of watercolored raindrops that had fallen from the heavens to bless our party.

Marti tucked the other box under the chair next to me and gave me a twinkle-eyed look of satisfaction. I knew what was in the box, but I didn't think Audra knew. She may have guessed. If she did, she remained composed.

We ate, mingling and chatting while Alex slept unaffected by the lively conversations. Sierra had left Ella Mae at home with Jordan. That piece of information prompted a round of comments about how we would understand if she had to dash out early. I heard Tess whisper, "Try to keep your shirt on this time."

Audra seemed to thrive among the chatter of the gathering of women. She was used to being with her many aunts. I wished I had thought to invite one or two of her friends, but once we all settled in our chairs around the circle, I knew that my early blooming daughter was more comfortable with the group being us. Just us. Women and not girls.

Marti, dressed in a beautiful, flowing top that looked like it must be silk, stood and took on the role Christy had given her as our mistress of ceremonies. "Audra, as you know, this party is for you. We are your women, and we have gathered today to celebrate you."

Audra sat up straight in her princess chair and balanced her china plate in her lap. She looked radiant. Her blond hair was clean, brushed back from her face, and tucked behind her ears. Her pale blue-gray eyes watched Marti's every move.

Marti had placed the box that was under her chair onto Christy's lap, and Christy slipped it under her own chair. Marti had an index card in her hand.

"Audra, we would like to each offer you a small thought." Marti held the card out so she could read it. "My thought for you comes from the Bible. It's from 1 John 4. This has always been my favorite verse. Anyone can memorize it. The verse is simply, 'God is love.'"

She glanced at the card more closely and continued reading, "A few verses later it says, 'Dear friends, since God so loved us, we also ought to love one another.'"

Looking up at the group, Marti added, "This is something the women in this circle do very nicely. They are loving and kind women. If you ever need some encouragement or have any questions . . ." Marti paused.

With a slightly nervous glance at me, Marti clarified, "Questions within reason, of course, we want you to know that we are available to guide you as you journey into this next season of life."

She squinted as she again looked at the card at the end of her extended arm. "Always remember that 'since God so loved us, we also ought to love one another.'"

"Thank you, Miss Marti." Audra had taken to holding court just a little too easily, in my opinion. I continually found myself marveling at the confidence she had for such a young girl. Or, as I needed to start reprogramming my brain to think, for such a young woman.

"My pleasure, Audra." Marti lowered her card, and with her free hand she made a sweeping motion around the circle. "Who's next?"

"I'll go." Tess stood up and handed a cute little gift bag with sparkly white tissue paper sticking out the top like the plume of an exotic cockatiel. "Go ahead and open it, and then I'll tell you my word of wisdom for you."

Audra pulled out a pretty tube of what looked like expensive lipstick.

Uh-oh. I should have told everyone about Trevor's strict opinions on makeup.

"It's the best clear gloss I've ever found," Tess said.

Clear. Good. Clear is fine.

"Whenever you use this gloss, I want you to remember that your lips are very special. Or, I should say, your kisses are very special. Don't give your kisses away recklessly. Save them. I've saved my best kisses for many years, and I don't regret it one bit. Keep your heart and your thoughts as clear and shiny as that lip gloss." Tess gave a silly, sweet, very Tess-like half curtsy to our reigning princess of purity for the day.

Alex stirred. Jennalyn took notice and stood to say her piece before he realized it was lunchtime.

"My mother taught me that the best use of any blessing you receive is to bless others. My gift to you, Audra, is to bless you with whatever you would like to learn about painting or creating art in general. It would be my honor to help teach you how to use your natural talents to create beautiful gifts for others."

Jennalyn handed Audra a watercolor paintbrush that had a dozen skinny ribbons hanging from the neck like a flowing rainbow.

"I want to learn everything I can from you," Audra said. "Thank you so much, Miss Jennalyn."

Christy stood next and held out to Audra a leather-covered journal with a white satin ribbon tied around it. "When I was on my journey into womanhood, God provided me with three important gifts. One was my mother." Christy glanced at her mom, and both of them teared up.

"The second gift was my aunt." Christy and Marti exchanged glances that seemed to be filled more with mutual respect than a deep sense of cherishing. After some of the things Christy had told me about learning how to release her aunt and her domineering ways, Christy's acknowledgment of her aunt's contribution to her life was powerful.

"The third gift was my first diary or journal. Whatever you like to call it. My uncle Bob gave me my first diary, and I still have it. I wrote in it whenever I needed to get my thoughts and feelings out so that I could sort through them and see what made sense. One day, I'll probably let Hana read my diary. It might help her to understand that the things she's feeling are normal."

Christy looked at her mom and her aunt again. "Since you now have in your life the same first two gifts I had during my entry into womanhood, I wanted you to have the third, as well, so I'm giving you your own journal. You may fill the pages with whatever you like. I hope some of the things you write will be prayers because the prayers I wrote in my diary are my favorite part when I read it now. They are like mile markers that show me how faithful God was and still is in my life."

Audra was a bit teary as she held the beautiful leather book to her heart and thanked Christy. I never would have thought to buy Audra a journal; I was still prone to pick up coloring books.

She needs all of us. Every woman here is giving her the pieces I don't have to give her.

I felt like I wanted to have a good cry before we went any further. But Sierra was next, and she had us all laughing with her opening line. "You, darling Audra, are a princess, and you know it!" Sierra made the declaration with lots of sass and a zigzag snap of her fingers.

"The thing about being a princess . . ." Sierra paused for effect. "And I should know." She flipped a cluster of her wild, curly blond hair over her shoulder. Grinning at her own joke, she continued, "The thing is, you can sometimes find yourself reliant on the affirmation of your adoring fans. Like all the uplifting words you're hearing from us today."

Sierra pulled one of her many gypsy-girl bracelets off her slender arm and presented it to Audra. "I made this gold bangle for you to help you remember that you must always live for your King, the King of kings. That's what this single pearl represents. He is the only one you need to hear affirmation from. You play for an audience of one. Only one."

"I love this, Miss Sierra. Thank you so much." Audra already had slipped the bracelet on her wrist and now gave it a twist so that the pearl spun around. She looked at Sierra. "Audience of one. I'll remember."

Mrs. Miller's presentation was the shortest. She stood before Audra, and Mrs. Miller's round, petite figure, clothed in a long, pale blue top, reminded me of one of the winged fairies in the Sleeping Beauty cartoon. I smiled, thinking how this presentation ceremony was similar to the way the fairy godmothers had all given their gifts to the little princess. If the similarity struck Audra, I knew she would love the comparison, since Sleeping Beauty was one of her all-time favorites.

Christy's mom had done as Marti had, and written out some verses on an index card. No notes for a speech. She handed the card to Audra and said, "The verses are from Psalm 139. One of my favorite parts is where it says that you are 'wonderfully made.' God has His hand on your life, Audra. You are wonderfully made." She returned to her seat.

Christy leaned over and touched her mom's arm. "That's my favorite chapter in the Bible."

"I know," her mom said quietly.

Watching the interchange between the two, I couldn't help but wonder what else Christy's mom knew about Christy by heart—small details that Christy didn't even know her mother had noticed, because that's how it is between mothers and daughters.

It was my turn. I felt nervous. Not because I was going to say something to Audra. I just always felt nervous in front of a group. Christy and I had talked about this part ahead of time, and I'm glad we did because I was clear about what to say and what to do.

Christy opened the box Marti had handed to her earlier. I lifted out the beautiful and fragrant head wreath of pink and white flowers. I heard Audra gasp, and my heart sang before I even looked at her.

Taking two teary-eyed steps to where my princess sat with her eyes wide and her lower lip quivering, I smiled and drew in a deep breath through my nose. "Audra, as your mother, it is my honor to celebrate this life passage with you today." I placed on her head the crown of rosebuds and tiny, fragrant white jasmine woven in between delicate fern leaves.

My voice was barely a whisper, but I pushed out the words. "Welcome to womanhood, my darling girl!"

Audra leaped from the chair and wrapped her arms around me in the biggest hug she had ever given me. We were laughing and crying at the same time. When she pulled back, her face was radiant. "Thank you, Mama. I love you."

"I love you too. So much."

Audra adjusted her mussed crown and looked to the other women as they all repeated, "Welcome to womanhood!" Once her crown was secure, Audra gave a regal curtsy to the group and went over to the table for a napkin, which she immediately used to blow her nose. Audra always was capable of blowing her nose with gusto. Today was no exception. The sound carried across the patio.

"That's my girl," Sierra said. "Keep it real, Audra. Audience of one."

The laughter spilled over the remains of the afternoon like ripples on a lake that had been gilded by the cool, silver light of springtime. We ate more macarons and then hugged Sierra gingerly when she popped up and said she had to dash. Audra asked Jennalyn to help her find the best way to preserve her wreath once the flowers dried.

Marti took me aside and said, "Emily, I do wish you would have told me that your husband was in need of a job and that he was such a superb salesman."

I had no idea why any of that information would have been necessary to share with Marti. Nonetheless, I automatically apologized.

"Todd told my husband the other night all about Trevor, and Bob said he wanted to hire him right away. He's been looking for a reliable real estate agent to come on board at his office so that he and I can do more traveling."

"But Trevor isn't a real estate agent," I protested.

Marti looked stunned that I should mention such a drawback. "He's a salesman, isn't he?"

"Yes, Trevor is an exceptional salesman."

"Todd told me your husband had at one point considered going back to school to earn his teaching credential. Well, if he was willing to do that, he should be willing to be trained as a real estate agent and eventually a broker, like my husband. He can have his license in no time."

I had nothing to say to Marti. I stood there, blinking at her, not daring to believe it could be that easy.

Marti patted me on the arm. "I don't know why you look so surprised. This is what my husband and I do. Since God so loved us and blessed us, we like to love and bless others. Especially young couples."

"Thank you."

She waved her hand, as if brushing off my words so they wouldn't land on her and ruin her hair or expensive clothes. I understood how Christy could have an ongoing adore/abhor relationship with complex Marti.

An hour and a half later, after everyone had gone and everything was cleaned up, I heard the front screen door open and scurried around the corner to see if I could read the outcome of Marti's predictions on Trevor's face.

He saw me, stopped, and with a crooked grin, shrugged and extended both hands, palms up.

"Marti told me," I said.

"Bob offered me an on-site service position for his rentals while I go through the training. I can start Monday."

"Is this what you want to do? Do you want to be a real estate agent?"

"I'm sure willing to give it a try."

"Wow."

"I know. Wow." He listened to the singing coming from behind Audra's closed door and pointed his thumb in her direction.

"She's happy," I said, by way of explaining why she was listening to her favorite music through Trevor's earbuds and singing along at the top of her lungs.

"I take it the party went well."

"It was perfect," I said.

Trevor pulled his phone from his back pocket and started a video of him approaching Audra's bedroom door, the volume turned up high so he could catch Audra's solo. I followed him and watched as he pressed his phone up to the slivered opening of her door. Audra was sitting on her bed with her back to us, wearing her floral crown and singing her heart out.

Trevor retreated, letting her finish her moment. I knew that soon he would sit on her bedroom floor and ask her to tell him all about her day.

My adorable husband was grinning and misty-eyed as he turned off the camera and followed me into the kitchen. "I'm thinking this will be the intro for the video montage at her rehearsal dinner one day."

I grinned back. "We can pair it with the video of her first dance recital when she was four."

"Oh, right. I forgot about that. The twirling daffodil with the bobbing flower that broke off."

"And yet, she kept spinning."

Trevor shook his head. "I don't want her to grow up."

"I know. Too late. She's not our baby anymore." I gave Trevor a side glance, waiting for him to say that we needed to have another one. Or that it was time to get busy and "make us a brand-new baby any way we can," as he used to say.

This time he put down his phone, stepped over to me, cupped my face in both his hands, and said, "Thank you, Emily."

"For what?"

"For bein' my wife. For bein' the mother of our daughter. For bein' all that you are."

Gazing into Trevor's eyes, I asked him the question I'd never dared to ask before. "Is it enough?" I blinked back a tear. "Am I enough? Are we enough? Just the three of us?"

Wrapping his arms around me, Trevor answered so convincingly that his words reverberated in the deepest corners of my heart. "Oh, darlin', yes. Yes. You, me, Audra, this life God has blessed us with—it's more than enough. Wouldn't you agree?"

I lifted my chin and answered with a lingering kiss.

We stood together in the middle of our little kitchen, arms entwined, forehead to forehead, nose to nose, heart to heart.

I had no doubt that we were actually doing that which had seemed so difficult to imagine.

We were confidently and joyfully becoming us.

Readers Guide

1. What do you think about the idea of a Favorite Things party, like the one Emily is invited to at Jennalyn's? What would you bring?

2. Do you resonate with Emily's feelings of anxiety about befriending Jennalyn, Christy, Sierra, and Tess, or are you the kind of person who feels comfortable in new relationships? Talk about a time when you found it hard to make new friends. What did you do—or what happened—to change the dynamic?

3. Have you experienced a situation like Emily did with Trevor's family when you felt the need to branch out to nurture your own family unit? How did you do this in your life?

4. In what ways have you been a haven maker in places where you've lived?

5. Describe a time when God brought someone into your life to remind you that you're not alone in a situation, like Emily's first meeting with Mrs. Miller.

6. Do you have someone in your life whose superpower is withholding approval or something similar?

7. What are some healthy ways you've learned to adjust your relationship with difficult people in your life?

8. By the end of the book, the DOE women have gone through quite a bit together. What are some experiences that have bonded you more deeply with friends? Have there been any surprising ones like Emily's experience with Jennalyn and the baby?

9. Can you related to Emily's losses? If you are a friend to someone who

has experienced such events, how have you tried to comfort your friend?

10. Which of the women do you relate to the most? Are you timid in new situations like Emily? Do you like to initiate get-togethers the way Jennalyn does? Or do you see yourself more in Christy, Sierra, or Tess? In what ways are you like them?

11. Why do you think Tess feels at home with this group even though she's not a wife or mother?

12. What aspects of Emily and Trevor's marriage did you enjoy reading about? What areas were you hoping they would change?

About the Author

ROBIN JONES GUNN is the best-selling author of nearly one hundred books with more than 5.5 million copies sold worldwide. Best known for her Christy Miller novels for teens and the Christy Award–winning Glenbrooke and Sisterchicks series, Robin's nonfiction titles include *Praying for Your Future Husband,* coauthored with Tricia Goyer, and *Spoken For,* coauthored with Alyssa Bethke.

Hallmark Channel created three movies from her Father Christmas novellas, which broke a record for the network by being the highest-rated and most-watched original Christmas movies.

Robin's love for storytelling and training writers has taken her around the world. She has served on the board of Media Associates International and has been a keynote speaker in Africa, Brazil, Europe, and Australia, as well as in Canada and throughout the United States.

Readers who grew up with Robin's books have written to tell her how the memorable characters in her stories have mentored and influenced them over the years. Robin and her husband have two grown and married children and live in Hawaii.

Go back to where it all began.
The popular Christy Miller series
is available in these
treasured volumes!

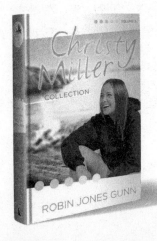

The heartwarming stories
of Glenbrooke

THE GLENBROOKE SERIES

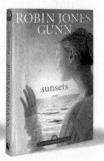

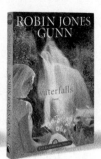

Stay connected to WaterBrook & Multnomah Fiction

Be the first to know about upcoming releases, insider news, and all kinds of fiction fun!

Sign up for our Fiction Reads newsletter at

wmbooks.com/WMFiction

Follow us on Facebook at

www.facebook.com/waterbrookmultnomahfiction

Join our Book Club at

wmbooks.com/BookClub

WATERBROOK MULTNOMAH

waterbrookmultnomah.com